Sidewall

David Graham was born in South Shields in 1919. He served
with the RAF as a fighter pilot during the Second World War
and later as a flying instructor, and has lived and travelled all
over the world. He is now technical author for a hovercraft
company.

Also by David Graham
in Pan Books

Down to a Sunless Sea

David Graham

Sidewall

Pan Books London and Sydney

First published 1982 by Robert Hale Ltd
This edition published 1983 by Pan Books Ltd,
Cavaye Place, London SW10 9PG
© David Graham 1983
ISBN 0 330 26942 9
Printed and bound in Great Britain by
Hunt Barnard Ltd, Aylesbury, Bucks

Sidewall: the twin vertical hulls joined by the main hull of the craft to form the modern hovermarine. Unlike the true hovercraft, the sidewall tips are partially submerged in flight, imparting the stability, ease of control and economy for which the hovermarine is justly famous.

This one for Hayley Jayne . . .

Author's Note

Inasmuch as at the time of writing there is only one company manufacturing sidewall hovermarines in Britain—and one which owns, in fact, most of the patent rights including the deep-sidewall concept, it should be made absolutely clear that the organisations and persons, both Governmental and private, depicted in this book are in no way intended to resemble any person or persons, living or dead, who have been or are connected with the hovercraft industry.

Further, any such resemblance, including choice of names, which may occur is purely fortuitous and coincidental. For example, the workers in the industry are honest and hard-working, and well represented by officials of trades unions. All references to the contrary, therefore, in this book should be regarded as poetic licence, in the interests of providing background material relevant to the story. I am deeply indebted to Mr Ted Tattershall, one of the pioneers of the hovercraft industry and an early associate of Sir Christopher Cockerell, for permission to use his deep-sidewall principle in developing the totally imaginary design of the *Albatross*.

At the same time, I am certain that, if the *Albatross* is eventually built, in one form or another, Ted Tattershall will have a great deal to do with its inevitable success.

Southampton, England
1979–1981

Beginnings

New York

March 2, 1993. Board Room—UNAM Building
Beyond the triple-glazed windows overlooking Central Park West some 135 floors below, the snow flurries streaked in oblique lines, white blurs against the grey skyline. Within, the temperature hovered around the 60°F legal maximum; most of the 24 people present wore friction-heated boots, dress coveralls, sealed at wrists and ankles. The air in the suite was glass-clear, thin and recirculated every three minutes by the wind-powered air-conditioners under each window.

Most of the occupants were familiar with the view, from previous visits. In clear weather it was heart-stopping, covering most of Long Island, from the tip of Manhattan, as far north as Yonkers. Unlike the first-timers rubbernecking at the windows, the old hands sat quietly around the long polished table, picking listlessly at bowls of candy, potato chips, relaxant lozenges. Most of all, they tried to invent some plausible reason for leaving the room, to find a quiet corner for a smoke.

European delegates, to a man, were non-smokers. Back home, there was a simple rule—drink and smoke to excess, and no-one would object. Providing one didn't mind being a social outcast with no rights whatever to treatment under national health schemes.

France, typically, had blazed the trail: with the highest incidence of alcoholism in Europe, lung cancer, chronic bronchitis and heart disease soaking up one third of the nation's medical resources, the French simply banned smoking and drinking from public places—and barred smokers and drinkers from State medical aid. Wine exports zoomed, tobacco imports halved and people lived more healthily in the meanest-tempered, most sarcastic and frustrated community east of Boston. America took six more years to see the light. It took that long to defeat the beer and bourbon lobbies. But the White House never convinced the crackpot organisations, who defended to the end a man's right to drink and smoke himself to death.

So the rubberneckers at the windows watched the propane cabs and the electricycles and pedal taxis and absorbed the historical fact that a New Yorker's definition of a pedestrian is a driver who's found a parking-place.

Immediately inside the sliding doors of the suite, a thin, tall red-faced man with broad shoulders sat at a plain table, checking a single sheet of paper. Each new arrival was stopped by a quiet word, identified and asked to clear the checkpoint: to enter the room proper, each was obliged to pass between two man-sized cabinets which burped to admit, bleeped to refuse.

The 25th man to enter was Walter F. Keyhoe, for whom no lights glowed, no 'beep' sounded. An athletic man approaching sixty, he wore an old-fashioned double-breasted suit in charcoal gaberdine worsted, into which a fine Body-Heat web was knitted; mini-generators built into shoe heels maintained a comfortable suit temperature indefinitely, and the outfit cost Keyhoe almost as much as his Rolls-Buick electro-gas hybrid town car.

Some of his friends—and all his enemies—called him 'Kipper' Keyhoe because, in their view, he was a 'two-faced bastard with no guts . . .' The accusation was false: it takes a special kind of guts to cheat, double-cross and crotch-kick one's way to the top and stay popular. He joined the old Panam outfit in 1970 as a trainee Traffic Manager; less than two decades later he was President and Chief Executive of United American, the single vast conglomerate of surviving US airlines. He sported the resurrected 'Dannemora Crop' haircut of the Gulf War vets, and over the years he developed a marvellous technique for dealing with those who didn't think 'the Keyhoe way'—he ignored them.

Men at the top of their professions or companies found they had ceased to exist in the Keyhoe world; behind his grotesquely large desk, he would make calls, receive other visitors, deal with underlings and finally stalk off to lunch. As a frog's eye can see only moving targets, the Keyhoe Blindness was famous; sooner or later, the offender went away and, if Walter F. Keyhoe was ever murdered, the N.Y.P.D could reckon on at least five thousand prime suspects.

The man Cody at the door set the Guarddog circuit on 'hold', switched on the room de-bugging system, nodded to Keyhoe and went away. Keyhoe stalked to the head of the table, leaned on the splayed fingertips of his hands and waited.

Conversation stopped. In a silence that could be tasted, the delegates took their places. Turned their heads Keyhoe-wards. Waited in their turn.

"Gentlemen—" the voice was harsh, almost a croak that seemed to demand he clear his throat instantly. He went on:

"My name is Keyhoe. Walter F. Keyhoe. Some of you know me, some don't. I run United American—which means effectively that I run the airlines of America. And I'm here to tell you it ain't easy. Most of you here occupy similar positions in your own countries—and I know that those of you who can't speak English are using pocket translators. Anything you don't understand, save it until I finish.

"So, between us, gentlemen, we operate some 95% of the world's remaining airlines. This meeting was my idea—and don't get thinking the US Government is involved, because involved it isn't. The Administration subsidises us, controls fuel supplies—and steals half our seat-capacity for official journeys. But it doesn't own us—not yet."

He was getting the standard Keyhoe reception for his speech: absolute silence and stillness.

"What I have to say doesn't go outside this room. It can't be bugged—so if anyone opens his mouth, I'll know about it the same day, probably within the hour."

Keyhoe allowed his pale hard eyes to drift speculatively round the table, meeting each man's stare directly, fleetingly, as if to assess his integrity, credibility, reliability. Their reactions, predictably, went into his mental file via an automatic shuffling process which left query marks over two or three faces. Later, he would remember them.

"We all know," he continued, "the facts of life in commercial aviation today. But I'm gonna run down the line quickly because it is important in evaluating the problem we have to face.

"In the last eight years, we have had to face what the egg-heads call a 'dichotomy' and what I call a goddamed tragedy. We thought once there would be an oil famine. But what do we have? We have a glut of the stuff, because people don't use so much. Now, today, it's cheaper at times to buy the goddam airplane instead of a ticket. You think that's funny? It wasn't funny when Panam and Transworld began selling off their ships. It wasn't funny when the Government took over oil imports, buying gas for the Air Force at bottom spot, and selling us the rest at top—plus tax. It wasn't funny when they went back to burning coal on the railroads to save money—and undercut intercity air fares by four fifths.

"Each time the price of aviation fuel is hiked, we lose passengers. We cut services—and the Federal commandeering of free seats takes up most of the remaining profit. We can't win—as of this time, our services are running at 12% of the 1985 level—and that was before the Gulf War started.

"If you think we've been sitting on our fat butts here, waiting for the Government to close us down altogether—forget it. Boeing at Seattle, McDonnell-Douglas in California are both working on flight reactor programmes—and they're getting close. The 797 stretched Jumbo is flying with four steam propeller-turbines, and they figure to crack the weight problem in a year or two. As of now, they can haul a reactor or passengers, but not both. But eventually the Westinghouse–General Atomics power plant will fly for 75 years—and cost less than the aeroplane itself.

"We still have to crack the second problem—designing that tail-mounted reactor so that it can be jettisoned in emergency. It's not easy, fighing off the anti-pollution fruitcakes."

"Mr Keyhoe—" the accent was almost—but not quite—pure Oxford; Keyhoe recognised Helmut Schafter, Chief Executive of *Alledeutshelufthansa*. Four years after the Polish–East German secession from the Warsaw Pact supported by world opposition to Russian intervention, Helmut's once-mighty fleet had shrunk to a score of aging Air Buses and 797's operating skeleton services along a handful of routes. "Mr Keyhoe," Helmut said tightly, "don't forget that nuclear power is not the only answer. In Germany we are working on hydrogen motors, and we know Japan is deep into diesel-electric hybrids using vegetable fuels. In any case, the Russians may beat us all to it—"

"You mean their orbital micro-wave generators beaming

power down to individual airplanes, Helmut? My research boys say they need another eight years, maybe ten, to work the bugs out of the control system. One of those beams wanders off target, they're into bad trouble. But you're right, Helmut: in just a few years, the breakthrough will come, but until then—we're in deep financial trouble unless we find a cheap source of power soon. It's no secret that UNAM will be in real trouble by the end of the year, even if no serious competition starts up. We can't afford the gas to fly one in a hundred of the people who need to fly. And once we stop operating for any length of time, it may take fifty years to wind up again from scratch.

"I mentioned competition. I want you to take a look at something." He walked stiffly to a wall cabinet, fished out a small gold key and opened the door. Reaching in with both hands, he brought over to the table a small but beautiful model made in plastic.

It was a ship—and not a ship. It resembled a catamaran, with a flattened main hull bridging the gap between two full-length sidewalls of remarkable depth; the lower edges of the sidewalls penetrated very slightly into the clear blue plastic sea on which the craft rested. At bow and stern, the tunnel formed under the hull, between the sidewalls, was sealed with black flexible skirts, and the bow skirt was split, each of two sections falling back at an acute angle from the knife-blade bow of a third 'centrewall'. The wide curved hull was sheer moulded beauty, painted smooth gloss white, and above the forward skirt a streamlined pear-shaped bridge moulded itself sleekly into the flowing lines, reminiscent of the flight deck and nose of a supersonic airliner.

High on each sidewall, row upon row of tiny round windows revealed the true dimensions of the craft: it was gigantic, easily as large as any transatlantic liner of the day. The men crowding round the model were startled into loud comment.

Keyhoe shouted them down, jaw thrust forward aggressively. "All right . . . so it's big. Now—shut up and let me tell you about this thing. It's a hovermarine—not a hovercraft. Those sidewalls, and the flexible skirts bow and stern, enclose an air cushion which lifts the thing almost out of the water. They've been around for a long time, in small versions—a British manufacturer has been building them for more than 30 years. And

13

they're good—don't ever sell 'em short. Mostly used for ferry work—short-haul stuff inland, in waterways, canals, rivers. Hong King has operated fleets of hovermarine ferries for years—twenty or thirty craft. They're running 100-tonne hoverbarges on the Rhine and the Amazon and the Nile right now We used Canadian-built craft of this type in the Gulf War evacuation. But they all have one problem—wave height. The smaller the craft, the smaller the wave height it can operate on. In rough seas, they lose the air cushions too fast."

He paused, eyeing the model, picking his words carefully.

"They're plenty fast, too. Use diesel engines with marine propellers. But they couldn't compete with the big jetfoils at first. Now, the foils are just as badly hit as us. They're looking for alternative fuels. Cheap fuels. Everyone is—even ship-owners. It ain't too hard to convert passenger ships, container ships, to coal—but who wants to go back to eight days trans-Atlantic, from eight hours?"

He had their attention now. He moistened his lips from the glass on the table.

"I want you people to take a real good look at this thing here. You're looking at the future—a future without the big trans-continental jets. We don't know much about it yet—but we will . . . we will.

"This hoverliner is being built right now—in Britain. Construction is well advanced. It cost us more than money to get hold of this model and the less you know about that, the better. But we began by scaling it up—and we don't like the answers we got.

"It will run out around two hundred metres in length—say, 600 feet, old style. Seventy metres wide, and the main hull, in flight, is thirty-five metres above sea-level. Atlantic rollers aren't going to faze this baby: they'll roll by underneath her, clean as a whistle. We figure the gross weight about 650 tonnes, passenger capacity about 2000—in regular airline seats, goddammit.

"Now, assuming it gets around the eighty-knot mark using conventional marine engines, it'll take about 48 hours for the Southampton–New York run. Too long for people to sit in an airline seat. In any case, we don't believe that 80-knot guess. For one thing, they'll never find a cheap fuel to run it economically.

"Secondly,—we took a very long look at these—" he used a gold stylopen as a pointer. "These are little old stabilisers—horizontal stabilisers, up here forward of the sidewalls, just behind the bow. Like little airplane wings—they're even swept back, as you can see. They rotate bodily, like the tailplanes of supersonic jets.

"It took us a little while," Keyhoe said presently, "to figure out what the heck they were. And what they do. These hover-marines keep their sidewalls in the water for stability, and use immersed rudders for control. But each time the bow or stern lifts, some air from the cushion is lost. They keep it pumped up with big fans. So the thing starts porpoising, gets very uncomfortable: drag increases the whole thing gets very bad. I am not getting too technical?" he demanded.

He was not, they assured him.

"Okay. So it was easy to figure that these things keep the attitude right—probably automatic and computer-controlled. All stabilisers are designed to do their job at a certain speed, at which they produce the required amount of lift. At higher speed they can be made smaller: at lower speeds they need to be larger.

"So we ran a computer study on these stablisers—and the answer takes some believing. This boat is designed to cruise at 300 knots."

The room erupted. Immediate reaction, predictably, was one of total disbelief. Expressed at around 160 decibels. Keyhoe let them sweat it out, sipping ice water with grim and obvious humour. Presently—

Four seats from Keyhoe's end of the table, a thickset Canadian stood dourly, waiting his chance to speak. His neck bulged over his collar and the white hair contrasted oddly with the deep tan of his skin. He watched Keyhoe closely, a small tic under his left eye twitching intermittently. At last—

"I guess you know what the hell you're talking about, Keyhoe. I doubt it, though. You think we're stupid, or something? There's no power source I know of that'd get that thing up to 300 knots on water. You can scratch marine engines and propellers, for a start. Water jets? They use more fuel than propellers. It might get up to half that speed using the latest ducted fans from Cargonauts—but I doubt it. So—what have they got?"

"What they have," said Keyhoe tightly, "is for us to find out. This model tells some of the story—but not enough. See here." He lifted the craft to show the underside: "These things usually sport two sidewalls—and never as deep as these. There's also this third 'centrewall' which is new—from bow to near the stern, on centreline. There's some sort of bulge here, aft, which we think is a propulsion unit of some kind. What? We don't know—yet. Right here, and here, she is fitted with waterjets—at the aft ends of the sidewalls. With rudders.

"My research boys think the stabilisers control the ship not only in pitch—raising or lowering the bow—but also in roll, by operating independently. So she travels straight, level, steady—and damned fast."

Claude Delange, boss of what had been Air France, voiced the question in every mind.

"Your computer, obviously, tells you how much power is needed for such speed?"

"Right. A million horsepower—maybe a million five. Convert it to kilojoules and it's still bad news."

Delange blinked. "Vraiment?"

Keyhoe grinned sardonically. "You ain't just shittin' blueberries, Claude." There were times, under pressure, when the raw original Bowery Keyhoe emerged involuntarily.

"It depends on drive efficiency, of course," he qualified. "It could be some kind of crazy rocket, chemical maybe. But they'd need two more boats like that to carry the fuel. No—we're guessing nuclear power of some kind—but what? No propeller can produce speeds like that. The British have come up with something new all right. And you can scrap all your trans-ocean jets if they make it work. It won't be worth running internal services, even. Eight hours to New York, with 2000 passengers? Hell, they'll charge less for the round trip than we do for flight lunches.

"We got it down to under four hours with the Concorde and the B1 conversion, before the cost of gas grounded them. Let this thing get into service—and we're finished."

He stared round the room, at the succession of frightened

faces. Between them—he did a quick mental computation—they represented an investment bigger than most average-size countries' G.N.P. He tried to imagine a world no longer linked by aeroplane. . .

"I'm almost through," he said at last. "Way I see it, we need time. Time to find our own solution—and regular income of a kind until we do. We have to find out what makes this thing tick—and we have to stop it. Stop it—or slow it down enough. Resources we have in plenty—money, contacts, power. So—we have to trust each other. All our asses are in a sling as of now: so I want a unanimous vote of confidence before we get through here today.

"One more thing—don't undersell those Limeys. You name any major development in engineering, and there's a Brit behind it. Steam railroads, the gas turbine, radar, the hovercraft . . . those smart sons of bitches invented them all, and more. Sure, they had a bad time in the Eighties, with their General Strikes and runaway unions and Reds in every goddam office. Okay—so they wasted North Sea Oil paying back loans to build City Halls—but it took only three years tough measures, to double industrial output. They've learned their lesson—If they fail on this one, it won't be for lack of trying.

"That's about it, I guess. Anything you can find out, I want to know. Personally! You'll be given a number to call by Cody, at the door. You'll get a weekly coded Radex report on progress, and I want absolute security. Why?"

He stared them down in violent silence.

"Some of you are wondering how far we have to go to stop this thing. The answer is—all the way, if need be. I want your personal support to take any and every action needed, to gain us the time we need so badly. Do I have it?"

He had it.

Keyhoe left them crowded round the model and walked to the door. It slid open and they gradually filed out after Keyhoe, past the thin broad-shouldered man who handed each a sealed envelope. Left alone in the suite, he locked the model away safely in the wall cabinet using a duplicate key: carefully, he recovered every scrap of paper in the room in a plastic bag brought for the purpose. Finally, he turned off the de-bugging circuit and went away, and, outside, the snow flurries turned to sleet and the low scudding clouds began to obliterate the tall buildings on the skyline, along Central Park West.

1   They Also Serve—

Savage lay face down in the shallow ditch bordering the British Hoverliner Corporation complex. Wet soggy grass, the salt night wind from Southampton Water reeking of mud, rotten garbage, unspeakable things. He shivered involuntarily: the damned suit was cooling off, too fast—sodding friction pads didn't last five minutes. In the dark night he turned his head slowly, listening, analysing; he felt nervous, brittle, edgy. Strange, he told himself—Security men were the most insecure damned people in the world. Because they lived through weeks of soul-destroying routine for every minute of action.

Yet, through the years of boredom, a man had to stay on high key every second: that 'real' minute of instantaneous, often bloody conflict could blow up any time—usually when cold, tedium, fatigue, took the edge off concentration. And there lay danger: cumulative stresses of inaction winding up that icy spring in the guts, tightening, squeezing, until a man just had to cough, sneeze, move—just to break the tension.

A lot of men died in that instant, Savage thought grimly. Ulcers? Hell, he'd probably end up with ulcers *on* his ulcers . . .

Maybe the Provos and UD's have gone home for good . . . relax for ten seconds and WHAM! Four hundred pounds of sugar and sodium chlorate let go under the Land Rover and you're flying wide and high over the hedge in four directions at the same time . . . rookie Private Donald F. Savage, back

*in 1979, sweating out his first tour, watching the men being
sieved out from the boys; you cut it one of three ways—you
coped, or you went back home a nervous wreck, or you went
back home ever so slightly dead. Savage survived, somehow—
and went back two years later for a second stretch, still Private
D.F. but drawing Corporal's pay in the S.A.S. Blooded the
previous year in the Iranian Embassy siege in Princes Gate,
London—emptied almost a full mag. into a terrified sallow-
faced man trying to hide among the hostages. Then ploughed
on into the smoke and noise, brain a sand-filled bag of
numbness.*

*Like they said in training: it happens fast at the time, doesn't
sink in: Savage was back in Hereford barracks, working his
way through a bottle of Hennessy Four Star when the shakes
hit him. They were bad: worse than the time he went out of a
Hercules over Abingdon and lost both chutes. No time to think,
with a double streamer—before he had time to realise he was
dead, he bombed feet first into a shallow lake off the main
road, stopped waist-deep in stinking mud, nearly drowned
before they got to him with ropes. Just a nose above water
. . . he shivered violently, remembering. They said later he had
a D-ring in each hand, wouldn't let go until they shot him full
of pentothal . . .*

*The third Belfast tour . . . his last, and worst. When news
broke, late in 1983, of the Thatcher deal with the Irish Republic,
the Prods went berserk. Paisley's Private Army went under-
ground along with the UDR and headed South, looking for
trouble: the Provos, IRA and Liberation Army together came
north, looking for Paisley—and Savage's troop were caught in
the middle. They went bush, living off the country, hunting
their senior officer targets on each side, hanging captured ir-
regulars with total impartiality from the nearest tree. London
announced the suspension of the Dublin Treaty—too late.*

*Savage survived because a cow farted. Later—much later—
he could see the funny side . . . but not then. In a wood near
Lurgan, he was trying to crawl under the bark of a sycamore
tree on the bank of a stream, feeling that crinkly-neck sensation
of someone behind him where no-one should be at all . . . his
wrist bug was vibrating urgently, but he ignored the rest of the*

19

squad; everyone had image-intensifiers, friend and foe alike, and his only chance was absolute immobility—welding himself to a tree and freezing.

Ten feet away—heavy breathing. His nose burrowed deeply into a crevice in the tree, and an eye muscle began twitching. The cow lifted an unseen tail and blasted; Savage jerked involuntarily, head tilting back. The 9mm slug went through the soft flesh of his shoulder, and out through the epaulet of his battle jacket, ripped a deep groove across the back of his neck and stopped thunk! in the sycamore.

He lay still, feeling blood spouting here and there, afraid to move. He could get a first-aid pad onto the neck, which felt the worst—but if he moved, the sniper would finish him. He could, of course, just lie still—and bleed to death. It depended on so many things—if an artery was hit, how soon the squad could clear the area. He lay quietly enough, thinking; around him, silent shadows moved—the squad going after the sniper. Come on, Savage . . . make an effort. Like a tourniquet round the neck? His belly heaved in a painful spasm of amusement; overhead, leaves rustled in the night wind and he closed his eyes, comfortably aware he was dying and perversely enjoying the feeling. He came round briefly in the Medevac chopper, vaguely aware of a toothy character emptying whole blood into him in quantity, between attempts to plug up the human sieve on the stretcher.

Savage checked his watch. 00.45. He sighed, shifted stiffly in the long grass, checked the portable screen under his chin. The scanner showed the long straight shoreline, the amorphous blobs of the factory buildings behind him, the bright blips of his team. He chin-keyed his radio.

"Eddie?"

"Yay. All clear, Don."

"Garner?"

The voice was muted, hoarse. "Yay. Something moving in midstream, Don. Small boat, maybe—"

Savage moved the range bar, checked the screen. "I have it, Sec Three. Sec One to all units—stand by. Garner, what's the source?"

"Number Three Camera. On the beach, south end."

Savage acknowledged, watching the tiny blip working steadily inshore. Fishing expedition? Jacks? Most likely Jacks—experienced thieves working at night with modern equipment: probably had as much sensor gear as the Team itself. He shrugged, waiting . . .

Ireland . . . long weeks convalescing in the Lake District . . . slow painful walks to remote village pubs. Repeated surgery . . . no talking for nearly eight weeks—Christ, that was rough! The last dressing removed from neck and chin, Savage could only mumble, tongue stiff and unwieldy. But the orderly grinned and said: "When are you going to stop malingering and get back to Belfast?"

The patient scowled, told him to fuck off, pull his foreskin over his head and to go sleep; the medic grinned, aware that his shock treatment worked every time . . . the Surgeon, hand at mouth, telling the nurse, "Not much wrong with this one, Sister . . ."

But there was. Not then—later. Much later. After four weeks sick leave spent trying to bang every girl between Plymouth and London, he went back. Found they had some weird sort of cease-fire going: about time, too—if the bastards who started wars had to fight, there'd be no wars. It was a crazy deal, from the start—crazy enough to work where all else had failed; in the end, they started to talk, after Paisley and the others went missing, and they worked out a plan for a divided Ulster, half Catholic, half Prod, topping up the Catholic half from the South until numerical near-equality was established. Moved whole local populations, built new estates, factories, created jobs. It cost billions—but still less than the twenty-odd years of Troubles.

Among that time, Savage recalled, some birdbrain thought up Jobsplit. The Shared Employment Act sounded fine in principle: every job was to be shared between two or more people. The employer paid part-wages, the Government and EEC the rest. For Savage, it was a disaster: all he knew was killing and avoiding being killed, and for a world at uneasy peace (ignoring the squabbles in El Salvador, Panama, Pakistan and the Ba-

hamas) such men as Savage were as popular as pork pies at an Afghan wedding . . .

In the end he drifted into Security. Mostly because a set of wheels usually went with the job—but that soon changed; the laws of supply and demand played cruel tricks. Higher fuel prices led to reduced consumption, forcing producers to hike prices again and again. Big insulation programmes cut fuel consumption still further and, when petrol became unfairly rationed by price and available only to the rich, individual power rationing became inevitable.

For ten years, Savage remembered, he drifted from job to job, gaining experience, becoming disillusioned, and in recent years he began to realise that all was not well with his health.

The harsh north-east wind scythed through the long coarse grass around him, and he felt the old familar numbness spreading through thigh muscles, the sensation of fatigue and weakness, tightening of the chest muscles. In the dark night, he grimaced, flexing each leg in turn. Months ago, the thing had progressed from mere aggravation to physical discomfort and pain; he set his jaw solidly and pulled down the image-intensifier for another look-see. Something was moving vaguely on the perimeter of his vision: whatever it was, he had a little time to spare. He found a little block of bran concentrate and lay quietly, chewing reflectively.

Late in 1989, Savage married Jan for no other reason than it seemed the natural thing to do. They were constantly on the move, trapped separately in an ever-deteriorating housing situation, and they figured it might be better to be miserable together than unhappy apart. At least, they could share it all. They had a place of their own; as Savage's duties involved increasing night work, Jan signed up with a Homeslot Agency and spent eight hours a day at the computer terminal in their living-room, processing an endless flow of invoices and orders.

Savage sucked gingerly at a hollow tooth. 01.00—Jan would be asleep in their tower block across the Water. What the hell was he doing here, lying in two inches of water, waiting for some stupids to make their move? He thought for a while about the imminent pleasure of kicking fourteen different kinds of shit out of someone very soon, and felt a little better.

Stirring, he checked the screen, opened up on the Guard Channel.

"Eddie?"

"Here, Don. Sixty metres from the fence on the shore side. I think they have a rubber boat. Wait while I move the camera—"

On short range, Savage got a good picture. "I have them now, Eddie. Sec One to points—do you have them?"

"Gamer—check."

"Tilley—yay."

"Caldwell—check."

"Okay. Eddie—I'm moving up. We'll wait till they make the fence; other points stand by."

He got up stiffly, with elaborate care, eased the gun in his forearm holster, went forward through the grass, knees lifting high, feet searching for solid ground each step, grunting rhythmically under his breath as thigh muscles stretched and contracted. In the lee of a fence post he stopped, watching the intruders on scope.

Two . . . wearing dark overalls; one carried a box, an indistinct green shadow on the miniature screen on Savage's chest. Close enough for nightscope again; he watched them crouch at the base of the wire fence, heard the snip, snip of cutters. Hand lasers were faster but too bright for night work, he thought: time for a quick call to Control. John Martin was awake and alert; Savage briefed him quickly on the situation and checked there was transport available.

On the Command net, he said quietly: "Wait till they're through. Garner—secure the boat. Tilley, take the tall one, Caldwell the other. Needles at half-power: we want these boys in condition to talk."

He watched, critically; the short figure in overalls crawled through the triangular gap, straightened, stared around.

"Go!"

The small man sagged at the knees, gently, as if very tired; the other toppled sideways ponderously, like a felled tree, and both lay still. Savage sighed contentedly; those air-powered needles worked about ten times faster than sodium pentothal—

before a man had time to appreciate he'd been hit, he was out cold, before he started falling.

"Sec One to Control—all secure, John. Send the jitney—two bodies, one small bag. They'll be out for an hour—I want interrogation reports on my desk by ten a.m. I think they're just a pair of bums out for what they can find, but check them out. Over."

"Will do, Sec One."

Savage watched in stark torchlight; he was right—petty thieves after valuable scrap, probably. No skilled tradespy would make such a cock of things, surely . . . Coldwell and Tilley went through pockets quickly, efficiently; after a while they heard the electric jitney whining up from the main Complex. It brought with it the relief squad and Savage realised, belatedly, that his shift ended at 1 a.m. As Security Chief, he could have delegated all night patrols; instead, he put in three nights a week minimum and it paid off—kept his squads on top line. He rode back sitting on the slumbering duo, enjoying a long-overdue Split, feeling the drive and bounce of the 15% grass mixed in tobacco—the maximum in law. Martin met him at the Guardroom.

"You want the local law in, Don?"

"Hell, no. Shove the sods in the pokey after you've done with them. And turn off the heating—if *I* have to freeze my arse off all night, so will they. Anything else?"

Martin shook his head.

"I've had it," Savage said numbly. "Four nights in a row we've had alerts. Don't these bastards ever learn? I'm for home. Anything in the Transport Yard I can use?"

"Sorry—" Martin sounded sincere. "All the electric jeeps are on charge. The night-shift electricians are using all the scooters. There's a trike with a new battery available—if you want to fit the battery—"

Savage exploded. "Jesus bloody wept, John! I'm not riding ten kays on a damned tricycle this time of night—"

"Better'n walking," Mr Martin said philosophically.

"In a pig's arse. Who owns this jitney?"

"Hoffman—the accountant."

"Well, up Mr Hoffman's. And up yours too, Martin. I'm gone." And he was.

The Civic Centre clock agonised four times. Savage stumbled into the apartment block foyer on legs of wet chalk and tried the lift: incredibly, it worked. What in the hell had the resident vandals been doing all night? He shook his head, amazed, and stood in the lift with bowed head, jaded, unwell, so tired he could hardly stand up straight. It occurred to him, absently, that there weren't many muggers around any more . . . maybe they were too scared of being mugged to go out nights.

He let himself into the flat quietly—not as much from consideration for Jan as from a disinclination to start a row at 4 a.m. After a few hours' sleep, maybe . . . he slipped off the friction boots at the door, wriggled out of the heated suit, still watersodden, and stood in the dark lounge for long moments, massaging aching thighs. The numbness seemed deeper, higher on the legs, and he bit his lower lip in a gut-wrenching surge of fear. In the blackness of the bedroom, Braille-clear after years of night walking, he stripped down to shorts, slipped into the sleepsac, zipped up the neck halfway and lay on his back, breathing quietly, trying to slow his pounding heart, trying to ignore the insidious loss of feeling in his upper legs, the stomach contraction which would soon rouse him from fitful sleep.

How much longer could he conceal this thing that was eating him? How long? Beside him, in the quiet room, Jan stirred uneasily on the bed next to his own; still deep in sleep, she mumbled, "Piss off, Savage . . . stay away from me . . ."

The recumbent man sighed. Home Sweet Home . . . it was cold, here in the bedroom—there'd been no heating since yesterday morning, for some reason he couldn't even be bothered to find out, and the place smelt musty, stale, the sleepsac damp and yukky . . . he turned over, pulled the zip all the way, rested his head on a forearm. Why in hell you bother at all, Savage, God knows. Four years in this shitheap boat factory, collaring sneak thieves and graffiti artists and guys building up their tool collections, poofs comparing sizes in washrooms, catching the girls in the word-processor pool spreading their legs for cash over the lunch hour, watching guys fiddling the time clocks and standing by, helpless, strapped down by rules . . .

Security Chief? Big deal, he thought drowsily. Twenty men on two 12-hour shifts, working three days a week a man . . .

time was when he could have held this place down tight with maybe six men. He was lucky, of course: he owned his job outright, in supervisor grade, slipping John Martin only 25% of his salary to watch the store when he was off duty.

He shivered again, spasmodically . . . fingers mauled at thigh muscles, as if to tear out the numbed ganglions and nerve fibres, to inject feeling once more into putty-like flesh. In the end, desperate, he found a self-heating warmbag in a cupboard, pulled the operating ring, wriggled back into the sac and pinned the heater between his thighs . . . nearly ten pounds a time, but what the hell—he had to get some sleep. Warmth spreading . . . relaxing, brooding, trying to remember when he'd last had a woman. Worse . . . trying to remember when he'd last *felt* like having a woman . . . any woman . . . and when

In mid-August, the year before, Savage surrendered to nagging worry about his physical condition. The deep scar across the nape of his neck was no problem; if his shoulder got a little stiff at times, it was no surprise—torn muscles rarely healed fully. What did disturb him deeply was what was going on within him: throughout that summer the numbing, prickling sensation had grown stronger, more persistent, spreading up from calf muscles into knee joints, on up into the lower thighs. There were brief but terrifying periods of sudden weakness and fatigue; more than once, he found shins torn and bleeding after unfelt impacts with sharp corners, alerted finally by the grisly accumulation of blood in his boots.

He found it necessary to concentrate on simply walking straight, without a limp, and a parallel fear grew alongside that already consuming him—the fear of discovery. Of losing his job and, with it, his home, such as it was. He would lose Jan too—but then, he'd lost her years before, when his sexual drive, inexplicably, began to fade. In the last year, he'd tried once— and failed totally, retreating into the kitchen and a bottle of genuine imitation Japanese whisky, to blot out the shrieks of mocking laughter from the bedroom.

In the end, he went to see a consultant in a dingy room at the corner of New Cavendish Street and Harley Street, in London. It cost him £1700 for the two hours—nearly £10 a

minute—and he told himself wryly he was in the wrong profession. Typically, the man refused to commit himself to an opinion.

"Mr Savage," he said reasonably, "I can only go so far in diagnosis from general examination. We need tests—a great number of tests—in a hospital ward. You drink and you smoke—so you're barred from any National Health treatment. Further, you say you can't afford private treatment. You have personal insurance, but you'd rather not cash in. Well, that's your decision and my opinion of it is immaterial. Let me tell you what we know."

Savage groped for a Split, changed his mind, clenched his hands in his lap and waited.

"Without exhaustive clinical and pathological tests, I can't be absolutely sure. But all your symptoms point to multiple sclerosis."

The man opposite him stared, ran a tongue over dry lips, waited.

"Do you know anything about this particular disease, Mr Savage?"

"No—" huskily.

The man in the white coat nodded. "Numbness of the lower limbs—periods of weakness—sensations of pins and needles—abdominal cramps. Sometimes slurring of the speech, as if the tongue was paralysed. These are all classic evidence: the disease attacks the nervous system, and it can be contracted at any time in life."

He paused. Savage said grimly: "Sounds bloody nasty."

"It is," the specialist said quietly. "Very nasty, Mr Savage. I have to tell you that there is no known cure for MS. We can only do so much with drugs."

Savage nodded, remembering the minesweeper rating in the hospital at Keswick: he'd had this thing, and eventually they moved him into a side room to ease tension in the main ward. Savage, remembering again, looked up sharply. "Listen, doc— you don't think it's anything to do with this . . . thing I got in Ireland?"

"The neck wound? No. I think we can rule that out. One other point I should make: there are one or two inconsistencies

27

*in your case. Things that don't quite fit . . . that is why I think
further tests are essential. I'm 90% sure I'm right—but I'd like
to make sure."*

Savage nodded briefly. "What'll it cost? Roughly?"

*The specialist looked up. "A lot of money. Two weeks at
least in a private hospital—one or two consultants—path lab
costs. You'd not get much change out of £8000, Mr Savage."*

. *"That's what I thought. No way, doc. This trip today drained
me dry. Listen—" he hesitated, thinking. How many times had
he seen this sequence on TV? How many times had he read it
in books? The corny dialogue that seems so unreal, the heroic
acceptance, the stiff upper lip? Hell, it was only one stupid
little question, and he was so scared he was almost zapping in
his pants . . . He said stiffly: "If you're right—if this thing goes
bad on me . . . I'm for the high jump, right?"*

*The specialist looked at him squarely. "We all have to face
that, sometime, Mr Savage."*

*"But some earlier than most. Shit, do I have to squeeze it
out of you, doc? How long?"*

*"If I'm right—nine months. Maybe a year. After that, you'll
be on your back. You're what—36? Modern medicine can keep
you alive a long time, Mr Savage—even if it can't cure MS."*

*The man in the patient's seat eased back into a better position,
groped for a cigarette; the specialist, normally paranoiac about
smoking in his consulting room, found an ashtray in his desk
drawer.*

*"You can make things a little easier, you know," he said
softly. "Go to your GP—he could arrange an emergency ad-
mission, when—"*

*"When I'm a bloody cripple, doc? No thanks. When I can't
get around any more, I'll push out into the country, find a
hole, crawl in."*

*"Your family?" The doctor's smile was gentle, under-
standing.*

"Forget it. There's no-one I need."

*For a long time, the little room was quiet. In the end Savage
got up, walked away from that place, hands deep in pockets,
a Split dangling defiantly from his mouth. He walked slowly
and painfully through a mile of London streets to his cheap*

hotel, *savouring deeply what could be the last long walk he'd take.*

On the way, he bought a bottle of Moet Chandon and a litre of four-star brandy with the last of his money. In his room, he slouched in front of a TV with the sound off, drinking steadily into the small hours. Eventually, when the building was still and the traffic at rest, when the sky to the east was pale grey behind the shabby curtains, he fell off the chair onto the floor, groaned once and lay still. His mouth was open, and he drooled thinly onto the faded carpet. On the crown of his head, the hair fell away, disclosing an incipient bald spot; at intervals, his legs twitched and, far away, some great bell scored the passage of the hours.

2 Storm Warning

Towards dawn, a great area of low pressure enveloped Southern England, bringing a wide rain belt down from the northwest; an advance guard of heavy grey-bottomed cumulus clouds marched southeast in stately formation, at a steady 50 kph, moving in a great encircling movement to swallow the sun, an hour away below the horizon.

In Hamburg, the New Baader-Meinhof operation exploded a device in a Government nuclear waste processing plant, spurting radioactive detritus into a half a million hectares of countryside: a black filth-laden tide saturated with slow agonising death.

In America, still wrapped in darkness, the War of Black Secession was in its second year; in the Atlanta-Augusta-Macon triangle, the Third Brotherhood of Carolina Regiment—high on grass and the sweet taste of victory—overran elements of the 43rd US Armoured Division, taking no prisoners.

In the Empty Quarter of Arabia, Dutch canal engineers prepared to detonate a chain of low-yield nuclear devices buried a hundred metres deep in the sand, connecting the Soviet-blocked Gulf to the Indian Ocean, bypassing the Straits of Hormuz.

In Eastern Nepal, Japanese climbers captured during the night the first genuine Yeti specimen; later reports through Reuter and UPI claimed the animal was capable of high-level communication.

Along the US-Mexico border, the US army strengthened its patrols against illegal oil-importers bound for the black market, where a gallon of high octane sold for $150.

In the deep ocean off Newfoundland, the third attempt to raise the *Titanic* failed, after an intruding Press Association minisub rammed a container of liquid hydrogen at 3800 metres.

In Hong Kong, gold hit a new high of $35,000 per ounce, and the Europound fell to $91.32.

In the high mountains of Laos, UN relief forces entered a landlocked valley containing some 3000 refugees, all infected with airborne anthrax dropped by Vietnam in the war with Kampuchea.

And in the darkness of the 14th floor apartment of a tower block overlooking Southampton Water, Donald Savage woke to the certain knowledge that this was going to be another bad, bad day . . .

He lay awake, feeling jaded, stale, unrefreshed; the telephone which had woken him sounded intermittent, far distant, and he turned his head, looking at the amorphous rectangle of the single window, behind the drapes. Already, his brain was racing across vast interlocking grids of thought, following neural geodesics into yesterday's problems, tomorrow's nightmares. The phone rang on steadily; he moved suddenly, reaching down to massage a stiff muscle, and Jan sighed, jabbed out a sharp elbow in unconscious rejection. Savage's face stiffened in anger, frustration, thinking of how it used to be . . . how long since . . .

No point going down that road again, he thought grimly. Through the years, they had passed through tacit condescension to growing impatience, the long silences merging into noisy and obscene warfare; with his commitment to the *Albatross* project, he had spent less and less time at home, and there were times when, stumbling in after fourteen hours or more caught up in some emergency, Savage would fall asleep in the middle of a meal and Jan would leave him there, head on sprawled arms surrounded by half-empty dishes.

Presently, he got up awkwardly, a lean ungainly man with a body dark with matted hair, clad in not-so-clean Y-fronts, and went into the kitchen to the phone.

"Savage—"

"Don? Johnnie Martin here. You awake?"

"No. I'm still asleep—you stupid sod. What time is it?"

"Ten before seven. Listen—we've got problems, Don—"

Savage shook his head dazedly. "Hold it, hold it. I have to crawl before I can walk. Wait a minute—"

He set the phone down gingerly, ran a half-tumbler of water, dropped a seltzer in it, took up the phone again and stood watching the bubbles rise.

"Now—slowly, for God's sake."

"All hell's breaking loose here, Don. Carl Wayne came in just after six, with a bunch of other characters—Navy, I think. He's called an emergency Security meeting for nine sharp and you'd better be there. I think it may be something to do with the—"

"Shut up!" Savage interrupted harshly. "For God's sake, Jackie—this is an open line—"

"I—sorry, Don. But something's brewing, that's for sure. When the Managing Director turns up at six a.m. in a flaming temper, he's not worrying about the canteen account."

Savage grunted. It made sense: the normally impassive Canadian wouldn't turn his head if the sky fell on him. He ran a probing tongue over dry cracked lips and was pleased he'd never been able to afford a visiphone; Martin habitually said what he thought, and this was no time to start a fight. Even if he did look as bad as he felt . . .

"You on your way, Don?"

"Yay. If I can catch a steam tram—that jitney's battery's flat, I think. See you—" he hung up, disturbed and worried. What now, for Christ's sake? Not those two apes last night; he felt a growing sense of foreboding and grimaced, standing there in the cold early light of the kitchen.

Yawning cavernously, he flicked the water-heater switch and shambled into the bathroom, crotch itching gratifyingly under scratching fingers, and stood at the wallslot, relieving himself, staring at the face scowling back at him. Stringy black hair, multi-spiked, over black brows bridging the beaky nose . . . you're a damned werewolf, Savage, he thought wryly. Bleary gaze, deep engraved lines at the eyes . . . he protruded his tongue, winced, put it back again. It tasted metallic, grainy—like the bottom of a baby's pram . . . all piss and biscuits. Early to bed, early to rise, you won't get red in the whites of the eyes? Like hell you won't, he thought sourly. The face disturbed him: it revealed changes so recent and drastic he could hardly recall how he'd looked, a year ago. The cheeks were sunken, eyes burning under grey shadows, and two new lines of pain bracketed the thin colourless lips.

Holy Mother of God, Savage . . . you belong in a knackers's yard. The *Albatross* project should be finished very soon . . . just a month or two, O Lord . . . give me a little time.

Hands shaking, he started chewing a dentatablet, creamed his face, wiped away the grey residue of beard with a tissue; a quick rinse and he was on his way to the kitchen. Fifty-five seconds . . . well outside your record, Savage. Filthy old sod—why don't you take a bath? No time, no inclination. He thought fleetingly of the Army's translation of 'NAAFI'—'no ambition and fuck-all interest' . . . a twisted smile crossed his face and he climbed into pants and shirt. Who cared if he smelt like a dead badger, anyway?

Filling a beaker with coffee, he switched on the TV, slipped his bunce card in the slot and watched the autofax morning paper printing itself, twice. He peered gingerly into the bedroom . . . Jan of the tousled hair and serpent's tongue . . .

"Coffee?"

"Sod off, Savage . . ."

"Thank you very much." He began singing, just loud enough for Jan to hear: "If I had to do it all over again, I'd do it all over yoo-hoo, dear—" He heard the bed creak, the door slammed in his face and he sighed.

"God bless our happy home . . ."

Holding the beaker in hands that trembled occasionally,

32

zipped into a grey heatsuit and old friction boots, he rocked to and fro steadily, applying pressure to the tiny heat generators in the heels. At the window, he watched whitecaps flecking the grey wastes of the estuary; patches of shade and light moved across the water, a pastel fresco etched by the cloud castles tacking overhead to maintain a southeast course. Two miles across the waterway, the British Hoverliner Corporation complex sprawled across thirty hectares of waterside; from his height, it seemed like a child's model, and he could even see the white blaze of the *Albatross* herself, lying in the dry dock basin. He'd watched her grow through the years, from nothing but a hole in the ground to a 200-metre ocean-going greyhound.

Down-water, towards the Isle of Wight, a supertanker edged into the Fawley oil Terminal, her two Navy escort frigates hanging on their heels in midstream—no tanker sailed alone today, Savage mused; not with cargoes worth ten times the tanker and escorts put together . . .

Behind him, Jan slammed down the percolator, filled the beaker on the worktop and ripped off the newsfax violently, leaving a sizeable segment in the slot under the commset. Savage turned, watching her nervously. He doubted very much that he could stand a full-blown row this morning; he took in the tangled hair, smeared make-up, creased and stained dressing-gown, and some icy hand squeezed his heart, recalling a ghost of a long-dead memory of the way she had been . . . where was that quick-silver beauty, that elusive and witty champion of all he did,—wife, lover, protector, mother-figure, resident whore, part-time angel? Had he really done this to her?

She stalked back into the bedroom without a word. He shook his head despairingly, replaced his cash card in the slot and dialled the datafax for Powerbank. The readout streamed across the tube, went into error feedback correction until the blue light flashed. He needed no print-out; with five days of the month left, they had less then 50 power-units left. The battered '89 Metro gas-electric hybrid down in the basement garage hadn't been on the road for six months—maybe it never would again. Savage scowled, punched in a series, converting his remaining 50 litres of petrol into house service: he got three full days' central heating, two days in the power circuit and a choice of any two lights at a time. He could afford to buy the whole deal—and it was the best offer he'd get all day, he thought.

Morosely, he left the apartment, shoved a £5 coin into the hall vending machine, opened the pack of half-charge Valium and swallowed two with difficulty. Standing in the elevator queue, he shifted incessantly from one leg to another, easing the burden. It would have been different, if they'd had kids . . . Looking back, he could hardly blame her. Jammed in the elevator under the CCTV camera, Savage frowned, tried to ignore the stench of sweat, bodies, urine, scented floor wash. What a lousy rotten world . . . he nodded bleakly at the TV camera, for the benefit of old man Collins, the Block Warden, and walked stiff-legged out into the open foyer, towards the road and the distant tram stop; no point even checking the jitney down in the basement: the red light had been on for the last four miles home. What the hell . . . he'd plug it in tonight, bill the Company for it.

The day was dank and chill and he shivered, feeling the rough texture of material sliding on his thighs; he stumbled a little, weakness undermining his sense of balance, and he leaned against a vandal-stripped sapling, staring up at the sky. The grey-white cloud blocks hustled onwards, on the strong wind, and he experienced once more the old sensation that the building was about to topple on him. One or two people stopped, eyeing him with concern; he shook his head doggedly, and they moved on, hesitantly, as if unwilling to turn their back upon him.

He started to sweat copiously, fluid running down his back in a dreary stream, and he stopped again, sitting on a low stone wall; presently, he got up, stared down the road towards the distant tram stop, occupied by a queue already too long by far. Savage said, "Shit!" bitterly and flagged down a passing twinrick.

The two runners were typical of their breed: big, raw-boned teenagers, baldies in paperthin leatherplas running hose, yellow windproofs, clearplas visors. They slowed, stopped, stared at him wide-eyed.

"You all right, Dad?"

Savage nodded tiredly. "Sure. It's a long haul—you fellers

fit?" It wasn't so much the money—he always seemed to hook crews who died on him, half-way.

"How long, pops?"

"Hythe. The BHLC complex—know it? About eighteen kays."

The tallest, around seventeen and sporting a fading Outlaw burn on his forehead, grinned.

"No problem. We have a good battery set. Only—you look sick, man . . ."

"I'm all right," Savage insisted. "Do we go?"

The lad nodded. "We go. Ten sheets to you—"

Fifty quid . . . pushing it a bit, Savage thought numbly. A day's pay for two hours' work. "Forty," he said flatly. "On delivery."

They looked at him, assessing, young eyes hard and calculating. "Forty-five. Up front."

"Half up front—and we go *now*!" Savage bent a little. They were young—and he couldn't stay upright much longer . . .

"Deal. All aboard—"

Settled in, draught sheet around his neck, Savage felt better—marginally. They began to work up speed, coasting the downhills with all feet off the deck, swinging on the rest bar, the single steering-wheel and mini-computer holding them a steady half-metre from the kerb. They made good time: 08.50 and the works traffic was pouring into the Main Gate past the Guardroom, crawling through Security check, the vehicles tailing back down the road. Savage climbed out carefully, groping for a little-used billfold: these boys dealt exclusively in cash. He looked at the tallest of the two.

"That burn mark—out of date now?" he asked diffidently.

"Uh-huh. Almost a year. What's it to you?" the boy said defiantly.

Savage said: "Just curious. What earned you that one?"

The teenager hesitated. "Aw—you know. This and that. Mostly a fire—the University."

Savage stared. "*You* burned that one?"

"Sure. I was only a kid—a couple of years back. I got six months' Grand Slam and a year on the beach."

Savage tried desperately to translate. These kids—a language of their own. "Run that one past me again?" he said slowly.

"*You* know—Oxford. The Bad Place."

"Oh." Belated understanding. The Correctional Institute . . . "Thanks—nice run. You can get coffee up the road a stretch—in the layby."

"Thanks, Dad—" the tall one stowed away the notes, and Savage watched them into the distance before walking stiffly towards the gate. Grand Slam—ripper language for the Psycho Correction Centre on a one-time airfield. Savage reflected that views had changed significantly in the past decade: rehabilitation was now a dirty word. Criminal tendencies weren't generated by bad environments, or bad parents; they were known psychological defects locked into the genes, and no amount of kind treatment was going to make a hooligan change his attitudes. It took deep-probing psychoanalysis and modern drugs, within a harsh and punishing regime, subjecting patients to permanent solitary confinement. The old-type associational prisons provided the best possible training for a criminal life—PPC was a straight choice offered to young rippers: several years' solitary, or a year at Abingdon.

Savage wondered what went on, within those walls; whatever it was, after nine years of operation not one inmate had ever gone back for a second helping. Which had to prove something.

He nodded to the Security man on duty and got in line for the Checking Gate. That Social Ostracism thing was something else, he pondered. No wonder so many kids took the short way out with drugs or a rope; to be totally banned from all public places, including transport, video theatres, football games, pubs, discos, was a terrible thing. So too was the strict reporting to the nearest police station, every hour, through the twenty-four; some of the yobs, he'd heard, actually slept on police station steps, afraid of missing a call—which stuck another month on the trip. But maybe the humiliation sessions really got the desired results: Saturdays, every city centre was filled with outlaws in yellow coveralls, pushing broom and trash-can, the harsh red 'V' surgically implanted on each brow. They all finished up there: the vandals, hooligans, muggers, amateur rapists, petty thieves—sweeping all through the long day, rain or shine.

He sighed, approaching the turnstile. It was becoming a stinker of a world—but the pressure-cooker lid had to be screwed down tight—the alternative was too frightening to contemplate. He slapped a palm on the read-out panel, said his name and works number aloud; the machine said 'click—beep—beep' and let him through.

Martin met him, walked with him towards the Administration Block. The tubby little man looked more than usually perturbed.

"They're still in there, talking, Don—" he gestured towards the Chairman's office on the ground floor. "Carl Wayne, two Navy types, David Perry, one or two others. The Telex machines are going crazy and they have two girls decoding nonstop."

"Any clues?" Savage said sharply, deliberately slowing his pace.

"Your guess is as good as mine, Don. I know they've got half the confidential staff files in there, with a portable computer terminal. Names'd make your hair stand on end. Oh—all drawing issues have been stopped—temporarily."

"Drawings? What in hell for?"

Martin shook his head. "Damned if I know, Don. Come on—we've time for a coffee before you go in there."

"Yay. There's a lot of activity on the old bird today—" Savage shaded his eyes, staring at the white superstructure towering above the rim of the dry dock.

The other stared, puzzled. "You forgotten, Don? They're activating the main drive today. The place is alive with nuclear engineers from EEC, the manufacturers."

"Oh, my God, so they are. You think that has anything to do with—?"

Savage grinned, a little shame-faced. They walked up to his office; Dee Purdy, the secretary Savage shared with David Perry, brought them coffee, and presently, when Martin was called away to investigate some petty theft, she hung on her heel, watching Savage, frowning.

"Don?" she said worriedly. "You all right?"

He produced a lop-sided grin. "Too much work, too little sleep. What's new?" The girl stared at him, her oval face a little pinched between twin strands of long silken hair. Short dark dress cut bleakly, fashionably; suede friction boots against the chill March weather, and the thin rubberoid-fabric gloves for paper-handling. She was as much a mystery to Don Savage this morning, as she had been on the day she first arrived, eighteen months ago. Her personal computer print-out said little: 24 years old, 57 kilos, height one metre seventy, unmarried, heterosexual, atheist, Grade Two breeding coding. Savage knew that she lived alone in a mobile home on Lepe Beach, four miles away; there were no adverse reports from previous employers and she shared the job with Gillian Fairbrother under Jobsplit regulations, handling the Monday–Thursday stint.

Dee Purdy was friendly but remote; almost a year elapsed before she and Savage reached first-name basis. Her face was rather plain, almost flat, with oblique, almost Oriental eyes, but her smile transformed her instantly into somewhat startling beauty; she was popular with the men, tolerated by women, and in warm weather she wore the fashionable short leather skirt, see-through shirt and painted nipples. Dee walked with a lazy, long-legged elegance which in the early days distracted Savage and most other men; he remembered spending hours watching her move around the office, but that was long ago, before the pressure built up, before *Albatross* began to take shape. The surveillance, he thought, went unnoticed—but he was wrong; Dee Purdy, very soon, began to think a great deal about the man himself, and in her lonely bed near the sea she fantasised to climax with visions of her boss pinning her to the top of her desk between legs flailing at the ceiling.

She was not altogether stupid. Her intuition sensed trouble in the Savage menage long before he—or Jan—locked horns. There was little she could do: only fill his needs at the office and take off as much pressure as possible. Normally, she would subdue her urgent need to know what troubled him; today, fear caught at her throat, settled ice-cold in her lower stomach. He was pale, unmistakably tired—lack of sleep was part but not all of it, for she had seen this condition too often of late.

"Don?"

"Huh?"

"I said—you look awful this morning—"

He grinned wryly. "Well, thanks. Now I've had my daily insult, I can start work. Don't worry, Dee—I'll survive. Bring the mail in—I have to make a Security meeting at nine. Anything else brewing?"

She hesitated. "David Perry's got a problem."

"So? Welcome to the Club . . . what is it?"

"That proposed visit by Members of Parliament—in April?" she said diffidently. Savage nodded. "Go on."

"They're coming today. Without warning—we had a Telex message a few minutes ago."

The Security man whistled. "My God. That's torn it. Today of all days. Arrival time, Dee?"

"Around eleven. Four of them—Ralph Bannerman—he's the Treasury man working with the *Albatross* project—you've met him?"

"I've met him. Checks spending of public money. But fair— very fair. Who else?"

The girl flushed. "That Weiskopf woman . . . you know . . ."

Savage knew the name by repute, the owner not at all. At 38, she was debatably the best-looking of the 100 women MPs now required under the Equal Rights legislation, sitting in the Social Democrat wing in North Commons. Savage's memory spewed up a distorted image of her Commons debut, wearing a red suedette dress split to the crotch, and six-inch heels. Foolishly, a doddering Tory MP had protested—and was howled down by the baying mob, and Betty Weiskopf's niche in history was assured.

Remembering, he grinned. "Who else?"

"Joe Pastorelli. Chairman of the Taxpayer's Union, or something. And that awful man Grainger."

Savage winced. That was a bad knock. Jim Grainger was notorious for many reasons—two expulsions from the House for obscene language; his spicy and libellous articles in the gutter magazines which earned him huge sums, and his scathing attacks on prominent people under the protection of the House, where they could not defend themselves. Grainger operated far to the left, exhibiting on every possible occasion his admiration for the Soviet Union; so much so that his home-brewed brand of Communism offended even Russia itself. Savage recalled stories of Grainger's private army of spies, informers, blackmailers, photographers, bug-men: little escaped the burly red-faced politician, and Savage swallowed hard. It *was* going to be a bad day . . .

Dee left him alone with his coffee and settled down at her desk to do some solid effective worrying.

In his office nearby, the *Albatross* Project Manager, David Perry, worked steadily on his fingernails, seeking unbitten areas with minimal success. He stood at the window and looked down over BHLC complex; it seemed to him that the pressures of responsibility, far from easing with seniority and experience, actually increased. Why did he feel, constantly, that he was wading waist-deep in liquid crap and getting nowhere at all?

Every time he solved one problem, two others popped up as replacements. In running a Design Project, Murphy's Law seemed to work fulltime: "If anything can go wrong, it will'. Invariably, changes of design became obvious *after* the main plans had been drawn; commonly known as the 'Now they tell us' syndrome. Further, the more innocuous any modification seemed to be, the greater its impact and the more involved the necessary changes became.

In the beginning, armed with a Design Study and Specifications for the *Albatross*, he believed, foolishy, that he might even finish her before deadline! He grinned crookedly, remembering how naïve he'd been . . . there'd been trouble with the Unions and trouble in deliveries. More snags with sub-manufacture and difficulties with supply. Changes in materials, systems, load factors and God knew what else. Without looking, he knew the state of the Progress Board on the office wall: the hoverliner was five weeks behind schedule—but it could have been worse.

He stared down at the immense dry dock, as large as two soccer fields end to end; a vast three-sided concrete box, sealed at the seaward end by steel gates so thick a roadway occupied the top, used by Yard transport. Within the box—*Albatross*: quiescent, immobile, most of her gleaming white superstructure in position. The 200-metre long triple hull rested on eight huge timer stacks; the pointed bow so like a jumbo jet aimed impatiently at the dock gates, as if straining to be free.

After two years, the sheer extravagance of the concept thrilled, yet appalled him: a slender 600-tonne glassfibre rocket, sliding through ocean waves upon a few feet of sidewall tip . . . a hurtling 300-knot juggernaut with tantalisingly accurate

control and stability. Perry rubbed his lower lip, lost in thought
. . . she resembled, in shape, an old-fashioned catamaran—but
there the similarity stopped. This bird would really fly . . .

"David?"

The designer swung round. "Yes, Dee?"

"Time for the Security meeting—"

"Ah . . . very good, Dee. You'll handle our calls?"

"Surely. Don't worry—" she smiled brilliantly, and he moved
out, heading for red-carpet country and the chairman's office.
Don Savage joined him on the stairs.

"Any clue what this is all about, David?"

"Search me. Dee says Admin Block's been in a frenzy since
early this morning. No-one's saying much—the only positive
thing I know is that the Print Room was told to suspend production of copy drawings."

Savage nodded. "So I hear, Dave. You know about Grainger
and Company?"

"God, yes. Trouble—with a capital T. Why hasn't someone
put a bullet into that man years ago?"

Savage humped a disillusioned shoulder. "Same reason bag-
pipe players march up and down—difficult to hit a moving target. Grainger's too damn smart to stay in one place too long—
they say he travels with half a dozen heavies for safety."

"You could be right . . ."

Carl Wayne was a big man—in every way. One metre ninety
tall, he could have served as a template for building a London
bus: broad, solid and a little worn at the edges after forty years
of infighting, wheeling and dealing. About hovercraft he knew
nothing; about running manufacturing companies, he knew it
all; he'd backed the first armoured troop-carrying hovercraft for
the US Navy as a private venture—and built a hundred just in
time for deployment in the Gulf War of 1989. They didn't stop
Russia blocking off the Straits of Hormuz—but they *did* haul
four US divisions out of Qatar and Kuwait before the gate
slammed shut. Wayne International operated out of the onetime
McGill University buildings in Montreal, but Wayne himself ran
the *Albatross* yard: it was his own baby, built half with his own
money and half from Government funds.

When Savage and Perry walked in, Wayne was in the centre of a tight group including Gabriel Wade, the Electronics Officer and Hoffman, the Chief Accountant. Two strangers were talking to Wayne: a tall Navy Commander in dress blues, and a civilian: short, brown hair surrounding an extensive bald patch, and dressed in impeccable pin stripes and black jacket. Friar Tuck in Whitehall, Savage thought whimsically.

"Don—David . . . you're late." Wayne smiled humourlessly. "Let's get to it."

Seated, Wayne wasted no time. "Meet Commander Chisholm—Ministry of Defence, Intelligence D2—and that's all you'll get out of him. A very tight-lipped gentleman—"

The Navy officer smiled bleakly.

"His friend is Mr Brewer, Home Office, attached to MOD-D2. I'm not sure what he does, exactly—"

"We're an obscure little department somewhere between MI5 and DI8—which may not help very much. I'm really only a civil servant, Mr Wayne—except that I specialise in the Soviet Navy." The man smiled deprecatingly.

Savage, with the others, stared curiously at the little rotund man. This was all very high-powered stuff—and there was only one area in which MOD were involved,—necessarily so, because they were putting up the money. Savage knew very little about RAZOR—the Radar invisibility research programme—but knew more than most people. He glanced at Gabriel Wade; the colourless eyes behind steel-rimmed glasses gave nothing away. Well . . . time would tell. Wayne was introducing his crew to the Navy men.

"Don Savage handles Security—very well indeed. David Perry—*Albatross* Project Manager. Garbiel Wade I think you've met—our electronics king. Our accountant, Bill Hoffman. And my secretary, Julie van Heusen."

Nods, mumbled greetings, inquisitive stares. Savage grinned.

"Commander Chisholm contacted me, late last night, with news concerning *Albatross* and parallel projects—"

Christ, Savage thought . . . the RAZOR thing is blown. Can't be anything else—

Wayne went on: "Julie, I'd like you to stay in the outer office until we finish here. No visitors, no calls. Understand?"

The girl nodded. Savage knew her basic history, as he did with most employees: efficient, experienced, imported by Wayne from the Montreal office. A plain, unobtrusive woman in her thirties, who avoided the heavy cosmetics bit and kept to herself. She smoked small thin cigars incessantly and guarded Wayne with the ferocity seen in nursing tigresses. She nodded impassively, got up and walked out.

Chisholm ran a lean forefinger along the trim grey moustache which matched his hair.

"Do all you gentlemen understand the provisions of the Official Secrets Act?" They stared back blankly, confused momentarily—but everyone nodded.

"Very well. This meeting is totally confidential: totally. I am based at HMS Vizier, Gosport—responsible for maritime security south of the Thames. Two days ago, London was contacted by Unistate—" he paused, eyed the puzzled faces surrounding the table. He sighed gently. "Unistate is the organisation formed by the Bush administration in the late '80s after public concern in the USA forced the dissolution of the CIA, FBI and NSA. One of their low-level Flash mini-satellites came up with something odd: its orbit covers a highspeed strip pattern photogrid survey of the Soviet Union, in random passes from Pole to Pole, with built-in irrational speed and altitude variation. The Soviets have tried—unsuccessfully—to knock the Flashes down—they are no bigger than a soccer ball and travel at Mach 10 or more around the 30-mile altitude.

"This—" he opened a buff envelope and extracted a stack of photographs—"is what it found. The area, about 5 square kilometres, is at Balyshin, at the north end of the Black Sea. Just east of Astrakhan—check it on the map, here. Note Print No. 1—clearly a small manufacturing complex near the port. Print Two, however, shows that the centre portion of the factory has a sliding roof, concealing a large dry dock. Print Three, infrared, taken at night, shows the roof open. There is something in the dock; does it suggest anything to you?"

Savage, with Perry, stared at the print between them. Across the table, Gabe Wade got out the pocket magnifier he used habitually. Perry said in a shocked voice:

"My God!"

Reaction varied; Wade sat back, print in hand, whistling gently under his breath. Hoffman, the accountant, tried to look surprised at something he knew nothing about. Carl Wayne sat immobile, like some giant dolmen stone in a silent jungle.

Savage leaned back in his seat, thinking hard. The craft in the dock was, to all intents and purposes, another *Albatross*: the long slender lines, the bow bridge, the aerodynamic stabilisers— a dead ringer. Only the aft superstructure seemed strange . . . He said as much.

"You're quite right, Mr Savage," Chisholm nodded. "It's a military version: that flat deck aft will take helicopters or jump-jets; the aft superstructure is probably a hangar. We think it carries a squadron of Bruins—Russian Harriers. We did the obvious thing and had our local sources investigate. These are much better of late, since the Polish–East German secession from the Warsaw Pact recently. However . . . a week ago, two workers in the Balyshin factory went on holiday to Albania, nipped across to Italy overnight and briefed our people.

"It seems the Russian version is near completion. The forward saloon now houses a number of Supersam missiles; the midships saloon some 400 Marines. They've fitted rocket torpedoes into the centre hull—they are Sharks. Cruise-type missiles which are fired underwater, take off and fly at zero feet to the target, dive to ten feet and wind up to high speed with rockets on final run-in. Altogether, a very impressive package."

Chisholm paused, waiting for the buzz of comment to die down. Wayne, Savage noted, sat in stony silence: he'd heard it all before.

"Two things," Chisholm continued, "are apparent. First, the general design, including main drive, is identical—which means that they have obtained our production drawings literally off the computer-board itself. They seemed to be about three months behind you people here—and with the problems associated with manufacturing special items, that seems remarkably good.

"Secondly,—as far as we know, and I say this with reserva-tions—they are not onto RAZOR. That project, as I understand it, is financed by MOD quite separately from the *Albatross* programme. Mr Hoffman?"

44

The accountant stirred uneasily. "Correct, Commander. I must say, Mr Wayne, that, while I have repeatedly asked for more information on RAZOR, this has been denied me. Surely it is essential that I know what our own money and that of the Government is being spent on. How else can I ensure we are getting value with minimum waste?"

Wayne said tightly: "The less people that know about RAZOR the better. Gabriel—how many people on your clear list?"

"Yourself, Glencannon—the MOD electronics liaison man—Bob Foster, my senior systems expert, Don Savage and myself."

Chisholm stared at the man in the steel-rimmed spectacles. "That all? Mr Wayne—anyone else?"

The Chairman's eyes glared under shaggy brows. "Julie van Heusen knows *of* RAZOR—but not what it is. No worries there."

"I see. Only the people on your list, Mr Wade, possess the computer access key code—right? Very well—let's keep it that way. I know you people are under great pressure to get the *Albatross* finished and on her way to New York—as a commercial venture. Obviously, a successful debut will lead to military orders. We know the Warsaw Pact, like everyone else, isn't short of oil—but what they have is very expensive, and exploitation of the Siberian fields is proving very difficult. For thirty years the major powers have used large jet transports for troop movements; surface troopships are totally vulnerable to air or missile attacks. Until such time as the alternate source is perfected, any highspeed movement of men or supplies over long distances will be a problem—and ocean-going hovermarines like the *Albatross* seem to provide the answer.

"We now know the Soviets can build such craft—but even highspeed hovermarines are easy targets for radar-guided missiles. RAZOR is a development of the Stealth research programmes started in America a decade ago; it provides total radar invisibility on all frequencies, plus a 90% probability of infra-red invisibility. Such a system will give the West a huge advantage—such that the future of the Free World may depend upon it. You see, now, gentlemen, why H.M. Government is so

45

concerned: we are under direct instructions from the King himself, through the Sea Lords, to push the programme through to full term.

"Two tasks before us: First, stop the leak, find the mole. The Soviets have had all the help we're going to give; from now on, they are on their own. Second—increase security around RAZOR. That is absolutely vital."

Presently, Carl Wayne said: "Gabriel, you'll have to change your computer access code at once. And brief your staff. My main worry is on the shop floor—anyone been asking awkward questions?"

"I think we are all right in that area, Carl. The metal web antenna was built in during hull lay-up, moulded into the fibreglass shell of the craft. Without going into detail, the antenna covers all exposed areas of the craft and senses incoming radar waves. It determines the wavelength and frequency, absorbs the impulses to prevent reflection, and transmits instead a radar image showing zero returns, back to the source."

David Perry said: "Zero returns?"

"We have radar scanners around the superstructure. If a probe impulse comes in from the east, the return signal shows an empty sea towards the west. The party at the other end receives an accurate picture on the correct frequency—except the craft is missing."

The designer grinned. "I like it. No wonder you've kept it under wraps, Gabe. Is that all there is to it?"

"The control box is ready for installation. It resembles an air-conditioning plant, so that's how it's labelled. Mounted in the forward electrical bay under the bridge, controlled from the helmsman's seat and the Captain's position."

Carl Wayne stood up slowly. "Don, I want maximum effort on finding our mole. I want a report twice a day—we may be too late for what's gone, but I'm damned if they'll have any more. Anything you need, you get—money no object. Bill, you hear me?"

The accountant nodded. "I hear."

"Fine. Don, any suggestions?"

Savage considered briefly. "A few. First, I want to dump all external security onto an outside firm—to man the gates, patrol

46

the fence. This leaves my men free for inside work. Costly—but necessary."

"Agreed. Next?"

"This suspension of drawing issues: I can't see that will help much. The shop floor needs the material. As I see it, we're deep into final fitting-out; all the main design work is finished. I think we're closing the stable door—too late."

"David?" the Chairman glanced at Perry.

"I'm with Don. Except half of my drawing office is working on the first military version—but the way I see it, those bastards are way ahead of us there."

"Okay," Wayne nodded agreement. "We'll release production drawing as of now. But we have to find this . . . this *person*—" there was a wealth of emotion in the big man's voice, and Savage became aware, in that moment, what this development meant to the Canadian, how deeply he was emotionally involved.

"Mr Wayne—the real problem is checking out every employee. We have around 1800 on the books—it'd take a small army to run a personal search on every one."

"Hire your army, Don. I told you—forget costs. Do it—"

"Right."

Wayne nodded his head and turned to Chisholm.

"Commander?"

"That sounds fine, Mr Wayne. Naturally, we'll be working on this ourselves. We have something going to slow them down a bit on the Black Sea—"

"Sabotage?"

"Something along those lines. Carefully applied, of course—"

David Perry said: "Won't that tip them off we're onto them?"

"Good point, Mr Perry. Naturally, we'll take care of that end. Perfectly normal accidents—no human involvement."

Perry said hesitantly: "You don't get my meaning. If we try that stuff over there, won't they do the same to us? I mean—if they're so near completion as you say, it's to their advantage to slow *us* down a little."

"We'd already covered that aspect," Chisholm said firmly. "We have certain arrangements in hand: there are some US Navy ships in Southampton we can call on for help. You see—"

his deepset eyes moved from face to face around the table—
"we know the Russians would gain enormous political advantage
out of launching first. They are quite capable of accusing *us* of
stealing their design—and publishing photographs to prove it.
If two people claim prior invention of a device, the world always
believes the first to show it works. Which all adds up to a very
big problem for you, Mr Savage—"

"You can say that again . . ."

Wayne said smoothly: "Don can handle it, Commander.
Believe me—"

*If he knew, Savage thought, agonizingly. If he only bloody
knew . . . After an hour in this damned chair, I'm going to fall
flat on my face when I get up. Jesus, how can I ever cope with
this . . . I'm a nervous wreck and half a cripple . . . with six
weeks to go to launch, I daren't leave the complex . . . have to
get a cot set up in my office. Jan . . . Christ, there'll be a row
when I tell her. First things first . . . just let me make my office
and I have a fighting chance. He began massaging a numb
right thigh gently under the table, flexing his leg, fighting to
restore circulation. Lord, he thought grimly . . . if You exist
any place around here, now's the time to show Your hand. All
I need is a pair of new legs . . .*

The meeting closed, Savage got up, stood for a moment waiting for the crowd to get clear and walked stiffly to the door.
Perry glanced at him anxiously.

"You okay, Don?"

"Sure. Touch of cramp. That damn chair was solid wood, I
reckon. Let's go—"

They went through into the outer office; Wayne had stopped
to talk briefly to Julie, and they waited quietly, unable to pass.
Savage's eyes moved incuriously around the office, waging a
neutral battle against the dull ache above his knees; abruptly,
he froze, head bent towards the desk.

The small audio box, elegant in natural teak, carried a single
switch alongside the combined speaker-microphone: the switch
was set to 'ON'. Without haste, he walked back into Wayne's
office, checked the audio box on the executive desk at the far
end of the room, clear of the conference table. The switch was

'on', too: he could hear Wayne and Julie discussing changes in computer access codes.

Savage stood there for a long time, absently rubbing a forefinger on the edge of the desk. Almost casually, he turned off the audio switch and walked out of the room; Julie was behind her desk, dialling a telephone number, and Wayne had gone, presumably with the Navy people.

The girl glanced up.

"Forgot my notebook," Savage lied.

She smiled.

Her audio switch was 'off'.

Savage nodded gently. "Have a nice day, Julie."

She sat for a long moment, forefinger poised over the phone punchboard, staring after him. Presently, she moistened her lips with a pink tongue, shrugged and turned back to the telephone.

3 *Too Late for Rommel*

The Capitol restaurant occupies a corner site in down-town Tunis, on the Boulevard Michel which borders the waterfront La Goulette section. Behind dimly-lit main streets lie hectares of dark and unspeakably filthy hovels, dirt roads, open sewers. Tunisia is oil-poor compared to Libya; secondary roads remain dark from one Ramadhan to the next, such that their inhabitants themselves are afraid to walk aboard after sunset. Streets reek of excrement, dead fish, rotting garbage, human sweat, unwashed goats; white visitors are as rare as Sahara blizzards.

A travel bureau fills the entire ground floor. It will—if pressed—make reservations, arrange tourist expeditions to Marrakech for those mad enough to travel, and charge exorbitant rates in the process. As a clearing-house for vast quantities of the up-country cannabis crop, it operates with coarse efficiency, receiving in its capacious back yard the trains of stolid camels which arrive throughout the hours of darkness.

The casual visitor to the Capitol enters via a side entrance barred by a heavy black-painted door adorned with polished brass studs and locks; such doors are commonly used in Casbah brothels, and all feature the tiny hinged surveillance panel through which callers are identified. Each has its Cerberus: the human watchdog serving the Capitol went under the name Ali Fawzi. But that was neither the name bestowed on him by his mother—whom he never knew—nor the name by which he was known and listed in police stations from Alexandria to Casablanca. Ali, it must be related, had a peculiar propensity for fun and games with young children—of both sexes.

Presently, he was preoccupied with the visitor who said his name was McDowd . . . In a country where white clothing was almost mandatory, the dark business suit and long black overcoat verged on the bizarre; the black Homburg hat was totally alien to Ali's experience. Nor was he totally at ease with the person contained in this strange clothing: grotesquely tall, thin as a rail, a gaunt, almost skeletal face with eyes recessed deep into grey shadows . . .

The doorman grasped the folded 10,000-franc note firmly and went through his routine with bolts, locks and keys intended to impress the tourist; inside, the man stood head high over the squat Arab, and climbed the stairs effortlessly, three at a time, long black-clad legs going like pistons. Ali stared after him, frowned, found a leaf or two of hash in his pouch and sat on the lower step, chewing contemplatively. A man to stay away from . . . Allah alone knew how a man like that would react to insults . . .

McDowd sank into the chair at the balcony rail, nodded curtly to the two men at the table and began watching the boulevard traffic below. There were fewer gharries, he thought, working the streets. The tiny ponies hauling four-wheel open carriages were walking skeletons, working a 20-hour day, driven in shifts by their owner-families. They hauled tourists until they dropped dead—frequently in heavy traffic—where they were left for the city knacker's yard to collect. The Irsihman frowned: how could people treat animals so? Horses, back home in Dungannon, were treated almost as equals.

There were many donkeys: once native to desert and mountain, they were increasingly valuable as town transport in a land where petrol cost the equivalent of £25 for 5 litres. A handful of cars—he could see a number of the economical but incredibly expensive French electric runabouts. The occasional gas-powered saloon with a billowing black rubber bag on the roof and the shit-machine mounted in the rear bumper . . . no shortage of fuel in Tunis. McDowd spotted one very long black Rolls-Cadillac with opaque-screened windows and armed scooter out-riders . . . a locak sheikh? More likely a Jewish oil broker . . . Across the table, the slim Frenchman stirred impatiently.

"Well, Macdow?"

"McDowd. With a 'D'—for the fiftieth time." The Irishman sighed.

"So—whatever." The other waved a brown hand disarmingly. A heavy gold bracelet swung at the wrist; all four fingers held incandescent rings, and McDowd's nostrils flared at the hint of body scent. "You have news?"

"The word," the Irishman said softly, "is 'go'. Immediate."

Jean Paul beamed, nudged Saif in delight and picked up his glass.

"Excellent! Salut, Macdow. And the money?"

"One million Swiss francs—in Kruggerands, split three ways. Plus costs . . . they wanted to pay in US dollars . . ."

The others hooted with laughter; McDowd's thin and elongated face, raddled with the sadness of his country's tragedy, relaxed briefly in a wry smile. Saif Ibn Achmed leaned over, laid a brown hand on McDowd's forearm. "Naturally, you refused—"

"Naturally. But they were generous with expenses . . . fortunately. We have equipment to buy, travel arrangements to be made. Listen—"

He broke open a pack of Splits, lighted the fat joint—half tobacco, half prime grass—and inhaled deeply. Slowly, he allowed the smoke to escape from flaring nostrils.

"Listen," he said again, "I have been here five minutes and

divil a drink I see before me. Nor a bite of food for a hungry man. I thought I'd trained you two better than that . . . damn yer eyes. I suppose you've already fed yer faces?"

They assured him, fervently, that they awaited his arrival.

The Irishman laid his coat on the rail, ordered crevettes, an entrecôte steak and wine; the Arab favoured some obscure and revolting dish of broiled goat intestine and sheep eyes, it seemed to McDowd. Jean Paul, who ate infrequently in public, settled for some wine and cheese. They talked quietly over the meal.

"Paul—" the Irishman dipped a chilled crevette into steaming mayonnaise and closed his eyes, savouring the superb Mediterranean shrimp at its best—"you must learn patience. There will be work in plenty very soon; I know Saif here is getting fat and soft sleeping with too many women. Whatever happened to the PLO, Saif?"

The Arab stared with ill-concealed anger. "You know what happened, McDowd. They settled for the Sinai—a million square hectares of desert—and the Jews' money. My people were fools . . . they should have kept fighting. Driven the Jews into the sea before they occupied Syria, Lebanon, Jordan. Now, their empire spreads like a cancer . . ."

"The Palestinians are doing all right, Saif, and you know it. Solar stills, plenty of water, irrigation projects. Why, they've even found oil down near Aqaba."

"We are fighting men, McDowd. That is why I am here, with you. Farmers do not need fighting men."

"Well," the Irishman said philosophically, "your cut from this operation will make you feel better. Starting tomorrow, we go to work. Not much time."

"How much time?"

"Eight days, Jean Paul. No more. After fitting out, one dress rehearsal—then we go to war."

"Equipment?" the Arab said curiously.

McDowd watched the thick-set man in the beige tropical suit with something approaching affection; those black expressionless eyes never changed. He had seen them gazing into the eyes of dying men held up only by Saif's knife in their ribs, and they seemed to be asking for answers to the eternal questions of Life

52

and Death. Only three, perhaps four, men had ever gained McDowd's unqualified approval: of those, only with Saif would he ever feel totally safe. The man was a professional with a tally of 30 or more field executions, excluding those many others killed in casual combat; moreover, he had one priceless virtue McDowd valued above all: he was quite immune to panic, always cool and in full control.

McDowd said: "How long since you two handled underwater gear?"

They glanced at each other: the Frenchman grimaced. "I can dive, McDowd—but I do not like it. Too many things in the sea with sharp teeth and an appetite for young French boys—"

Saif's teeth flashed. "Out of the sea, also, McDowd. You should see his Italian woman . . ."

"All right—" the tall Irishman finished eating, pushed his plate away, lighted a Split. "The job," he said flatly, "involves Plastique UD. Know what it is?"

"The new cutting explosive?"

"Right, Paul. Saif?"

"I know of it—I have not used it."

"O-kay," McDowd extended the prefix syllable comfortably. "UD is a uni-directional polarised plastic, packed in sealed polythene sausages half a metre long, weighing around ten kilos. A contact adhesive strip down one side allows the stuff to stick to anything—in or out of water."

He drew heavily on the Split, the end glowing like charcoal. Then—

"The bag is slit with a knife after being fixed to the target. Insert a detonator quickly and the outer skin of the UD hardens into a tight molecular bond which resists, for a micro-second, the force of the explosion. Clear so far?"

They nodded in mute concentration.

"The UD explodes inwards along the contact face—where it is needed. Excellent for safe-blowing, opening up security vans and high-speed amputations—we don't use shotguns these days."

He squashed the butt of his cigarette, wiped his face with a clean tissue; the night was becoming warm, humid.

"We meet two nights from now on the beach at Bahdour Point, twenty clicks south of Tunis. Half an hour before midnight, local time. There will be a boat, with equipment, to meet us. What we have to do will take perhaps an hour. When we have finished, the boat takes us to France, to a beach near San Tropez; we take the electric train to Le Havre. There we collect our main equipment. The target is in England."

Jean Paul said softly: "Ah. England."

"I know," said McDowd, "that you are wanted there. Don't worry—we don't land at all. Questions?"

"Only one," Jean Paul smiled brilliantly. "Money?"

"When we've earned it, me boy. When we've earned it. Now . . . I think we might try another bottle of that wine . . . it's rubbish, an' I'll be glad when I've had enough. However . . ."

Saif said quietly: "It is a defended target, McDowd?"

"It is not," the Irishman said explosively. "It'll be so easy I might feel guilty taking their money . . ." He grinned wolfishly.

"You didn't say who is paying—" the Arab toyed with his glass.

"That I didn't—and 'tis no concern of yours, Saif. I'll tell you this, though—they're not short of a million or two. It's like money in the Bank of England."

Jean Paul said: "I seem to remember the Bank of England went broke years ago . . ."

"Figger of speech, ould lad. Figger of speech. Drink up, now . . ."

Night. Dark, moonless, glass-clear, starlight pale incadescence on purple. The constellations burned overhead, rich glowing flares in a bottomless universe, totally oblivious of the existence of a minor planetary system round a small 'G' type star, far out along a spiral arm of a galaxy lost in a billion similar systems. Jean Paul Marin, enduring the discomfort of a rocky ledge, nursed a lacerated shin, craving a cigarette he dared not light. The harsh rock and shale coastline paralleling the black tarmac road was moth-eaten with bays and coves almost inaccessible from the mini-cliffs; from the point at which they left their rented gas-driven Renault truck, he and Saif had fought their way down through the tamarisk groves, following a path fit only for mountain goats, between man-high cacti with lethal spines.

The rock upon which he sat was black, porous, volcanic: armed with a thousand cutting edges—the sea, a hundred metres distant, washed and thundered on the shingle and he could smell the rank untreated sewage which polluted half the Mediterranean.

When McDowd came—*if* he came—he would smoke, Jean Paul promised himself. Beside him, further along the ledge, Saif Ibn Achmed sat immobile; as still as the rock itself. It was unnatural, Jean Paul thought irritably, that anyone could remain thus without moving, for ten, fifteen minutes—but then, *merde*—the man was from some filthy country far to the east, full of nothing but snakes and sand and shit . . . what could you expect?

He checked his watch again. 23.37 . . . the Irishman was late. Jean Paul began once more to search the shoreline, seeking the black shape that might be a boat; the grey-white foam wavered eerily in the half-light of the stars and he shivered, pulling his windproof closer about him.

An inch under his right ear, a small circle of flesh felt abruptly cold, under pressure; he started violently, the gun-muzzle following his withdrawal as if glued in place. The Frenchman froze into shocked immobility, a thin stream of urine on the inside of a thigh.

"Now," an Irish voice breathed in his ear, "where would yez be, me bucko, if I'd been after being someone else? Somebody nasty? ALL RIGHT, SAIF! RELAX!"—the Arab had slid fluidly into the shadow as soon as McDowd spoke. Two metres away he slid the knife back into a forearm sheath and said reprovingly:

"One of these days, McDowd—you will risk too much!"

The tall man laughed softly. "Maybe so, Saif. But it's business we're about. As of now, we're on war footing. If I catch either of you sitting scratching your arse when you should be looking for trouble—you'll find it. This is for real, and cock-ups I will not have. Not in McDowd's Foreign Legion. Clear?"

Jean Paul said stiffly: "Clear. You will not catch me like that again—"

"I'd better not, young fella. Now—I got here first. The boat dropped our gear down the beach and put out to sea. Exactly two clicks out from that point, on a heading of zero eight two magnetic, a ship lies in nine fathoms on a sandy bottom."

"Fathoms?"

"About twenty metres, Saif. 'Tis a German supply ship, sunk in 1942 on the way from Sicily with stores for Rommel. Now— we go out to her under water. You'll find a target square on the hull; Jean Paul carries the UD, Saif the detonators.

"Now, listen carefully. I'll only say it once. Strip off the sealing tape, stick the plastique along the target line. Cut the bag, insert the detonator quick. The UD hardens very quickly. Clear?"

"Go on, please."

"They are standard US Navy Mark sixteen detonators, radio-activated, working on a 5-band interlocked coded trans-mission to avoid accidents. You arm them by rotating the head a quarter turn and pushing down hard—you'll hear a click. They'll be detonated from the boat at exactly 1 a.m. local time— which gives us an hour to make the trip and reach the boat. Which will be 500 metres due east of the wreck. Compris?"

"Yes—"

"Right. I have my wet suit on already; I'm going to the wreck to watch. Follow instructions very carefully—I'm too young to die but old enough to be nervous. Don't forget your compasses . . . 62 minutes to detonation. GO!"

In the darkness, the one-time IRA man grinned widely. There were two empty holes in the air, recently vacated by his col-leagues; he walked slowly down to the surf, slipped into harness, bit on the mouthpiece, slid down the mask. Flippers on, he waded out until the cream foam washed around his waist, ducked and vanished.

Jean Paul cursed silently. The mad Irish had mentioned the sandy bottom but omitted savage currents, streaming kelp, poor visibility. Burdened with explosive, fighting his way onward, shoals of slim fish ballooning on the rim of visibility: he checked the time again, worriedly. Beside him, Saif grasped a rocky outcrop, waved a hand . . . Jean Paul pointed at his watch, punched a fist forward twice and ploughed on.

Almost by accident, he rammed up against the old rusted hull encrusted in weed and barnacle, and stopped, waiting. He pointed at himself, waved left; pointed at Saif, waved right. Pointed to his watch, held up two fingers and pointed downwards. The Arab nodded, comprehending. They parted; Jean Paul began working his way down the hull.

The ship—probably about 5000 tonnes—lay on her bottom, but listed heavily starboard; he found a massive hole amidships, shone his torch into the blackness and decided to leave well alone. The big conger was prior owner and gaped wide in challenge.

Five metres on, a patch of hull, roughly cleared, displayed a three-sided square of white sticky paint which glowed dimly in torchlight. He motored back and found Saif and they hung motionless in the slack water, each wondering what dead cargo lay within those steel walls. How many men slept eternity away here? Down with the fish and the weed and sand?

His watch said 39 minutes had elapsed; Jean Paul slipped off the lethal garland, waved Saif off with the detonators, sweat breaking out afresh in his hair. He ripped away sealing tape, slapped a plastic frankfurter along the white line, went on to the next. With all in contact, he waved Saif forward, slashed the first package open; the Arab rammed in a detonator, twisted and pushed, grinned at Jean Paul through his visor and on to the next, the UD changing colour to a deep angry red as they progressed, assuming a glossy sheen and feeling rock-hard to the touch. They took a last quick look, turned and moved off to the east, legs going like pistons, arms flush at their sides, to put maximum distance between themselves and the horror behind.

They climbed slowly to the one-metre level, reluctant to sacrifice speed, pausing briefly once to avoid trouble with blood nitrogen; nine minutes later, they picked up the dim light suspended from the anchored motor cruiser and surfaced and, almost before they were aboard, the two big MAN diesels roared throatily. The boat began steady acceleration up to 40 knots, turning slowly north.

On the shadowy aft deck, illuminated only by a blue sea light, they stripped off, staring furiously at McDowd, immaculate in blue jacket, white slacks and yachting cap. He held out two large whiskies and beamed down at his troops.

"McDowd! Pig! Pervert! You filthy—" Jean Paul groped for the words he wanted, shaking visibly with rage. "You were not there! You let us do this thing alone!"

On the unseen horizon, night became day. A deep red balloon emerged from a dazzling white flash, climbed steadily, writhing like some living creature in mortal agony. Seconds later, a stunning pressure wave followed a dull resonant explosion, reaching out for the speeding boat, laying her on her beam ends. The helmsman fought the wheel, brought her out of it, and they surged onwards into the north.

"Now," McDowd said mockingly, "now you know why, me lads. With all that nasty stuff down there, why—a man could get himself hurt. But I knew you two decent men could handle it all right, all right. And so yez did . . ."

The Frenchman accepted a lighted cigarette from a crewman with trembling fingers and glared at McDowd. "That explosive— it is very strong—"

"It is that," said Mr McDowd smugly. "Of course, the other stuff down there helped a liddle bit . . ."

"Other stuff?" Saif Ibn Achmed said sharply.

"Didn't I tell yez, now? Surely I did . . ." McDowd said innocently.

They stared at him, straddle-legged, balancing with ease against the motions of the launch. His eyes glowed, reflecting the dim blue running light.

"'Twas a supply ship, d'ye see. For Ould Rommel himself. He could have done with that ammunition, no doubt at all, at all. So he could—"

"Ammunition?"

"Isn't that what I'm tellin' ye? About two thousand tons of it." The Irishman stood tall and stark, and they could sense, rather than see, the sardonic grin on the thin face. "Here, now . . . have another whisky. Put a bit of lead in them ould pencils of yours . . ."

4 *The Body Politik*

The day started well for Savage. Jan was away on a three-day computer course; he had slept on a bunk in the Guardroom the night before, using the evening to clear a vast amount of paperwork. Earlier, he had called a briefing session of his crew and it had gone well, he thought.

Yesterday, after the meeting, he and Perry walked back to the offices, talking desultorily about the problems facing them: Perry deeply perturbed about the visit of the politicians, Savage about the new situation.

"I don't see what you have to be worried about, Dave," Savage commented. The noon-break whistle was sounding; men and women gravitating towards the works canteen, walking, half-running. "They're only bloody MPs after all. What can they do?"

"They can cost me my job, Don. That's what."

"You're crazy! How can that be?"

Gradually the story came out. Unknown to Savage, the Design Office had gone through a traumatic period in the past six months; Perry found his time schedule falling further and further behind, until the beginning of October, when he found the shop floor was waiting for production drawings—literally. Several systems including electrics, hydraulics and machinery foundations were actually at a standstill.

The basic problem was Jobsplit. Like every other company, British Hoverliner took on additional labour, sharing jobs between two, three, sometimes four, people. It made sense in an Alice-in-Wonderland fashion—but gave managers constant headaches. Perry explained.

"Don, in ordinary manual jobs, no problem. Carpentering, laying up fibreglass, producing system components. But how in hell can you get two creative people like design draughtsmen to work on a system together? Listen—ask ten designers to work out a system and they'll produce ten different designs. They'll all work—some better than others, some more costly, others heavier—you know what I mean. Talk about rows! All through last summer we had arguments, stand-up fights—I spent most of my time arbitrating between pairs of crazy people determined to see their own ideas on an automated design screen. We were getting more and more behind deadline . . ."

He stopped, opened his door and walked in. Savage followed and they sat waiting for Dee to bring in coffee. The Security man shook his head. "That's the craziest thing I ever heard, Dave. Hell, it's like forcing two painters to work together, or asking two musicians to play the same instrument. I mean—with a piano, okay—but a saxophone, or a flute? It's madness!"

Dee came in, glanced concernedly at Savage and decided whatever she was going to say could wait; she dumped the coffee in front of the men and stalked out.

"What the hell's wrong with her?"

Perry ignored the question.

"In the end, Don, I decided to sort the thing out myself. Look, I know the basic idea of job-sharing is good: even if a man only works two days a week, at least he has a job. It's a question of pride . . ."

"So—what did you do?"

"I told all the two-men teams to decide who would drop out. There was no way I could sack them, but quite a few had had enough of the arguments anyway. Others had work they could do on the side; still others were overdue for a break anyway. I ended up with about thirty draughtsmen working a full day, and a similar number at home doing nothing. Carl Wayne helped— he found the extra cash to pay the working crews; since then, we've caught up on the programme—we're even a little ahead. Everyone's happy, and the place ticks over like a sewing machine."

Savage held a hand to his head. "I don't get it. You iron out a problem like that and you say it may cost you your job?"

"Don't be a clod all your life, Don. Who do you think introduced Jobsplit, five or six years ago?"

"Huh? Oh my God—don't tell me. Let me guess. Grainger?"

"Dead right. You know what I think? I think he's got wind of what I did—and he's come to chop off a few heads—mine included."

Savage said thoughtfully: "Outside of the drawing office, who knew about it?"

"Carl Wayne, of course. Bill Hoffman—the Accounts section arranged payment, but he's a decent sort, Bill—he wouldn't talk out of turn. He arranged to pay the design crew himself via the payroll comptuer. I suppose quite a few people in the works caught on, too."

Savage nodded. "I'm thinking about the union people—"

"Sinclair's the ASTMS and TASS man in the works: he liked the idea."

"Really?" Savage grinned. "I wonder why—"

"Because he's a design draughtsman himself, on the team!"

"It figures," Savage nodded. "It figures. So now what?"

Perry said glumly: "So now Grainger and that red-haired cow'll be in here soon to have my guts for garters. Anyway— what the hell? The design task is virtually complete—my job's about finished any time now. And you know what? The way I feel now, I don't give a damn. When I think about those bastards over there pinching every bloody drawing as it comes off the computer, building that thing step by step along with us if I knew who did the dirty work this end . . ."

Savage said softly: "I may be able to tell you, soon."

"What?"

"Our little friend Julie van Heusen needs watching, Dave. When we were in that meeting, she was listening to every word through her audio box. Now, it may be just feminine curiosity— but I doubt it."

Perry stared at the lined, ravaged face in front of him. "You're kidding!"

"I kid you not, feller. She's my number one suspect. Loyal to Carl Wayne she may be—but she's working for some other party as well. Look—I have to go. Your bloodhounds'll be arriving any moment. They can't go on the craft—you're fitting the main drive reactor in the morning, right?"

"Yes. But—"

"So I'll get my little men out with red flags and seal the boat off. You can show 'em the works canteen and your own offices and the factory toilets—but that's all."

"Don," Perry said warmly, "you're a genius. Get to it . . ."

Around two o'clock, Savage called a war party meeting in his office with Eddie Caldwell, Jack Martin and a few of the others. They listened bleakly to his briefing and were at no pains to hide their anger; as Martin pointed out—

"They've made bloody monkeys out of us, Don. It's our job to make sure things like that don't happen—"

"Check," Savage said tightly. "Carl Wayne didn't say the same thing—but he didn't have to. I feel just as bad as you. Point is, now we know—and we can do something. Eddie, I want you out of the factory for the next few days. Take a list of all employees—and I *mean* all—and hire private investigators wherever you can get 'em. We want fast results, cost no object; see Bill Hoffman and he'll give you an open cheque. We have about 1800 people; you need about 90 operatives, taking about 20 people each. I want a full run-down, with emphasis on anyone spending above their means, people with left-wing interests, people spending holidays in Redland. You know the form— questions?"

"No questions."

"Right. Report to me noon and six pm daily on the phone. If you strike oil, I want to know the day before. Got it?"

"Way ahead of you, Don."

Savage grinned. He was feeling better already. "On your way, then—"

Jack Martin looked at his boss curiously. "I thought you'd give me a job like that. I worked with several of the big London outfits before I came here."

"I have something special for you, matey. Listen—" Savage gave his Number Two a run-down on Julie van Heusen. At the end, Martin whistled.

"Lucky break, seeing that switch."

"Sometimes," Savage said bluntly, "we need a break—and never more than now. I want you to have some firm in Montreal take her to pieces, up to the time she came over with Wayne— two years ago? Three . . . okay. Make that a priority. Next— I'm handing over external security for the complex to Blood-hound Company in London—they'll have three dozen men here four hours after I call. Thereafter, all our people have just one job: internal security. They must watch everyone, everywhere, all the time: if a garbage man farts, I want to know before it drifts downwind. In particular, you keep everyone away from Gabe Wade's section—I'd like a man for each of his people, and two on full-time duty aboard *Albatross*—he'll brief you on that. Next—you watch our little Julie yourself. I don't care how you do it—I want to know everything she does, everyone she speaks to, everywhere she goes. Sooner or later, she'll make contact with someone—and that's who I want. I want him so bad I hurt. Do I make myself clear?"

It seemed he did. They went into details; Garner came up with a good point.

"Boss, you say most of the design work is done. Chances are, she won't risk taking any more chances: she'll figure it's not worth the candle."

"So?"

"So—I spend most of my spare time fishing. How about dropping a little groundbait in the water?" Garner pressed.

"I—think I see what you mean. We should—"

"Sure! Suppose we have the Drawing Office issue an urgent instruction that something isn't quite safe—say, something to do with the main drive. How do they handle that normally?"

Savage thought quickly. "They issue something called a D.A. Sheet—Design Alteration. They give them various priorities . . ."

"So if Julie saw a D.A. demanding urgent changes in the design, for safety reasons . . ."

"She'd break her back to pass the message on. Joe, you've earned yourself a dirty weekend in Paris for that. I'll go see David Perry right away—"

He didn't get to see the Project Manager right away. Dee Purdy stopped him in the corridor, face pale and set.

"Don, you can't go in. There's the most frightful row going on . . . those MPs are in there . . . David's keeping hold of his temper—but only just."

Savage smiled. "You can hear from your office?"

"Every word . . ."

"Lead me to it. I got an axe to grind here . . ."

Dee was perfectly right. Savage straddled a chair near the connecting door and listened . . .

"My Perry, do you deny you refused thirty design engineers the right to work?"

"I do. I gave them the option of working or taking a sabbatical. The choice was their own, Mr Grainger. And incidentally—how did you get to hear about this?"

"That's immaterial," Grainger roared. Savage thought his voice sounded just as it did over Parliamentary radio—rough, uneducated, egotistical as all hell. Heavy feet tramped the floor in the next room. "Under the Shared Employment Act everyone is entitled to share in available work. You've spent a great deal of money paying men to be idle—taxpayer's money—"

"Not true, Mr Grainger; that cash came specifically from the BHLC contingency fund. Eventually, out of profits—if we finish the craft on time. Six months ago we were months behind schedule, because you'll never get creative men to share creative work. Now, we're only 5 weeks overdue—"

"Aha!"

"—due entirely to delays in supply of sub-manufactured items from other factories—factories where, I should point out, job-sharing is forcibly applied by the trades unions—"

Betty Weiskopf barged in, furious and fairly stuttering with emotion.

"It's obvious you hate trades unions, Mr Perry," she snarled.

"Here's my TASS membership card, ma'am."

Savage clapped a hand over his mouth . . . David needed no help . . .

"And less of the 'madam', young man; I don't run knocking-shops for a living and don't you forget it . . ."

There was a long pregnant silence in the next office; Perry was floored by that extraordinary statement, just for a moment. Then—

"Mrs Weiskopf, I have no strong feelings either way. One thing I do know—most workers in this country work up to ten hours overtime. Every four workers steal the job of a fifth who really wants work. If they all worked a straight 35- or 36-hour week, you could reduce unemployment by a half. But that's by the way. Let me give you some figures: the design task has been completed on time, because I have shown that job-sharing is good only for non-creative jobs. If we launch on time and make New York, there'll be jobs for tens of thousands of people, building the hoverliners and military hovermarines of the future. We'll have gained all that—by bending a stupid rule just enough to give us room to work. Now—if you want my job, or my head, you go right ahead. We've made it—and be damned to you."

Savage waited. Presently, he heard a new voice. Pastorelli?

"You know, Jim . . . there's some sort of sense in all this. Sure, Mr Perry's broken the rules—and if he'd failed to produce we could skin him alive. But he hasn't: he's succeeded in making something which may mean a lot to this country. I'm not saying he'd have failed, by sticking to rules; just that it would have taken a great deal longer to get there. And that would have cost us dearly in the long run. I would say on the face of it that you two seem to be the only people dissatisfied with the whole business. You can raise this in the House if you like—but don't blame me if you get a fruit pie in the face."

Betty Weiskopf hissed: "I don't believe what I hear, Joe Pastorelli. Your Taxpayer's Union have put a lot of money into this project and I don't believe the thing will ever reach New York. You know what you have here, Mr Perry? Another *Titanic*. Who ever heard of travelling 300 miles an hour—"

"Knots—"

"Nuts! You hit anything at that speed and it'll fall apart. The Government made a bad investment, Pastorelli—and your Union's cash'll go down the drain. Now—let me get out of here—"

Without warning the door crashed open, and Savage sprawled his length on the floor. The woman with the flaming red hair stopped in mid-stride and screeched:

"Get out of my way, you . . . you Peeping Tom!"

Dazed but happy, Savage got up, grinning, and watched the others trail out after her. Perry saw them to the door; Pastorelli turned, shook his hand.

"Don't you pay much attention to her, son. She's at that sort of age—you know—?"

The howl of rage from the corridor made Perry's face blanch, but he mustered a smile. "Thanks, Mr Pastorelli—"

"My pleasure, son. Anything you want, you call me at the House. Okay?"

They watched the party from the window, trailing across the Yard towards the gate. Perry wiped his face with a handful of tissues.

"My God—I never want to go through that again . . ."

"David, you did just fine—" Dee said jubilantly.

Savage supported her. "Damned right. You put a flea up their backsides, Dave. It was beautiful . . . listen—can you talk right now?"

"Fluently," the designer grinned. "Never felt so good. Give me five minutes—"

Dee and Savage went back into her office; he sat down, relaxed and unreasonably happy, watching her fix a hot drink. There was something exhilarating about seeing the mighty brought down to ground level . . .

The girl sat on the edge of her desk, legs swinging, watching him closely. After a while, Savage had had enough.

"Well? What's on your mind, Dee? Let's have it. Either piss or get off the pot—pardon the expression . . ."

She was silent for a long time. Presently—

"What's wrong with you, Don?"

"With me? Not a thing. I feel fine—" he beamed at her—unconvincingly.

She said slowly: "I watch you, you know. I see things. You have to rest half way up the office stairs. You rub your legs all the time. And there are times when I wonder if you've been drinking, the way you speak."

He stared at her, sullen and withdrawn.

"Nothing for you to worry about. Listen, I don't want people poking their noses in . . . I get a touch of cramp now and then—so what? I'm an invalid? Get off my back, Dee."

She said softly: "I don't want to be on your back. I just want to help. It's not only that you're not well, Don . . . I think you're terribly unhappy."

Savage said tightly: "Dee, I don't want to hear any more of this. Bloody hell, don't you think I can handle my own problems? I've too much on my plate to get involved like this . . . I know you mean well, but—" he broke off, embarrassed.

"But I should mind my own business? Maybe you're right, Don. Only . . . if there's anything I can do? Any time?"

"Yes, yes," he mumbled impatiently.

"Promise?"

"Oh, for Christ's sake," he flung at her, "leave me alone, Dee."

He got up, stalked into Perry's office and slammed the door. The girl sat back in her chair, a hand laid against one cheek, watching the door; presently, she shook her head until the yellow hair went flying every which way, blew her nose and started work.

David Perry was still in a state of shock. Savage's proposals to set up Julie van Heusen didn't help. "My God, Don—you're talking about laying a trap!"

"You're dead right, chummie."

The designer sighed. Things were happening today which passed all comprehension: first, the Soviet craft—and that unholy row with Grainger; he hadn't heard the last of that by a long chalk, he told himself. Then this hot head Savage comes in talking about trapping Julie van Heusen into . . . Perry went a little cross-eyed trying to adjust his attitude to Wayne's secretary: if the truth were known, he'd always been attracted by that trim slim figure . . . little on the small side, but who cared? Some said she was about as pretty as an Irish navvy—but who looked at the mantelpiece when poking the fire? Guiltily, he recalled his two abortive attempts to talk her into dinner somewhere—and that awful Company dance when he tried to make her in an upstairs cloakroom . . .

Savage said: "Problems?"

"No . . . not really."

"Listen—if I'm right, that little bitch almost ruined us. Chances are, she may even do it yet. And you're sitting there picking your nose! Honest to God, I don't understand you sometimes, Dave. Now let's get down to it: can you do what I ask?"

"Push out a phoney Design Alteration? I suppose so. I expect you'd like a drawing or two to make it authentic . . ."

"That sounds more like it . . ."

"Suppose we disclose a calculation defect in the structure diagram for the main power plant. I could even put off the plant installation tomorrow—that's going to create a lot of talk. You think it'll work?" Perry said anxiously.

"You have to make it work, Dave," Savage told him firmly. "It has to be for real—but push out a very small number of copies—mark it confidential. And a copy to Carl Wayne, marked 'very urgent'. That should do it."

Perry said hesitantly: "You think she'll move?"

"Move? Her feet won't touch the deck until she gets where she's going," the Security man said comfortably. "And we'll be with her all the way. How soon can you do it?"

"I can have the D.A. notice ready in a few minutes. The dummy drawing—half an hour. It can be on Wayne's desk by three o'clock."

"Dave," Savage said carefully, "don't be a damn fool. It'll never reach Wayne's desk. It's going to get lost . . . very quickly."

Perry stared at the other man glumly. Savage was perfectly right—but why do I feel bad about it, he asked himself? Julie? I just don't believe it. Anyone could leave a switch on . . . maybe he should ask her about it . . .

5 *The Wet World of Suzie Wong*

Deep in the earth below His Majesty's landlocked Ship *Vizier*, close by Lee-on-the-Solent, the DAMSEL unit functioned quietly and efficiently. Four air-conditioned control rooms, inter-connected by corridors, were served by a network of support facilities and a permanent staff of 120 men and women who came to the surface one week in three. The complex was in the highest security classification: after four years of operations,

only a handful of people on the surface base knew of its existence—to everyone else, the group of buildings behind a tall
electrified fence was left in peace willingly. The large notice at
the locked gate read: "NUCLEAR WEAPONS COOLANT
RECYCLYING AND CLEANSING FACILITY—OUT OF
BOUNDS TO ALL PERSONNEL". To which all personnel
responded promptly—few would touch the fence with a barge-
pole, let alone enter.

Visitors—rare creatures—were checked in at the Main Gate,
scrutinised carefully and driven into one of a row of four garages
in the corner of the compound. With the doors closed, the
concrete floor sank smoothly for 20 metres to operational level.

DAMSEL has three main areas: the control room complex,
a deep salt-water tank connected to the open sea by a two-
kilometre tunnel and the Administrative complex. Each operations room is unique in design and purpose; the largest is the
Master Control Room which, in addition to the sixteen control
consoles, contains the Operations Desk and Communications
Centre.

Three of the walls contained consoles; each was equipped
with an array of flat and stereo TV screens in colour, a computer
terminal and an operator's seat. The fourth wall of Main Control
was covered by a huge map of Southern England and the Channel as far south as the Spanish coast. The map was overlaid by
a glowing green grid; a smaller screen to one side permitted a
blow-up of any grid square to be displayed. The Channel sea-
ways showed numerous blips and contacts, each electronically
coded and constantly in motion.

The sixteen operators, while wearing Navy working rig, were
extremely young—between eight and sixteen, male and female
in rough balance. Their screens showed oddly tinted green views
of underwater contours, weed streaming in unseen currents,
jumbled rock mountains, flat rippled sandy bottom. In many
cases, screens showed only a dark translucent opacity which
swirled and eddied in vague vortices with random fluidity.

Each controller wore an intricate array of headphones with
multiple connections to the computer input bank and communications racks; each wore, instead of the conventional throat
microphone, a neck harness carrying something very similar to

a child's tin whistle—some 25 centimetres long and fitted with an electronic pick-up device. The weird and unrecognisable sounds they produced were modulated by the computer, changing their frequency, time length and signal strength into sounds inaudible to the human ear, which functions only in the 14- to 16-kiloHertz band. But totally audible to other, non-human organs . . .

Eighty kilometres south of Ventnor, on the Isle of Wight, in the dark silence of the sea fifty fathoms down, the streamlined blue-black shadow with pale underbelly drifted slowly with the current.

Suzie Wong was 11 years old. She knew not that her name was such; she knew only that a specific and individual sound applied to her—and her alone. On dry land, she would weigh at least 125 kilos: a superb specimen of *Phocaena phocaena*— the bottle-nosed dolphin. Born in captivity, she spent most of her life with men, not dolphins; in many ways she considered herself human and, in a strange inverted snobbery, she could never understand why men had such difficulty in travelling in the sea. She and her kind had inhabited the oceans of earth for millions of years—yet still she bore the vestiges of mammal ancestry: her flippers contained all the bones of the hand, wrist and arm, still identifiable. Bones near her anal region were once pelvis and lower limbs; her skin was smooth, the shape of her body aerodynamically clean as a fighter jet. At speed, the skin itself wrinkled and folded to induce a laminar flow of water over itself—a principle hailed as a breakthrough in aviation less than 50 years ago. Thus, she could surge along at more than 70 kph, for long periods of time. Unlike a fish, her symmetrical tail moved vertically, powered by the massive caudal peduncle located each side of her vertebral column.

Suzie's eyesight, in and out of water, was superior to that of both man and fish. She could overcome effortlessly the parallax error which occurs at the air/water interface, and the fields of vision in each eye overlapped extensively both forward and downwards, producing a fine stereoscopic presentation. The eyes themselves were mobile, glowed with intelligence and that single miracle which distinguished her from all other non-human mammals: a fully developed sense of humour.

She swung to the left slowly, listening intently; at intervals, she emitted short staccato bursts of sound, picking up faint echoes on her natural sonar. She was relaxed but alert; presently, reassured, she slid onwards, noting absently the gritty oily taste of the water, the fleeting flavour of some far-off bed of kelp.

Suzie remembered, vaguely, the start of her training, almost seven years ago; time, of course, held no meaning for—if she thought about time at all, it was in relation to past events: the period when she almost died from some corrosive overspill from a wreck, the two occasions she had been allowed to mate.

She remembered clearly the primitive exercises—pressing a button to open a door, retrieving objects from the tank floor, working through ever-changing mazes. And the day when the manfish, black skin smoother than her own, came to her unafraid in the training pool. Nervously, she allowed him to approach her, caress her . . . together, they moved in the cool depths and over the long weeks and months she came to love him as another dolphin. Yet she knew truly that he was no real dolphin—that they could never mate in the green valleys of the sea floor to relieve that savage urge which racked her body time and again; it drove her to still closer contact, moving upon him in the water with frustrated urgency.

The manfish taught her to think. To thread the mazes, to deepdive to anchored sonarbugs, replacing exhausted fuel cells, retrieving them for recharging. He taught her to carry the unknown things he strapped around her dorsal fin, but, most of all, he taught her how to communicate. To understand the greaty mystery of numbers—she could count proficiently, do simple sums . . . many times, she had the oddest feeling that these things were already know to her, those and many others . . . it was as if she was on the brink of recalling some great secret buried in the minds of her race since time began . . .

Best of all, she learned the meaning of pleasure. With a growing vocabulary and the novelty of hearing her language from the manfish, she began to receive rewards: from a thing

71

upon her back, by which the manfish talked in her head, came waves of great ecstasy when she succeeded in a mission. Sometimes, nothing—when things had not been right. Once or twice—a surging vibrant pain, when she abandoned a training mission to go hunting the shoals of mackerel.

The dolphin/machine/man end-product was a highly sophisticated cybernetic module, perfect for its designed purpose. She could work in depths up to 400 metres, in conditions of total darkness, navigating with remarkable precision. Her sonar operated around 150 kiloHertz, receiving echoes of "clicks" produced by muscular action, much as a human throat produces sound; her own hearing apparatus was not her ears—small atrophied holes behind her eyes—but her entire lower jaw, by means of which she obtained directional confirmation of the sounds she heard.

Now Suzie hung poised again, head turning, mouth slightly agape. Presently, she slid obliquely into deeper water, sensing fleetingly the change of temperature at the thermocline; she heard-tasted-sonared a shoal of foodfish out in the gloom to her left and abandoned—reluctantly—the impulse to hunt, to hurl herself from the water in long joyous leaps in pursuit of the mackerel. There would be food aplenty in Homepool tonight . . . and no pleasure if she disobeyed the voice of the manfish.

Her patrol area, covered three times a week, 6000 hectares of Channel, was as familar as Home Base itself: she knew intimately each current, the taste, the feel, of the water; deep within her, the natural homing beacon of her kind operated constantly, and she knew instinctively—accurately—in what direction Home Base lay.

On her back, the small green hump moulded around the fin was no burden. Through the long years of training and operations, she first ignored, then forgot, it. At the mission's end, she would slide into the release slot, wriggle free leaving the pack in the rig. She understood very well that the manfish spoke through the finpack; free of it, her handlers thought her incapable of understanding human speech—but they would have been surprised . . .

The pleasure . . . she sensed that the night's mission was almost over and surged onwards vigorously; she craved rest and security and the sensational vibrations of the pleasure . . . the sound in her head made her name.

"Suzie . . . go right . . . go down . . . go fast . . ."

She moved into top gear, dark arrow flashing through midnight vault; at intervals the voice guided, encouraged. Far away to the right, she detected the faint echo, heard the muted buzz of machinery, tasted the harsh tang of metal; she emitted a series of muted whistles in sheer excitement.

The Voice again: "Good Suzie . . . very good . . . calm . . . slow . . . go left . . . steady—"

She slowed, angling in closer, felt the pressure wave pass through and around her and knew a Big Fish was near. Her backpack turret rotated, stopped, glowed gently; she came in closer and needles of fear sent the adrenalin flowing, heart action speeding up, brain alpha rhythm fluctuating violently . . .

"Easy girl . . . very good . . . calm . . . calm now, Suzie. Big Fish friend . . . Big Fish good . . . no fear . . . very good, Suzie . . ."

Soon the Voice took her away from the Big Fish and sent her on a homing heading, turned her loose to find her own way home, and the pleasure came flooding . . . flooding . . . She went for the surface like a blue rocket, bursting from the green Channel rollers in a leap of sheer exuberance, flashing unseen on a lonely sea under a pale moon, and the voice talked to her of many things on the journey home under the dark waters.

The controller, all of fourteen years old, feet barely touching the floor, slipped off his headset wearily, pressed the call-button and sat back, stretching mightily. Old Suzie . . . a smashing ride tonight . . . he was pleased, satisfied, exhilarated. They made a good team . . . so they should, after nearly five years; after the Testing Board found him, on a routine school test for parnormal faculties, they gave him Suzie as a young raw animal straight out of Training Tank; each would never work with any save the other. He was, the Board President told him, one of the rare ones: a natural, with a strong affinity for animals . . .

some day, he told himself, he'd talk to Suzie without the gob-stick; there were times, homeward bound from missions, when he would change microphones and talk to her in English—tell her about people and things and places she would never see. He would tell others in the crew that, somehow, she seemed to understand—but they laughed . . . he'd show them . . .

"Randy?"

"Huh? Oh—yessir!"

"Make your report, lad—then off duty. School tomorrow—"

"Yessir. Thank you, sir."

The lad bent over the computer terminal, tongue protruding slightly.

TIME 04.22 ZULU. CONTROLLER ONE NINER WORK-ING DOLPHIN SUZIE WONG ON GRID SEARCH PAT-TERN 12 REF 993638 DASH 71. UNKNOWN INTERCEPT IDENTIFIED AS UNITED GERMAN REPUBLIC KRIEGS-MARIN UNTERSEEBOOT U906 DRESDEN CLASS NUKESUB HUNTER KILLER, PROCEEDING ON AU-THORISED PLOT TRANSIT TO BISCAY AREA FOR WATO EXERCISE LONGSTOP. FULL PLOT DATA TRANSFERRED TO COMBANK ANALYSIS FOUR. SUZIE WONG DID A FINE JOB AS USUAL. REQUEST BONUS DOZEN FRESH GREY MULLET FULL SIZE. NONE REPEAT NONE OF THOSE FROZEN TIDDLERS. CONTROLLER 19 LEADING HAND BINNS, RANDOLPH.

The Deputy Controller concealed a grin with an effort.

"You'll have to cut out those unofficial titbits, Randy. You know the Old Man—have my guts for a necktie, he will—"

The boy stood up, ran fingers through tousled hair and yawned.

"I don't care, really, sir. Let him try to handle Suzie himself—see how far he gets. I mean, she does all the work and they give her awful meals when she comes home. She says one of those fish last time was—"

"Never mind that. I'll have a word with the Storebashers' Mate—but I'm promising nothing—understand? Just remem-ber—stick to standard reporting procedure—just for my sake?" coaxingly.

Randy grinned tiredly. "All right, sub. I'll try."

The DC nodded, walked upstairs to the Chief Controller's office, laid the comprint copy down and went away quietly. The Old Man put in at least one night watch weekly, he would read tonight's reports when he came in later in the day. The Officer Commanding DAMSEL would never pull rank and ask a junior to take his watch—he liked protocol—and hated abbreviations with pathological obsession. The unit painter needed three days to finish the gold-lettered door to his office: COMMANDER PETER JAMES MACDONNEL, R.N. OFFICER COMMANDING DOLPHIN-ACTUATED MACROSONAR ELECTRONIC LOCATION UNIT.

Abbreviations, the Old Man insisted, characterised a tendency towards haste—and "haste makes mistakes", he said very frequently. Besides, he would point out: with at least 40 nations possessing nuclear weapons and at least half prepared to use them at the drop of a hat, mistakes could result in very loud expensive noises which produced no echoes. Because, he said, to hear an echo requires that one is alive at the time . . . a very unlikely possibility . . .

6   *Ground Bait*

"Don, you can't cover *every* possibility!" Martin said plaintively. "She could try a hundred different ways along the line, to make contact—and she's no fool. Julie van Heusen's a smart girl."

Savage gnawed his lower lip. "Jesus, I know that, Jack. You don't have to keep going on about it. Perry's going to ring me when he's ready to go—which leaves us less than an hour. He's holding the match till I tell him to light the fuse, but I'm worried to bloody death that she might move sooner. I mean—she heard every damn word of the meeting: she knows we'll be watching everyone within five miles of this place. Look at it this way—

she knows the ballon's gone up, but what matter? They have almost everything they want."

"You think she'll make a run for it?"

"Dunno. But she must think she's safe—I mean, if she was really blown, she'd be in the Guardroom now—and she knows it. No—I think she'll sit tight and sweat it out, Jack. We have to be damn sure that, when the bait is set, we can cover her every damn way she can go. Let's look at it logically . . .

"If she reports to anyone else in BHLC, no problem. She's being watched every second of time. Four of the team have remote microphones: unless they talk in a bloody cupboard, we'll hear what they say. Well?"

"So far, so good," Martin nodded.

"If she leaves the factory, we have that covered too. She drives that little Citroen hybrid—Wayne sees that she has plenty of fuel—but she'll find it won't start. Now—in that situation, what's left?"

"Public phones?" Martin hazarded.

"Exactly. Which is why we sent out two lads to cover every local call-box within a mile or so. If she uses one of them, we'll be hooked in—"

Martin frowned. "A hell of a lot of people use those phones, Don—"

"Carl Wayne kept her in his office for ten minutes—I had Garner nip in and wire up her handbag. Women take their bags everywhere—even into a phone-box, Jack. Don't worry—we'll hear what we want to hear. And record, it too; I want to nail every one of the bastards . . ."

By mid-afternoon, Julie van Heusen's shakes had subsided to occasional tremors, and she was able to work with some semblance of normality. There was, of course, no question of risking further action; that man Savage had said the Soviets had almost everything they needed, and she was damned if she'd do any more. She began to think about Savage again, and that made her feel much worse; in her core, she was terrified of the gaunt dark-haired man who seemed to limp with both legs; of all the people in BHLC, he alone was the enemy incarnate—he whose task was to root out and punish such as she. Hands shaking, she lit another small cigar, and quailed at the terrible imagined sequence of events which would follow her discovery; the man was raw, bitter, ruthless, with a terrifying inner ferocity that hinted at fearsome consequences . . .

Her entrapment, a mere three years previously, had been traditional, almost old-fashioned, in the mould of historical KGB methodology—some perverse sense of masochism had led her to the libraries of Montreal and New York, and it seemed to comfort her in some measure, that she was neither the first nor the ten thousandth to be caught so simply. Walter van Heusen, himself enmeshed in a vicious circle of soaring inflation, growing family and static income as an executive officer of the Brunswick Mutual and Trust Bank in Montreal, began appropriating funds for his own use in small measure at first. The leak grew into a flood: some $100,000 dollars worth, before the external auditors arrived. Now, it was Walter's good fortune and Julie's bad, that the senior auditor was a KGB sleeper trained specifically for this work: there was a rich and continuing harvest of men who had been tempted and found out, and the injection of money to cover default was no problem for the Soviet Union. Such men, once bought, stay bought.

So it was that Julie, working blissfully in the Wayne McGill building in Montreal, received a visit from two soberly dressed and impeccably spoken gentlemen who went to some lengths to prove their case. They did not want, they stressed, anything criminal performed. They might, as a matter of fact, never have to call on Julie at all. It was simply their way of making business contacts and helping people; provided she did exactly as she was told, there should be no reason why her father's little peccadillo should ever become public knowledge.

For almost two years, she lived in a void of anticipation and anti-climax; as the months went by, she began to believe that they had forgotten Julie van Heusen, that perhaps she had imagined it all, that it was really too ridiculous to worry about . . .

Until she came to Britain with Carl Wayne.

Eventually—sooner or later—she would have to make one final contact, simply to tell them that the thing was finished, that there was nothing else she could do.

It would be totally unwise, she told herself, to make any move at all: the risks were too great, for one staggeringly simple reason. They did not know that she knew the name of her contact—there was just a telephone number and a voice at the other end. But she knew . . . there was only person it could be.

Not that she cared: the men from Montreal had told her she would be free, once the task was completed, from future pressure—she had paid her debt, squared the account.

She ground out the cigar, flung the butt into the wastebasket, tried to do a little work, but her thoughts kept intruding. Was she in any real danger? Had anyone spotted the audio switch? Wouldn't they be here now, questioning her, if that was so?

The audio buzzed.

"Yes, Mr Wayne?"

"Come in, please, Julie—a few letters—"

"Yes, Mr Wayne."

It all sounded so perfectly normal . . . she sighed with something approaching relief and picked up her stenorecorder.

At 3.35, the long-haired youth from Central Registry barged into her office, typically without knocking, dumped a sheaf of documents on her desk, winked cheekily and exited without breaking his step. Slimy lout, she thought viciously . . . these British kids were as bad as . . . she glanced desultorily through the small pile of paperwork, stopped, re-read and sat immobile, staring out across the Yard, bright and busy in spring sunshine, with unseeing eyes.

Holy Mother of God . . . I can't . . . I won't . . . but if they find out—Father, why aren't you here when I need you so much . . . we must make quite sure—

She read the document again. Installation of the main drive nuclear reactor postponed . . . stress calculations reveal weakness in structure around the mounting . . . fresh drawings in progress . . . Over the years, inevitably, Julie had picked up a considerable amount of technical knowledge, much of it unconnected, much of which made no sense unless the full context were known. But this—this made dreadful and ominous sense. If she failed to pass on what she now knew . . . and they found out . . . after some awful accident . . .

78

She got up suddenly, went to the window. The *Albatross* . . . so clean, glistening white, streamlined bullet . . . she felt a tremendous surge of pride, in that she had had something to do, however remotely, with such an acheivement; if things had only been different . . . she was seized by an impulse to walk herself halfway to his door, pulled up short, aghast.

Conflicting thoughts churned through her mind in searing waves, the back of one hand jammed against her mouth . . . her head felt as if it would burst, and she knew that she had to share this burden with someone, anyone . . .

There were, she had been told, two other friends in the BHLC Yard. One who would watch her activities closely and report; the second a back-up contact channel to be used only in dire emergency. Quite early in the game, she decided that the "monitor" simply did not exist. If he did exist, he would have to be one of the people in Administration with whom she worked closely—and after much inner debate she decided there was no-one who could possibly fit the bill.

Which left only the emergency contact. The implications turned her belly to ice with fear: if she was being watched, the contact would be blown totally; further, they would be given no opportunity to pass information. Mary Mother of God, help me . . . if they *were* on to her, and she tried to leave the complex, she would be stopped. There was nothing for it but to try both ways . . .

"Mr Wayne?"

"Yes, Julie?"

"I have to go out for half an hour. And I have some internal mail for the factory—I can do both together?" She left the vital question unspoken.

Wayne looked at her blankly. "Why not? Take all the time you need."

"Thank you . . ."

Did he suspect? Was there . . . something . . . in his eyes just now? She bit her lip in a paroxysm of uncertainty and in the end she slipped into her jacket and walked out along the plush carpet of the corridor. She knew the man she wanted by sight; but not where to find him. She feared to wander round asking for him—sure to cause curiosity . . . she walked out across the

Yard with long hasty strides, heading for the *Albatross*; on her left, the long blue-painted façade of the Stores Building, on the right, identical in size, the Production Engineering Shed. By the very nature of his job, her man could be anywhere in the complex—but where?

Where the narrow aluminium bridge from *Albatross*'s main entry port rested on the lip of the dry dock, a Security guard in the standard pale-blue zipsuit watched her approach.

"Yes, miss?"

"Can I go on the craft, please?"

"Sorry, miss. Work in progress on the main drive assembly. Anything you want in particular?"

She smiled briefly. "Not really . . . I have a little spare time on my hands . . . I've never really seen her close up. Just a thought . . ."

The man stared at her with expressionless blue eyes. "You're Mr Wayne's secretary, aren't you, miss?"

"Yes. Julie van Heusen."

"I thought so. Very sorry—wish I could help. Tell you what—you could take a ride down to the bottom of the hole, look at her from there—"

"The . . . 'hole'?" she said faintly.

"Sure. Take the elevator over there—takes you right down to the floor of the dock. Fabulous view—you can walk all round her . . ."

Maybe she could get on board from below . . . worth a chance. She thanked him prettily and moved away; behind her, the guard pressed his throat mike switch and spoke briefly.

Julie had to share the lift with half a dozen workers and a mass of strange components; she stood in the corner enduring the half-concealed sexy jokes, the crude looks and winks. Presently, she was free to walk away along the sloping, wet concrete expanse into the shadow of the giant hoverliner; despite her agitation and fear, she found her imagination caught by the classic lines and sheer mind-shattering size of the craft. The forward skirts which entrapped the air cushion generated by huge fans were partially lifted; they swept back at sharp angle to fill the apertures between the knife-sharp sidewall blades and the centrehull. Far above her head, she could see the needle-shaped bow and bridge, and the twin aerodynamic stabilisers which would maintain the craft in perfect alignment to the water surface, eradicate any tendency to roll. The sidewalls, she knew, were double-shelled, the outer skin moving hydraulically to keep a bare metre or so of the sidewall immersed in the water; in this way, loss of air from the underhull cushion would be minimised.

She moved round under the bow, searching for her man in the horde of workers milling around; the vast tunnel under the hull was brightly lit, and far down the dock she could make out the black curtain of the aft skirt, stretching from one sidewall to the other. The centrehull stretched away into the distance; at its far end she could see dimly the massive bulge of the main drive module; she knew what it was, but now how it worked— very few people in BHLC were privy to *that* secret.

Walking back to the service elevator, she struck oil. The man she wanted came past, clipboard in hand, white safety helmet jammed on the back of his head. He saw her and knew her; he frowned deeply, shook his head minutely and walked away, engrossed, into the shadow of the starboard sidewall near a timber support pile. She followed, heart in her mouth.

"For God's sake—what are you doing down here?"

"Mr Chaffey—you have to listen . . ." she began.

"Listen be buggered!" he hissed. "You were told never to come near me except in emergency . . ."

Her temper flared. "Shut up! What the hell do you think I'm here for? A goddam sherry party? Now listen—"

Chastened, he stared at her when she was done, but he seemed calm, undisturbed; Chaffey had spent too many years as a shop steward fighting shop-floor battles to be worried by anything less than an earthquake. "What do you want me to do?"

"We have to get word through—you know that. I can't use the BHLC phones—and they may be watching me anyway. I have to try for an outside phone—but if I don't make it—it's up to you. Here—" she fumbled in her bag— "this gives full details. Give me until . . . noon tomorrow. If I don't check back with you, or I go missing, it's your problem all the way. Can you handle it?"

"Don't talk bloody stupid. Of course I can. Just one thing

. . . if you're caught, and blow me out—I'll cripple you. Wherever you are, I'll find you. Seventeen years I've had this job—smash me up and you're horse meat, you mare. Now—get out of here before you do any more damage."

The girl hurried away, heart pounding and mouth suddenly dry; she was caught between Savage and Chaffey and she did not quite know which she feared the most. Nothing mattered now but reaching the main gate . . . getting to a telephone . . . she'd drive far away, into the City, to find a quiet place and a telephone . . .

"Don?"

"Yes, Jack?"

The voice sounded jubilant. "We're off, I think. She left the office—the D.A. sheet's missing, as you predicted. Carl Wayne says she asked permission to leave the Yard for half an hour—but she went over to the craft first—and tried to get aboard."

"The devil she did! Go on—"

Martin said carefully: "She was looking for someone, all right. I had three men covering the dock—two up top, one down below. The man she found—Chaffey."

"What—the shop steward?"

"None other, Don. Apparently he was livid because she approached him—but she calmed down soon enough. She passed him a paper of some kind—"

"The D.A. notice about the power plant foundations?" Savage guessed.

"I would think so, Don. Anyway—she made a beeline for the car park and her Citroen—"

"Which wouldn't start—?"

"Which didn't start! I watched her from the Purchasing Office window—Jesus, was she ever mad! Slammed the door and kicked at the thing until she hurt her foot. Stalked off into Hythe, madder'n a cat with eight tits and nine kittens."

Savage grinned. "Beautiful . . . beautiful. Where is she now?"

"Halfway to town, I think. Take her a little while to reach a phone."

"And she's wired up?"

"That she is. We set one in her handbag, one under the collar

82

of her jacket. Sound-activated bugs—they'll transmit when she talks and not before."

"Keep me posted . . ."

"Will do, Don."

Savage put down the phone carefully, leaned back in his seat and began making church steeples with his fingers, absently. Jack had things well in hand—he'd have at least two men on Chaffey all the time. Chaffey, of all people! Savage thought he was a little out of his depth in all this . . . Christ, Chaffey was one of the BHLC originals—been with the firm since he got out of Tech College. Why in God's name did people have to snarl up their lives like this?

He got up, extracted Chaffey's file and began to read. Strong Labour supporter—that figured. Savage lighted a Split, flicked the match at the waste-basket, missed, grimaced, went on reading.

Chaffey went way back, he found. Member of the Revolutionary Workers Party in his early years—probably caught up in the wave of support after the backlash against the British Nazi Party riots. Resigned two years later . . . officially—but then most undercover people started serious work by severing contacts with the front-line organisation. Shop steward . . . the man's trade was officially a metal-worker—but he did very little real work. Access to every part of the complex on union business . . . perfect. No wonder the Reds got a steady supply of working drawings hot off the printer!

The phone again.

"Don?"

"Yes, Jack. News?" Savage said.

"You're just not going to believe this—"

"Try me—"

"She made her call—from Hythe. London number—we checked it out. It's a shifter—you know?"

Savage knew. The original call activated an answering device which shifted the contact to any of fifty random numbers—it made call-tracing very difficult.

"No luck, Jack?"

"That's what I'm trying to tell you. You said we should call your Mr Brewer in case of trouble—by Jiminy, that man works fast! He came back to us with the final number even before we'd finished playing back the recording of her call. Know who her contact is?"

Savage sighed. "You'll get round to telling me eventually . . ."

"Grainger!"

"WHO?"

"You heard! Grainger—the MP! I tell you, Don, I almost pissed myself with surprise. Listen—what's 'Razor'? The girl was talking to Grainger about it—something to do with radar. Couldn't understand what she was talking about, but it sounded important. So I rang Brewer again—suggested he roped Grainger in pretty damn quick."

"Makes sense—" Savage began.

"Wasted my time. He said there was already a team on the way to pick him up, and he'd had Grainger's phone disconnected. Seemed to think the bastard wouldn't have time to contact anyone—it should be okay, Don."

Savage gulped. Said thickly: "You ever get the feeling everything's happening too fast these days, Jack?"

Fat chuckle. "Bloody right. You have to sprint like hell just to stand still. But we're winning. What else is new?"

"I'll tell you what's new. I'm going to sleep tonight, for a change. Where's van Heusen now?"

"Walking back from the village. Our lads are keeping their distance—what do you suggest?"

"I don't quite know," Savage admitted. "Have to think about it. We can't take any more risks—I think we ought to get her under wraps. But that'll only tip off Chaffey—and Chaffey may have other friends on the shop floor. The way I see it, they'll be more confident, now she's made contact. The problem's out of their hands—they've done their bit. I think we have more to gain than lose by letting them run loose for a while—but not too loose, Jack."

"Right."

"Have a word with Carl Wayne—he has to carry the ball as if nothing's happened. It'll be hard, but I don't want her scared away."

Martin was silent for a moment. Then—"And Chaffey?".

"Keep watching. I want to know everything he does, everyone he talks to. Most of it'll be routine—but if he as much as scratches his arse, I want to know about it. Can do?"

Mr Martin's reply was coarse and to the point; Savage 'grinned and hung up. He got up, went to the door.

"Dee? How about a drink?"

"Coming up, Don."

He hesitated. "Dee—"

"Hm-mm?"

"I was rude—bloody rude—this morning."

She flushed. "It didn't mean anything—you've been under a lot of pressure lately. I shouldn't have said anything . . ."

He walked into her office, favouring his right leg a little; her eyes clouded over, and he cursed himself for an idiot. He stood before her, hands in trouser pockets, looking down with affection he found difficult to conceal.

"You're all right, Dee—you know that? I mean, I never talk like this as a rule, but I appreciate the way you beaver away in here. You take a lot of the load off me at times. Look, when this boat's in the water and things calm down a little, I'm taking a break. I know of a Welsh stream full of trought who've never seen a fly. And there's a little family hotel and stretches of mountainside yellow with buttercups. All I need is to sleep for a week solid, a few good meals, some exercise. And company— nothing else, understand?"

She smiled tremulously. "I thought you were going to make a rude suggestion."

"No way. I can't—I mean—Oh, Christ, do I have to explain?"

"No. I've know for a long time you have—trouble at home. But I don't want to know about it, Don. Only—"

"Only what?"

"Promise you'll go to a doctor—after the launch. Now—don't get mad again. There is something wrong with you, Don—everyone knows that. But—at times, you're so unapproachable— no-one can talk to you about it. Promise?"

He stared down at the pale face, filled with concern. "Okay. Keep on nagging like that, you'll make some bloke a good wife one day. Now—go find me a cup of coffee."

She smiled broadly, and once again something caught at his

heart, to see the emergence of the butterfly of beauty from the chrysalis of plain features. Dee said sternly: "You drink far too much coffee."

"Sure, sure. Sometimes my back teeth are awash. But coffee keeps me going—you know where?"

"Don't be coarse," she laughed. He watched her move away and went back into his own office, vaguely aware that some kind of milestone—kilostone?—had been passed. God knows what lay round the bend of the road, but whatever it was, he could handle it . . . he didn't have to fight alone any more.

7 Banker's Order

Newport News is America's Portsmouth. Anchored firmly where the James River enters Chesapeake Bay, it was steeped in naval history long before John Paul Jones carved his name with pride. Together with sister town Hampton, straddling Hampton Roads and the twin towns Portsmouth (US style) and Norfolk, Newport offers a permanently open door to sailors of all ages and sexes. Outside the big dockyard and Navy base, there is a ripe and roaring town fitted, kitted and titted out to attract the dogsbody gob sailor, complete with white pillbox and navy blues.

The town suffered a depression of sorts in the '80s, when the US Navy was contracting at roughly the same rate the Soviet Navy was expanding; it took an Iran, a Pakistan, Panama, Cuba and the Gulf War to reverse the trend. Today, the town is lavishly equipped with sailor-traps including strip, clip and flip joints catering respectively for sex, gambling and drugs. Since the majority of such establishments are owned, directly or indirectly, by the senior echelon of the Newport Police Department, operations proceed apace with minimum interference—especially when the Fleet comes in.

It must be recorded, regrettably, that at such times a sailor hurries ashore interested in only two things: his stomach—and what hangs on the end of it. It seems to make no difference—officer or enlisted man, crap-shovelling rating or a CPO with 20 years' service. The only regulating factor seems to be the existence of families in the base quarters—a retarding influence on a small but resigned sector of the Navy personnel list.

CPO Warren F. Hardy possessed a number of advantages denied to his shipmates on the USS *Sherman*. Married, he was separated from his wife by 3000 miles, two years and a major at the USAF Edwards Air Force Base, California. Further, he seemed to have inexhaustible supplies of the $100 gold pieces coming into circulation as the result of soaring inflation. Properly approached, he would stake a man for amounts up to $50,000 at the very reasonable rate of 50% per month; scuttlebutt said half the wardroom of the *Sherman* was in hock to The Banker, for anything from a pound of flesh from the buttocks, up to a quarter of a million dollars.

Known throughout the Atlantic and Pacific Fleets, The Banker had long since lined his own nest; he never regretted the heavy cash outlay to the Assignment Branch of the Washington Personnel Department. Originally a missile guidance system technician, he refused to fill in commissioning papers, pointing out that he was already earning more than the Admiral so what the hell?

He was a far-sighted man. Seeing the eventual obsolescence of all surface warships and the comparative safety of the new type of semi-submersible missile cruisers coming into service, he settled for the *Sherman* as an ideal base for the final run up to retirement.

As warships go, the *Sherman* was the first of her type and quite unique. Her 14,000 tonnes carried a wide range of radar, infra-red Doppler, surface-to-surface and surface-to-air missiles, conventional and nuclear. Secondary banks of anti-missile missiles guarded her flanks, but her greatest asset was her ability to submerge until only a tiny fighting bridge remained above water.

With sealed upper works and retractable "Christmas-tree" antennae mountings, she could survive virtually anything but a direct nuclear hit within a hundred metres. She could even, given five minutes' warning, sink completely to a depth of 50 metres from a stationary position.

In sort, the *Sherman* offered The Banker as safe a refuge as he'd find anywhere, afloat or ashore—not least because she could fire low-flying supersonic Cruise missiles with built-in radar capable of seeking out any surface ship within 1000 kilometres, delivering a conventional explosive or nuclear punch of quite amazing capability.

All things considered, The Banker mused, *Sherman* was home from home. Ashore, it was his habit and pleasure to occupy a corner booth at the "Dying Whore" saloon—not the most select joint of the hundreds in Newport, but one in which anything went—and frequently did. Dining in solitary state, The Banker held court, transacting business without interrupting the finest steaks on the East Coast; later, he might graciously allow one or two of the resident hookers to tickle his fancy and anything else they could reach (save his billfold) and settle back to watch the floorshow. At such times, one might find a short queue of hopefuls proposing to put the bite on The Banker for a couple of hundred or so; others, anxious to unfold a proposition guaranteeing universal profit, would wait their turn patiently until the stripper, the song-and-dance man, or the brace of bored lesbians finished their act.

This particular evening, four or five potential customers waited in line, drinking genuine imitation Taiwan vodka and chatting amiably; all showed signs of puzzlement and anger when the tall man with steel-grey hair walked up to the hallowed table, wearing a long black coat, carrying a rolled umbrella. This last item he levelled and prodded The Banker unceremoniously in the ribs; the audience waited expectantly for the sky to fall on him.

"Chief Hardy?"

The Banker stared in total disbelief. In the queue, Yeoman First Class Harvey T. Kraus stepped up and shoved a fist under the long sharp nose; had he been nearer sober than drunk, he would have noted the cold bleak stare in the fish-like eyes. The stranger grabbed Harvey's own nose between vice-like finger and thumb, propelled him backwards until his legs hit a table, mouth agape in surprise.

The stranger hauled off and let Harvey have an open-ended slap heard clear down to Pier 16: a veritable shotgun blast of a slap. Harvey made two good sideflips, landed flat on his back and took no further interest in the proceedings. Still clutching his umbrella, the stranger started off from scratch with the poke and question routine—forewarned, The Banker pushed the prod to one side and growled:

"You crazy or something?"

"Chief Hardy?"

The Banker shook his head, incredulous. "I jus' don't believe it. Who wants to know?"

Black Coat sat down calmly and curled a finger which attracted a waiter as if it was an electromagnet. "Two whiskies. *Real* Scotch—or I'll ram this thing so far up your arse you'll have a sore throat—"

Depart one terrified waiter. Presently—

"Now, Mr Hardy—let's talk business," the stranger said jovially.

"Business? What sort of business?" The Banker's voice held a measure of respect. Anyone capable of walking into the Dying Whore and throwing a handful of shit into the fan fifteen seconds later couldn't be all chicken-crap and bilgewater.

"Ten-million-dollar business?" the man said casually. Hardy swallowed convulsively, temporarily bereft of speech. Then—

"How's that again?"

Black Coat laughed, accepted a drink from the waiter, sipped, threw the contents into the man's face and said firmly: "I said real whisky—"

They watched the tray-jockey fade into the distance, and The Banker grinned.

"Tell me, friend—what are you like when you lose your temper?"

"You wouldn't like me at all."

"That's for sure. You said dollars?" promptly.

"Any currency you like. Or gold—"

"Shee-it!" said Mr Hardy, shaken to the core. "Show me the bottom line—"

Black Coat said blandly: "Not here. Let's finish our drink—if I ever get one in this dump—and go to my hotel. I have a bottle of Harper's Bourbon—1971."

"With the square cut-glass stopper?"

"That's the one."

"Bullshit!" Mr Hardy said explosively. "That stuff's been off the market 14 years."

"So it has. Nevertheless—"

The Banker was suddenly a Believer. Anyone with *that* kind of booze just might have the odd million bucks on one side. Waiting for Warren F. Hardy to show up. It could be a heap of ripe slok—and it could just possibly be a deal . . .

"Okay. Why not?"

They stood up. The waiter arrived with his next offering—just as Harvey T. staggered to his feet. The Man tasted, grimaced, flung it in Harvey's face.

"He's drinking it," he told the waiter. "He'll pay for it."

Dazed, CPO Hardy followed the stranger out; on the sidewalk they hailed down a gas-cab and The Banker slapped the other on the shoulder. "You know, I think we might do business—"

"You'd better believe it. Get in and shut up."

Once aboard: "I know we can do business, Mr Hardy—because once I explain my proposition, you'll be one of two things—"

"Which are?" Hardy demanded.

"In or dead. Your choice."

To give him his due, the Navy man had no yellow streak. "You're snowing me—"

"No. Not at all. I know a good deal about you, Mr Hardy. I know about your accounts in First National, Citibank, Western Trust and Mid-West—all in different names. I could give you the balances to the nearest cent—in fact, I could give the IRS even more. We know about your loan-sharking, your safety-deposit boxes and the seven whore-houses you own in Newport, San Diego and L.A. We even know how and why a certain sailor called Maskell came to fall off the dock in Galveston a year or two back—how a piece of wire strop around his neck came to have the other end stuck in a bucket of cement. And how his wife finally paid off what you called his 'mortgage' out of his insurance money."

Warren F. Hardy sat quite still, staring out of the cab window, jaws working. Common sense suggested the immediate elemination of the threat this man represented, but one little word stuck in Hardy's throat: "we". Who? It was a million to one against this guy's working alone—and he must have a lot of clout to find out such information. Such as—only two people knew about Maskell: Hardy and Mrs Maskell—the concrete-mixer had met with a fatal accident a week later; Hardy believed in covering tracks.

They rode on in silence. Hardy, because he knew he had to go all the way to check this character out; Black Coat because he'd said enough to ensure full attention. They walked past the bored desk clerk, up four flights of stairs flanking a dust-filled elevator, into the typical American hotel room, right down to the dead flies in the window and the air-conditioner that didn't work.

Great Godfrey, it *was* the real thing! Hardy sipped once more, to confirm, let the silky fluid sneak its way to heaven and relaxed, feeling the fire igniting two inches south of his belt.

"Man—this stuff is worth a thousand bucks a bottle—" ecstatically.

"I paid exactly twice that, Mr Hardy. Just for you—"

"Listen," The Banker said forcibly, "who are you? Huh? Who's your boss?"

The other regarded his guest whimsically, a long green cigar in one hand, clippers in the other. "Why," he said carefully, "do you think I'm not working simply for myself?"

"Because you're a fifty-fifty bet, that's why. Half muscle, half brain. Anyone steaming into that joint the way you did doesn't run $10 million games: no, sir. Second string, maybe—but you're one floor down from the penthouse. Maybe two."

Black Coat grinned, unoffended. "You are a perceptive man, Hardy. Let me put it this way—I'm in the top three of our Company—and we have nearly a million employees."

"Which means," Hardy commented, "you can afford to buy

the legs you needed to pull my record. And just for the record, who tipped you off about Maskell?"

"Immaterial, irrelevant, unimportant," Black Coat said quitely.

"Who are you, anyway?"

"You," said Black Coat primly, "can call me Cody."

"For Chrissake," Hardy said despairingly. "Like—Buffalo Bill? Sheesh!"

"Business now?"

"I'm all ears, Cody."

"I had noticed," said Cody, "but this is 'Let's not be Rude to our Friends' week in Newport; let us proceed. Questions can wait . . ."

He paused reflectively, as if gathering his thoughts.

"Now . . . Warren F. Hardy. Born Miami, Oklahoma, June second, nineteen and fifty-four, to Fred. K. Hardy of Pitcher, Oklahoma, and Charlene May Hardy, née Endicott of Tulsa, Oklahoma. Age now—48, give or take a month. Retiring in two years; substantive rank Chief Petty Officer. Grade: Electronic Warfare and Countermeasures Technician First Class. Decorations—Navy Medal, Iran Cross—were you in that snafu too, Hardy? Me too. 89th Airborne. Where was I? Ah . . . wife Betty Lou Hardy, née Anstruther, married Kansas City, Missouri, March tenth nineteen and eighty-one, separated December twenty-fifth four years later . . . I find that date of interest, Mr Hardy?"

The Banker, listening to his own life story, sat up and refilled his glass—again.

"Huh?"

"Why Christmas Day, of all days?"

"Oh—that. Well, sir—I came home kinda sudden four days after we sailed from Diego on the *Robert F. Kennedy*—Betty Lou saw me off at the jetty—bound for Honolulu. We blew a boiler and came back to Diego in time for Christmas."

"And caught your wife with a man, I suppose—"

"Three of them, buster. Say—if I'd had a video camera I could have made a million bucks. I mean—everything but swinging on the chandelier—you know? Except we didn't have no chandelier. If we had—"

92

"I see—" Cody eyed the Navy man with obvious disapproval. Hell, the man actually seemed *proud* of his wife's gymnastics!

"You're with the *Sherman* now. Guided Missile Semi-Sub. Crew two hundred ratings, forty officers. We know about her armament—I'll come to that later. You carry a number of Cruise missiles, right?"

"Right."

"Nuke or conventional?" Cody pressed.

"Both. Listen—why . . ." Hardy was not allowed to finish. He was seriously worried now: somehow, he'd been suckered into something stinking . . .

"Just a moment—" Cody broke in. "I told you when we started, Hardy—in or dead—remember? In or dead."

"Whaddya mean?"

"We took the precaution of coating the inside of your glass with a slow-working poison cooked up by our Dirty Tricks department. You've had roughly four times the lethal dose: no pain for maybe an hour, but then—"

"Then—?" Hardy felt a vein throbbing enormously in his head, a fearful dryness in the throat; he could not continue, staring at his tormentor with mouth agape.

"So," Cody resumed cheerfully, "we have plenty of time. I have what our Dirty Trick boys hope is an efficient antidote stowed away around here some place. No—don't ask me where, old buddy. If you decide you're in, fine. If not—well, I'll have to organise a bucket of cement myself—specially for you. Clear?"

The Banker nodded, sat down heavily. Jesus H. Christ! This was worse than Iran, the time he fragged his Lieutenant with a grenade . . .

"Now," Cody went on, "your job aboard *Sherman* involves target assessment and firing computer programming. Tell me— if you wanted to . . . dispose of a single small ship perhaps two hundred kilometres away—with minimum hassle and backlash. What would you use?"

Hardy sat quite still, a small, seemingly shrunken figure. He tore his thoughts away from thinking how bad he was feeling already. "Cruise missile, conventional warhead, proximity fuse, random high-level approach under command radar, lock-on at twenty miles. Final run-in under rocket power from five kilometres."

Cody beamed. "There now! That wasn't so hard, was it? How long to set up a programme?"

"An hour, maybe less. Longer if we have to change the warhead. Each round, that is."

"We should only need the one," said Cody modestly, "with a guy like you in charge."

Hardy peered up under bristling brows. "How big is the ship you're after?"

"About a thousand tonnes, maybe less. You can handle the main target computer?"

"No sweat. Those birds are satellite guided to the target area—we're locked onto at least four any one time."

The red-faced man got up and started walking around the room. Then—

"Accuracy, Hardy?"

"You gotta be joking. We can hit a rowboat five hundred kilometres away with a dummy warhead."

Cody grinned. "With one hand tied behind your back? Never mind—just a thought. Now—just for the sake of argument—"

"Who's arguing?"

"Shaddap. Listen. Suppose you wanted to take over the *Sherman* at sea. Could it be done with a hundred men, fully armed?"

"You'd never get 'em aboard, fella."

"Leave us to worry about that. With the ship secure, you'd need a team to fire missiles. How many?"

The Banker considered, chin in hand. "Listen, I'm not talking any more until you get that damned antidote . . ."

"You feeling any pain?"

"No—but . . ."

"No buts, Banker. How many men?"

It wasn't easy to figure but they finally agreed on a total. The steering and engine controls were fully automatic, the bridge designed to be conned by as few as three men in emergency. Hardy figured he needed nine, maybe ten, men to work the firing sequence—once he had the safety keys from the Captain and First Officer.

"Can you find ten men?" Cody said sharply.

94

"Depends what it's worth, right?" Hardy thought his tongue was swelling—or maybe his mouth was shrinking? "How much?" he asked.

"Shall we say $5 million each?"

Hardy stared suspiciously. "I thought you said 10 million bucks?"

"So I did," Cody said neutrally. "You want a share too, right?"

The Banker did a little mental arithmetic and had trouble in focussing his eyes—they kept crossing. Presently—

"Lay it on me, man. What's this ship? Who are you trying to take out? The President?"

Cody's laugh boomed out in the quiet room. He leaned forward, refilled Hardy's glass. "The less you know the better, friend. I can tell you this. We can take over the ship without violence. No-one gets hurt. We hand her over to your team and you do your stuff. You get to be flown off by a Chinook helicopter and a few days later you're anywhere you want to be, with false passports, your families or girlfriends and all the money in the world. Now you tell me—in or dead?"

Hardy stared at his brimming glass. "You don't think I'm going to drink any more of that stuff, do you? I'm in, right? Now—gimme the antidote!"

"What antidote?"

"For this goddam poison, you ape!"

Cody said serenely: "What poison?"

"What? Why . . . you lousy stinkin' pig-faced . . ." all of a sudden the Banker found he was laughing, great gusty gut-laughs from all the way down in his belly, and he picked up the glass, drained it and threw it at Cody's head.

The red-faced man straightened up, grinning. "Okay. Let's clean it up, Hardy. This operation is scheduled for early May— we don't have a date yet. We know that *Sherman* is lined up for a Fleet exercise in South American waters with the Brazilian and Mexican navies around that time—" he gave Hardy a new glass.

"The hell you say!"

"A fact not for general publication—even your Captain doesn't know yet. You have about six weeks to do your homework, line your men up—collect their passport photographs, locations they want to go to live. One other thing—you all get to have plastic surgery as soon as you arrive—after which you get updated passports. If you ever wanted to look like John Wayne, Hardy,—now is your chance."

Mr Hardy held out his glass, eyes a little bloodshot. The bottle had suffered severe damage as to liquid level; he watched the liquid gold accumulating and tried to imagine a life in which he could afford liquor like that every day. He stared up at Cody.

"You son of a bitch," he said solwly. "I always did like the Dook . . ."

8 *The Legless Runner*

Savage slumped in his office chair, fighting off all the waves of despondency which threatened to drown him. He thought he'd almost cracked it the night before: the worst stand-up fight he and Jan had ever had, because he was so little at home; she'd torn into him mercilessly, screaming in rage until she could hardly speak, spittle running down her chin. Until she realised, quite suddenly, that he was saying nothing—just standing, watching her with the oddest expression in his eyes, like some wounded animal in a trap watching the hunger approaching. He had turned away into the bedroom, dragged his battered suitcase from the closet and began packing, and in that instant she knew she had lost him forever.

The mere thought of being left alone was sufficient to channel her into some semblance of sanity: from purely financial considerations it would be a disaster. She would not be allowed to live alone in a flat large enough for a family of four, and it takes time to go to court, arrange alimony. Further, the way Savage looked in that instant, she was doubtful that he would ever pay anything towards her comfort again; for the first time in her narrow, twisted life, she had seen the glare of genuine hatred in the eyes of another human being—and it was terrifying in impact.

Apologise—impossible. Plead—never. The most she could force herself to do was offer a hand of conciliation: a truce, a cease-fire, but not the end of the war. Savage was not persuaded to stay, but merely not to go right then; it was the best compromise either could hope for, and both knew that a new era had begun, a time of compromise—the minimum possible compromise to avoid out-and-out bloodletting.

The whole episode extracted a terrible toll from Savage himself; Jan's fiery uncontrolled tongue had mouthed insults neither would forget—foul, slanderous accusations which were, she knew, quite untrue: Savage had never looked at another woman, nor, she believed, in his present state, would he ever do so. She understood, in an uncaring, unforgiving way, that something was seriously wrong with the man; she did not care enough either to enquire or sympathise. He had not been, had been unable to be, a husband to her these six months or a year, and this she could never forgive; phyisical condition never entered into her assessment. He was no longer a man.

If she thought about it at all—an unlikely proposition—she put his condition down to overwork, nightwork, lack of sleep or any combination of the three. She had thought to arouse him by tantalising, mockery, and insults—to no avail; it was as if he had resigned himself to being virtually a block of wood and, in retrospect, she believed herself guilty of a serious error of judgement in letting her raucous laughter loose, the last time he failed totally. Men, she knew, could not stand ridicule of any kind; applied to their virility, it became a two-edged sword. Like most wives, she had acclimatised herself to sex with but one man, and it would have been easy enough for her to simulate affection, if that was what it would take to re-establish some kind of acceptable relationship—but she had begun to realise that any attempt at immediate reconciliation would be suicidal: she would only succeed in provoking him into one last try, followed by certain catastrophic failure.

In the end, they went to bed silently, either side of a chasm with dimensions quite unrelated to the space between their beds; silent, they lay awake into the sharp grey hours, and silent, they parted in the morning. Sitting there at his desk, brooding, Savage began to wonder if he would go home that night; if she would be there when he arrived; if they would speak ever again—the world seemed to be a swirling tide of uncertainty and indecision, and he faced the day with less enthusiasm, tired, jaded and unwell.

The telephone roused him from lethargy . . . an hour had passed and he had not even read the neat pile of reports Dee placed before him; he had looked up only once, to shake a weary head at the suggestion of coffee, and she went away, torn with indecision, knowing she should call the Company doctor, fearing Savage's reaction if she did. In the end, she did nothing.

"Don?"

"Yes, Jack. Whatever it is—can't you handle it?"

Martin's voice was concerned. "You all right? Christ, you sound bloody awful—want me to come over?"

Savage made an effort. "No—don't fuss, Jack. Bit short on sleep, that's all. What is it?"

"Terry Williams just called in on the phone. He's one of the men on Chaffey—"

"Yes—go on."

"Chaffey is up to something, Don. He went into Main Stores by the side door ten minutes ago—Terry and young Bobby Skelton went with him, all the way. They lost him inside, somewhere. Well—we got a man on every door within seconds, and ran a search straight through the building. Nothing."

Savage said irritably: "What do you mean—nothing? He can't vanish into thin bloody air."

"No? Listen—we picked him up twenty minutes later—walking through Production Engineering as if butter wouldn't melt in his mouth."

"Hold on a minute, Jack—" there had to be a simple answer to it, Savage thought desperately. If Chaffey didn't come out of any of the doors—there had to be another way out. Trouble was, there was no other way: Savage knew that building better than the lines on his palm and it was as tight as a duck's arse in winter—he'd stake his job on it. He grinned twistedly: maybe he had.

"Jack? I'm coming over. Side door, about five minutes."

Martin was waiting; Savage nodded to the guard on the door and followed his man inside, eyes irresistibly drawn upwards to the soaring tiers of storage racks overhead. The concrete floor was painted red in the walkways; they walked to the end of the section to talk to the storeman waiting.

"Chaffey? Yes—I saw him. Half an hour ago—went down the far end. I think he was making for the Valuable Items Store—that aisle is a dead end there."

Savage glanced at Martin. "Good enough. Come on—"

The storeman was right: the walkway terminated at a red-painted steel door, set in heavy corrugated asbestos sheet walls.

"You got a key to this place?" Savage demanded.

The storeman nodded.

"Well—open this damn thing up! Does Chaffey have a key too?"

"No, Mr Savage. Not officially—" the man flushed guiltily.

"For God's sake—yes or no?"

"I think he does have one. He keeps the union cash-box in their, nights—he doesn't have an official office."

Martin nodded. "That's right. Trust him to pick this place—ah—now we can see," and shouldered his way into the small enclosure. Perhaps ten metres a side, backed up against the vertical asbestos sheet outer wall; heavy wire mesh formed a roof of sorts. Savage had visited the place once or twice, on each occasion to investigate apparent theft of small items, and he stared round with narrowed eyes. The racks were loaded with items too costly to be entrusted to open storage—clocks, instruments, compasses, first-aid kits—whole shelves of these: the *Albatross* carried eighty large kits plus scores more in the many life-rafts. There were stacks of the expensive long-life batteries used in life-jacket safety torches; ingots of specialised metals and alloys—he recognised the expendable platinum-alloy anodes which minimised corrosion due to differing electric potentials between various parts of the hoverliner.

At length—

"All right, Jack. Are you going to tell me Chaffey came in here—and vanished?"

"All I'm saying is that he didn't come out of any ordinary door, Don. And Frank Mellor here saw him making for this place. Come on—there has to be an answer somewhere—"

There was—but it was thirty-five minutes before Jack Martin, clutching at straws, took a long close look at the metal grille in the main wall. It was barely half a metre long, half that in height.

"That's a standard de-humidifier, isn't it, Jack?"

"It is just that. But there's something odd about the grille, Don—look: these screws don't hold it secure at all—they're all dummies! Hang on—" the Security man pushed and pulled a little; in the end, he grunted with satisfaction and lifted the wire grille clear of the wall. The black rectangular face of the power unit and fan stared blankly at them; Martin grasped the box and pulled tentatively. It came free with surprising ease, and he set it down, breathing heavily, knelt and put his head and shoulders into the hole. The second wire grille had been modified to swing upwards, and Martin wriggled through—to find himself standing outside two massive polyester resin storage tanks, and completely hidden from the road.

He peered back into the store, grinning. "The Chaffey patent door," he said jubilantly, and Savage grinned back at him.

"Come on in again, you fool," he ordered. "Want to tell the whole bloody works what we've found?"

Martin clambered back and they took a long slow look at the modified unit.

"Jack," Savage said at last, "no wonder our pilferage rate is high. Mellor, you'd better nip off to your office and bring back an inventory list for this place: I want to see what's missing, if anything—and why our Mr Chaffey's so interested."

"Yes, Mr Savage."

They began a systematic check of contents; within minutes they found four cartons of torch batteries, empty, resealed and hidden at the bottom of stacks. Two stopwatches and four digital clocks, destined for the passenger saloons, missing. But Mellor, the storeman, claimed the honours.

"Mr Savage—take a look—"

"What is it? A can of oil?"

"Very special oil. Five litres of it. I know this stuff—it's the special high-temperature lubricant for the reactor control rods. EEC—the reactor people—supply this themselves. Two cans came in a week ago. But look here—"

Savage looked. Mellor had unscrewed the shining outer stopper, disclosing the thin alloy sealing cap beneath; there were two small round holes in it, each surrounded by a mini-bubble of green oil.

"Jack? What do you think?"

"Damned if I know. Let's have a look at the other can—Mellor?"

"It was issued this morning, eight thirty, I think."

Savage stared down at the container; deep at the back of his mind there was something screaming to be let out but he couldn't quite think . . . think what it was . . . where the other . . . Jesus Christ!

"Jack, for God's sake! They're commissioning the main reactor this morning, aren't they?"

"Eh? Well—yes. You mean . . , oh, no . . . he couldn't . . . you think Chaffey stuck a needle in each can, drew off some of the oil and refilled with something else? Oh, sweet Jesus, no . . . Don?"

He was talking to empty air.

After four or five strides, Savage knew there was no way he was going to make it in time. Halfway down the long walkway to the exit he damned himself for an impulsive fool: he could have reached the craft by telephone from the Stores offices—and here he was running the wrong damned way! And why hadn't he stopped to brief Martin?

The truth was that he was hideously afraid he could be too late by mere seconds; he knew that Perry and the EEC reactor crew had started the fire-up programme some two hours ago, that quite possibly—even now—those hellish control rods might be sliding into the reactor pile . . . he ran on, arms flailing, chest heaving for breath, through and out into the glare of spring sunshine, angling out across the concrete desert towards the *Albatross* access bridge. Some remote part of his brain was running a constant check on the straining body, and now he could no longer feel calf muscles, or the flexing knee joints; a tightening band of constriction was compressing his chest, each breath a major effort—and not yet halfway . . .

Voices far behind him . . . pink haze masking the perimeter of his vision . . . his feet, it seemed, were huge equine hooves, solid, unyielding, clumsy. Across the shaking flexible bridge, two figures in black overalls leaning far out over the rails to afford him passage . . . Savage began to lose all sense of sound, his ears filled by a gargantuan pounding, the massive *booo-oom booo-oom* of some timpani, and he smashed forward into the lateral gangway below and behind the bridge, equipment and technicians scattering, loose electrical leads reaching to trip him, angling left to stumble on down the starboard companionway, into the main saloon, teetering between piles of passenger seats awaiting installation. Everywhere heads turning, mouths wide, hands reaching . . . down the long tunnel between starboard auxiliary engine room and midships saloon, bursting into the rear saloon and hurling aside the two guards closing in on him. They recognised him, belatedly, and he knew that running feet were pursuing him, voices screaming . . . there was no feeling now below his groin and sheer animal instinct propelled him forward to the stairway leading down to the main engine room.

The place was a solid glare of light and noise which seemed to fade, in the space of a microsecond, into absolute silence and time began to slow down, such that his fall from the sixth-lowest step to the glassfibre deck resembled the gentle drift of a child's balloon. He caught flashes of white-clad figures with strange glass-fronted helmets clustered before a control panel before he crashed onto rubbery knees, palms sliding on oil-slick floor, and the light began to diffuse, darkness closing in until only a pinpoint glow remained and finally that too was gone and he was sinking, drifting deep into a black universe which contracted upon itself until . . .

Donald Savage awoke briefly, experiencing very short periods of lucidity, during the journey between BHLC and the radiation treatment annexe of Southampton General Hospital; there remained nebulous memories of whining sirens, the stroboscopic sequence of light and darkness passing through some woodland stretch, the movement of hazy figures around him. There were other vehicles in the convoy, rotary linear motors on all four wheels at maximum torque: batteries were expendable, lives were not. There were images of suspended bottles of dark fluid, firm hands manipulating his wrists, and he tried to speak with a tongue four times as large as his mouth until the dark tide washed over him once more.

They rushed Savage and nine other suspected cases of contamination into a sealed ward; they stripped him, burned every scrap of clothing and subjected him to interminable baths: soap, scrub, rinse and soap again. Vats of warm oily detergents drained away before jets of clean sterilised water until they were satisfied and began intravenous feeding of concentrated vitamins. Once in bed, they changed his blood again completely not once but three times, and, towards midnight, they allowed him to come slowly out of sedation, to sleep naturally.

Typically, on wakening to a lighted ward and dark-skied windows, none of the nurses would answer questions; a team of totally deaf doctors, it seemed, ignored his pleas and ordered a sequence of pathological tests and X-rays which lasted until early evening.

When Jack Martin arrived with an incongruous bunch of flowers, rather like a reluctant bridegroom, Savage managed to produce a crooked grin.

"They'll think you're queer, Jack—flowers for a male patient?"

Mr Martin said four very rude words and laughed. "So what?" he said cheerfully. "It's the bloody thought that counts. Do you feel as bad as you look?" he said curiously.

"Fug off, you old sod," the patient said thinly. "I'll see you out, you doddering old swine. Listen—for God's sake—what happened?"

"You mean you don't know?" incredulously.

Savage took a deep breath. "You don't know what it's like in here . . . they just don't listen. Do this, do that, do you want a bottle—last thing I remember was getting to the main engine-room—"

"You mean falling into the engine-room . . . I was about two minutes behind you—I stopped to bash in a fire-alarm. David Perry's in the next ward—mild case of burns but nothing serious. I talked to him this morning. Whatever Chaffey put in those oil-cans, it nearly worked . . . the control rods, apparently, were being inserted automatically—they used the lubricant before starting. When you arrived, temperatures were already off the clock and they couldn't figure why . . . then you fell down the ladder, crawled over and fell on the can of lubricant—"

"I did? I can't remember—"

"Fell on it? They had to prise it away from you. But the EEC engineers got the clue, abandoned the whole thing and dumped the rods. There was a very hectic five minutes putting out the fires—burning oil everywhere. Seems there was phosphorus in it . . . Chaffey has a lot to answer for, Don."

"Anyone badly hurt?"

"We'll never be so lucky," Martin told him. "Minor burns, some radiation problems but nothing really serious. Hell, you'll be out of here in a day or two—"

Savage nodded weakly. "See Jan?"

"Your wife? No. The sister says she's telephoned several times. Carl Wayne sends his regards—too busy to come in just yet."

"I don't wonder. *Albatross*—much damage?"

Martin shook his head, grinning hugely. "Minimal, they say. Maybe a week to sort out the reactor, let the place cool down a bit. The EEC boys are still shaking—they say the whole damned thing could have melted and dropped through the keel into the dock. You can smell burnt oil all over the Yard. Lucky? You could fall into a sewage pit and come up smelling of Chanel Mach 3. Here—move your legs—"

"Move—?"

"When you came in, you couldn't move your legs at all, the sister said. They all right now?"

Savage experimented cautiously. "Seem okay. Bit of cramp, pins and needles—been getting those for months."

Martin eyed the patient reprovingly. "I know. The whole Yard knows. Why in hell didn't you go see a quack?"

"None of your damned business. What about Grainger—and the van Heusen woman?"

"We had a call from Brewer—the Intelligence feller in London?—seemed really topped up. Apparently they put a crew into Grainger's London flat to monitor his phone—did a fantastic trade roping in people who called. Grainger's been at this for years, apparently; usual Swiss numbered accounts, stacks of money under the mattress. The girl—we held her in the Guard-room and two birds from MOD collected her."

"And Chaffey?"

"Under surveillance," Martin said slowly. "Now, don't get worked up, Don—we know what he did—but proving it is some-thing else. I had a word with Mr Wayne and he agreed: no evidence, other than the fact that Mellor in the Stores saw him making for the Valuable Items Store. I told Mellor to keep that fact quiet and I increased the team watching Chaffey."

Savage was tiring quickly. "So he's not sure if we're onto him, Jack?"

"I don't think he does. He'd expect to be picked up quickly and put through the mincing machine—by now he's got his confidence back. I thought we might get lucky if he contacts anyone else."

Savage nodded slowly. Somehow, things were settling down . . . Martin was doing a fine job and it was nice just lying here, relaxing . . . he'd discharge himself from this place tomorrow, maybe take a few days off . . . sort things out with Jan . . . maybe—

Jack Martin looked at the silent figure in the hospital bed. You poor old bastard, he thought affectionately . . . you've had a right beating the last few days—on top of whatever it is wrong with you . . . He glanced involuntarily at the long thin legs outlined under the sheet; they twitched, jerked spasmodically even in sleep, and he watched Savage's hand near his thigh, moving ineffectually as if to nudge the limb into life . . .

Outside, he found Jan Savage waiting, recognised her from the photograph on her husband's desk.

"Come to see Don?" he said brusquely.

"Yes—you are—?"

"Jack Martin—I'm holding the fort while he's away."

"Can I go in?"

"Best see the sister. He's asleep at the moment—what he

105

needs is rest. Plenty of rest and quiet. Nothing seriously wrong—a few little burns but they think they got all the radioactivity thing cleared up. That's not what worries me, Mrs Savage—"

She stared at him with hostile eyes, lips twisting in agitation. He said:

"There's something else wrong with him. Has been for months. You know what it is?"

"No—he never talked much about himself."

He nodded grimly. "That's Savage all right. Nut-case. Chances are he's let it go untreated too long. It's his legs, isn't it?"

The colour rose like a tide on the pale cheeks. "Yes—I think he has trouble breathing sometimes as well. And—" she broke off sharply.

"And?"

"Nothing. Nothing important. I'll come back tomorrow—maybe the next day," and she turned away, walking quickly towards the main corridor, heels clacking on the painted concrete floor. Martin watched her go, frowning. He had gained the odd impression that she was more afraid for herself than for Savage—and that didn't make sense . . . worse, he sensed that there was no deep concern about her man's condition—only an interest in self-preservation . . .

They came to Savage in mid-morning—the ward doctor, two consultants he had already seen, the sister. Within the curtained enclave, he sat up, against a pillow-stack, eyes wary.

Gillespie, the older of the two consultants produced the stereotyped bedside smile. "Well, now—Mr Savage. How do you feel?"

"Not too bad—" cautiously.

"Let me tell you about your condition," the doctor said comfortably, "and we can talk about possible treatment. Now—" he glanced at the case clipboard on his lap—"we can eliminate any difficulties with your burns . . . a few days and you won't know they were there. Contamination—I think we were very lucky in that respect. You had seven complete changes of whole blood, plus a quantity of plasma, within an hour of the accident, and I think we'll have no subsequent problems there.

"I think you know," Gillespie said, reprovingly, "that your

general condition is not good. Further, you appear to have pushed yourself to the absolute limit just before the accident, and this has resulted in strain to the lungs and heart—"

He held up a reassuring hand. "But nothing to cause concern, Mr Savage. In short, a week or two and you'll be as you were before the incident occurred. And that is what we want to talk to you about."

Savage thought grimly: I might have expected that. Nosy bastards . . . they know, all right . . . Christ, I may never get off this damned bed again . . . that quack in London—a year, maybe less, he said. A bloody sight less . . . oh, God, that bastard Chaffey—but for him . . .

The doctor watched impassively.

"Well, Mr Savage? You realise that when you arrived here, you had lost the use of your legs? We suspected spinal injuries—it seems you fell down a flight of steps—but X-rays of the lumbar region show no evidence of that."

Savage stared balefully. There was nothing to say; let them dig it all out for themselves; he'd be damned if he'd help them railroad him into a wheelchair.

Gillespie said gently: "I think you know quite a lot of this, don't you?"

The man in the bed turned his head away. The doctor went on talking, and slowly, painfully, the story began to emerge. In the end, Gillespie turned to his colleagues, read the expression in their faces.

"Whatever you may think yourself, Mr Savage, it is certainly not multiple sclerosis."

"Not—?" Savage's face was a mask of emotions—confusion, surprise, disbelief—even a trace of hope, Gillespie thought absently.

He went on: "It is true that MS affects the legs and the nervous system. It is, in fact, a neurological disease which attacks the nervous system, but in your case there are a number of important symptoms which are absent. In addition, there is no onset of the wasting of muscle usually associated with MS. You seem to be a naturally thin person, Mr Savage—tell me: has your weight fallen significantly in the last year?"

Savage was still feeling totally disorientated, trying to come to grips with an entirely new situation. "No—only in the last month or two . . . a kilo or two . . ."

"During which, presumably, you have been working very hard?"

The patient nodded.

"Very well. At the risk of seeming premature, I think we can write off MS—the immediate objective is to find out exactly what it is. That scar on the neck and shoulder interests me . . . a bullet wound, I think?"

"Yes. Ulster."

"Hm—mm. Take your jacket off . . . fine. Lean forward . . . do you recall which way the bullet was travelling, Mr Savage? I mean—through the neck and into the shoulder muscles—or the other way?"

"Other way—" Savage grunted, head between his legs.

"Hm-mm. Yes. And this was some eleven years ago. Your symptoms began appearing—when?"

"Huh? Oh . . . early last year. Fifteen months . . ."

Gillespie nodded offhandedly. "Any pain around the neck at that time?"

"More of an ache—"

"All the time? Or periodically?"

Savage thought about it. "I suppose all the time. Got used to it after a while."

"And the numbness in the legs, difficulty in breathing, all started at a later date?"

"Yes."

The consultant told Savage to dress again, talked briefly with his colleagues. Then—

"Mr Savage, we're not entirely happy about that neck wound. We're going to take some pictures, perhaps make an exploratory incision—see what is happening in there. I think we both know there are problems—would you like us to try for an answer?"

Savage said hoarsely: "You're joking . . . you can take my head off and stitch it back on again if it'll help."

The medical man smiled thinly. "I doubt we'll have to go as far as that, you know. One more thing . . . can you remember what you were wearing at the time you were shot?"

"Oh, God . . . uniform. The usual—combat jacket—helmet. An eye-eye—"

"An—I beg your pardon?" Gillespie stared.

"Image-intensifier. Ammo belt. My gun. Radio. Emergency rations—Christ, I was a walking Christmas Tree. We all were. Why?"

"Only a thought. My first guess was a steel splinter of some kind, possibly from your helmet—but the trajectory rules that out. Don't worry about it, Mr Savage; let us do our little tests and you can go home for a while. And rest—you understand?"

A sheepish grin. "Okay. You're the doc—"

"That's right. I'm the doc. And I have many other patients— good-day to you, Mr Savage."

He went out, with his entourage, leaving a very confused patient to grapple with the concept that, just possibly, things might not be so bad as they seemed.

9 Interdiction

South of the Isle of Wight, the sea was dark, oily-smooth, long regular swells running up-Channel with the tide. There was virtually no wind: the high-pressure area centred over Southern Ireland, free of frontal activity, produced a fine clear night of ethereal beauty during which surface temperatures fell steadily as the heat of the earth and sea was radiated into space. Overhead, the arched vault of infinity framed the glowing tapestry of island universes, and a slim crescent moon climbed a shadow gradient into the west.

On the skimming French-built hovermarine heading north, the pilot sat hunched over his wheel and radar screen, maintaining a steady sixty knots at half throttle. He would be long gone before sunrise; the timing was right but not impossible and, with his passengers gone, engines silent and the craft off-cushion and low in the water, there was little fear of radar detection. The Hirondelle carried ballast tanks and could submerge until the main deck was awash; the tiny glassfibre wheelhouse would be invisible to probing electronic eyes.

Further, he told himself, the battery-powered lift fans and water jets left no discernible trace on infra-red screens; Messignac sighed, lighted another Gauloise and checked his position.

On the flat aft deck, braced against a buffeting slipstream, McDowd and Saif Ibn Achmed squatted in the wheelhouse lee, examining explosives, scuba gear, depth gauges; Jean Paul Martin, already in black wet-suit with identifying blue legstripes, bent over the subtug lashed to the deck. Perhaps three metres long, a metre in diameter, it was a long sleek cylinder with pointed nose, a tail propeller in a protective duct. Forward, near the bow, a small clearplas screen gave protection to the driver's position; on each flank, similar screens had hand-grips for passengers. Behind the cockpit, an open access panel revealed a stowage compartment, in which Jean Paul stowed away spare air-bottles, torches, a portable welding/cutting pack.

Saif walked across the deck, a little unsteadily, lips moving in silent curses, and began passing rolls of plastique to the Frenchman.

"How long now, Paul?"

"About thirty minutes. Our drop point is five clicks south of the Nab Tower—you remember that on the chart?"

"Surely. I think maybe it is too far from the target—?"

"About twenty minutes—" the slim Frenchman stared across the deck at McDowd, lighting a cigarette between cupped hands. "You trust that one?"

"As much as I trust you, dear Paul," the Arab said softly, and his teeth gleamed in the starlight, as they had done that night off Tunis.

The other one grinned. "How nice to have friends, Saif . . . don't worry: this steel fish does all the work—all we have to do is hold tight. The pilot will detonate at exactly 2 a.m. Greenwich Time—when we are half-way home."

The Arab grunted, unconvinced. "And McDowd—this time he goes, too?"

"This time he goes. Most assuredly."

Saif nodded. "It is well. I told the Irish I do not wish to find myself standing under the camel's legs again . . . we were pissed on in Tunis, but never again."

"The Irishman," Jean Paul said thinly, "has many faults—but through him we have become rich, Saif. After this, we do not need to work again—"

The Arab shrugged philosophically. "Yes. But money is not all. Sometimes I think how I shall kill McDowd, if ever he . . . it would be almost as good as the money, Paul."

"I would keep such thoughts to myself, Saif. Time to get dressed—"

"I do not like these rubber suits," the Arab said bitterly. "It is like sleeping with a long-dead whore . . . in thick mud."

"You should know, old friend. In any case—these are free—unlike whores."

Saif laughed quietly. "True. But with this money I shall buy the most beautiful women in the world and live in some far place . . . I grow too old for such exercises as this."

"You'll never retire, Saif. You like the danger, the excitement . . ." The other made no reply, struggling into his wet-suit. But again and again he would stare up into the starry dome, as if to imprint upon his mind an image that he would never see again.

The craft slowed to hump speed, allowed its bow wave to overtake it and settled on the surface like some giant water-beetle. The tide was running free and strong; Messignac was obliged to head into the northwest on partial power to maintain position. The deck was dark; to the north, the muted glare of Southampton City.

It required the efforts of all five men, including the craft mechanic, to ease the subtug into the water; McDowd straightened up, breathing hard, to fasten the painter to a deck bollard. He stared around intently: darkness, broken only by some far-off flashing beacon, the pale glimmer of moon-light. They moved cautiously over the side in full diving gear, settling into position;

111

McDowd, driving, glanced at the others, lifted a hand in salute to the hovermarine and eased forward slowly on the power lever. The tug slid away, sinking gradually, until the waters closed in a swirl of foam and it was gone.

McDowd felt reasonably optimistic. He had done everything that planning and foresight could accomplish, but in all such operations one needed a little luck, a commodity he had found in plenty on many similar expeditions. The inertial navigation system would deliver them accurately to a point within a metre or so of that specified, cruising at the five-metre depth in a randomised zigzag heading to avoid the straight lines abhorred by nature. He hummed occasionally snatches of ancient jigs from a childhood in the villages of Kilkenny, bare fingers tattooing an accompaniment on the wheel.

After a few minutes, Saif and Jean Paul found it necessary to change hands frequently, massaging away the cramps; when the tug drifted to the bottom and came to rest after nineteen minutes cruise, they were stiff and chilled to the bone. For McDowd, the journey existed only as an interval between places, not times: they departed, they arrived. Had the trip taken nineteen hours instead, no complaint would have crossed his lips. Nonetheless, he thought sourly—there had to be easier ways of making a living . . . fifty years on and still no viable way of heating a wet-suit? Holy Mother of God, 'twas as well this was the last time.

With some satisfaction, helping to unload the subtug, he began calculating the exchange rate in Krugerrands at the current price of $2200 each . . . pity about Marin and the Arab— they'd made a good team for a handful of years, but there came a time for all partnerships to be dissolved.

The dissolution he planned was carefully orchestrated: the £3,000's worth of specially modified scuba gear came out of his own pocket, but a good investment, all the same . . . when pressure in his partners' bottles fell below a certain level, a valve would open, admitting potassium cyanide into the system— about the time they'd be halfway back to the French boat. The stuff worked very quickly, which pleased him: he would not want them to suffer. Not too much, anyway—he was essentially a humane man, McDowd . . .

The tug shifted uneasily in the quickening tide; McDowd tightened the bow anchor a little, turned, and adjusted the intensifier circuit in his visor. The tug showed as a sleek green shadow; Jean Paul and Saif, two hovering shadows on the edge of darkness.

McDowd checked: they were loaded for bear and ready to go; he switched on the subtug homing beacon, raised a thumb in query, nodded and headed out slowly to the south-west, flippers pounding a steady cadence.

"Confirmed unknown hostile, sir!"

"All right, Bailey. Calm down—there's a good chap. What fish are you working?"

"We started with Lucy, sir. She's watching the hovercraft. Operator Seven reports it is drifting slowly north on the tide— two men aboard. No identification marks but it's a Hirondelle commercial electric bulk carrier."

"I understand. And the sub-tug, Bailey?"

"Jack the Ripper's watching it, sir. He's the best we have for close surveillance, and Denise Crowley knows what she's doing. Three men aboard—moving up Southampton Water at about 20 knots. No markings, again—we have it down as a standard Westinghouse Surveyor—oil rig inspection module."

The Commander scratched his chin thoughtfully. "Whatever they're up to, I don't like it. Out to do someone a bit of no good, I'll be bound. Position now, sub?"

"Abeam Fawley Refinery, sir. If that's the target, they've left it damned late. I have two standby fish half a kilometre behind— I thought it best not to interfere until you got here, Commander."

"Quite right, Bailey—quite right. Have you signalled Admiralty Ops.?"

"Yessir. Copy of the Radex on your desk, plain language, sir."

The Commander sighed gently, looking at the master screen. "There's precious little moving, sub. What the devil are they after? What's that reference blip DKN5, south of Selsey Bill?"

The sub-lieutenant glanced at his notes. "Tanker, sir, inbound from Hamburg to Fawley with heavy crude—not due in for about twenty hours. The Oil Terminal's free, too—nothing discharging or sailing. I say—do you think this might be a dry run for something later on—?"

The Commander thought not. "Negative, Bailey. They'd be mad to make two runs—double the risk. Why doesn't that French thing off Bembridge show up better on radar?"

"Good question, sir. I've been thinking about that myself."

"Um. Look—can we get The Ripper close enough to see what that tug is carrying?"

"Stand by, sir." They moved over to the girl Denise: she was slim, teen-age, hair blue-black in the diffused lighting, and the Commander wondered for the hundredth time why it was only the adolescent, the very young, who had this magical faculty of communication with animals . . . And why did the talent diminish with advancing years, to finally disappear? What was it in modern society that seemed to grind away the innocence and purity of youth? They were lucky to get ten years from the best operators—and they were coming in younger all the time. Little Peter Snell was barely ten, with two full years of service already.

If Denise was aware of the officers standing nearby, she gave no sign. The contraption in her pursed lips bleeped and warbled softly, the sounds disappearing into the electronic nightmare which converted them into concepts understood only by trained dolphins. Bailey deftly lifted the lobe of an ear-piece, whispered. She nodded; slowly, the small screen image wavered, tracking, lines condensing from the murky background, and they watched in silence the hazy green images of the men aboard the tug.

The Commander said nervously: "Can they see our fish, Bailey?"

"Negative, sir. Poor visibility—what we see is computer-enhanced, of course. Less than a metre or so down there—three of four times that using Nighteye equipment—that's those odd bulbous visors they are wearing. In any case—if they do spot him—he's only a fish."

The Commander grinned. "Some fish! Scare them fartless, I would think. Too much like a shark—sorry, Denise—"

"She can't hear you, sir. Hold it—they're slowing down—on the bottom now . . . what do you make of that, sir?" The lieutenant's voice rose a tone in excitement.

"I don't like it, whatever it is. Bring up your standby fish, Bailey—smartly!"

"Aye aye, sir!"

They watched in silent, almost painful concentration. The camera followed every motion, zooming in to close quarters to inspect the equipment being removed from the stowage compartment; as the swimmers moved off in single file, the Commander straightened up and stared at his subordinate.

"Anything from Admiralty yet?"

"No, sir."

"Set up the situation on the main screen, large scale. Where are they now, sub?"

"Just off BHLC, sir—Christ! The dock gates! Can't be anything else!"

The Commander said thickly: "I hope you're wrong, Bailey. Get those other fish in close, now—are you getting this on videotape?"

"Standard procedure, sir. Wait . . . something showing—it's the gates all right. The leader has a marker of some sort . . . Orders, sir?"

The Commander's personal file specified 'High Personal Initiative' . . . it told no lie.

"Hit them hard, Bailey! All of them! That's explosives they're carrying!"

Deep down, near the base of the steel wall, where a breach would do most damage, McDowd outlined a set of soccer goalposts three metres wide in waterproof chalk, motioned the others in. Jean Paul slipped a loop of plastique loose, stripped the tape, rammed it onto the marked line and reached for another. Two metres away, Saif hung horizontally, hands moving deftly.

First charge in position . . . McDowd slit it lengthwise, reached for a detonator, jabbed it deep into the hardening goo ready for priming. He turned the red-painted knob a quarter circle and pushed down hard.

He felt only the surge of the pressure wave in the green silence punctuated by heavy breathing, streaming bubbles; no time for analysis: something crashed into the small of his back with stunning force, and he was forced bodily against the steel wall, dislodging the primed charge.

It drifted slowly down, until checked by his failing leg; the impact adhesive made contact and locked on.

Turning over slowly, shocked into temporary paralysis, he saw Jean Paul Marin whirling in the water like some demented pinwheel; the pointed beak of a great fish had caved in his chest and thin grisly streamers of lung tissue drooled from the gaping mouth of the dying Frenchman, mask blown clear away by explosive exhalation.

McDowd caught sight of Saif's body, drifting face down in a red haze of blood and small bubbles, and he knew his only chance was to feign death, before that damned fish hit him again. He allowed his body to slacken and drift towards the sea-bed, turning randomly like a discarded doll; he was painfully aware of the dolphin, poised on the rim of vision, and noted absently the dorsal equipment pack, the black eye of the TV camera.

His back . . . it was broken, sure to God . . . waves of pain swirled over him and he screamed silently into the echo chamber of his face-mask, slumping into the mud, right arm outstretched half under the massive gate edge. The dolphin hung motionless, metres away, watching for movement with bright intelligent eyes; vaguely he was aware of other fish, circling, inserting beaks into scuba webbing straps, and he watched through half-closed eyes. The bodies of Marin and the Arab moved away into the darkness, herded, prodded by sharp beaks.

His own sentinel moved slightly and McDowd froze in a frenzy of fear: he remained quite still, and the dolphin turned slowly in the tiderace; the diver felt tentatively with his right flipper for the under-gate slot, held on stubbornly with his right arm, sobbing with pain. The fish came closer, probing an experimental beak into his harness loops; the attempt failed and the thing backed away again, as if under orders. It stayed on point, facing him like some hunting dog, and he realised it was watching the thin stream of bubbles from his mask—betraying the existence of life.

The back-pack rotated; the black eye pointed; Mary Mother of God, could he do it?

McDowd took a long searching breath, exhaled. Another. And another . . . in his youth he had held his breath for more than 60 seconds—but now? Here?

He took a last breath and froze. He began to count—his watch was far under the steel gate. Thousand-and-one. Thousand-and-two . . . there it was again, devil take it . . . blue-black angel of death . . . thousand-and-six . . . seven . . . keep still, McDowd, for your life . . . don't move an eyebrow. Forget about breathing . . . it's a luxury . . . you don't need it . . . thirty-four . . . he could hear a great and ponderous thudding in his ears, as of some giant diesel engine, booom . . . booom . . . fifty-three . . . fifty-four . . . time and again, he fought the temptation, the craving for air, and knew only the endless ache of his chest and the fiery pain centre in his lower spine . . . sixty-two . . . sixty-three . . . Holy Father accept my spirit . . . sixty-six . . . he felt the swirl of water and raised his head. Through a pink mist, he saw the dolphin was gone and he drew in great shuddering breaths, cool, life-giving . . . was it really over? McDowd lay there for long moments, accepting the danger of the dolphin's return—slowly the red haze faded, the heart rate subsided to mere panic frequency and a twisted smile flexed stiff facial muscles around the mouthpiece.

Slowly, with infinite care, he moved away from that place of death, hugging the bottom, seeking deeper water, pulling with strong arm strokes, legs trailing uselessly behind. Presently, exhausted, he stopped, hung slackly in the dark sea, switched on the tub homer, turned the device until intermittent beeps faded into a continuous note. Taking a quick compass bearing, he headed off again, kicking slowly this time. Waves of nausea were breaking over him; eventually he stopped, spat out the mouthpiece and contrived to vomit, almost drowning in the process. After a rest, he tried again, more successfully, ejecting the sea water he had swallowed.

Moving slowly, he tried to analyse body sensations. His whole being seemed numb from the waist down—he was quite unaware of the roll of plastique jerking along behind him at the end of its tape; the right leg seemed unwilling to move at all, and in the small of his back there was a great burning vortex of agony, near the kidneys. He began to urinate in the suit, feeling the hot flow, the clogging thickness of blood in the dispensing tube. That damned fish had ruined his kidneys . . . and the operation. It seemed not to matter very much; his whole world had contracted to a mouthpiece, a mask, a compass heading.

Would he sleep on the bottom, this night? And forever? The darkness ahead became less intense, and he stopped, hugged the bottom, moved forward cautiously. Aft of the tug, a metre or so above it, a dolphin hung poised, head down, a subdued green glow from the backpack spreading through the water. Two others moved around on slow patrols, tails thrusting leisurely to hold position, orbiting the tug. McDowd absorbed the scene dully, impervious to disaster superimposed upon catastrophe; he considered briefly swimming back to the hovercraft and pain seared his back, just thinking about it.

In any case, he reminded himself, the French boat would be long gone before he . . . chances were, it was being watched, too. These people seemed to have an inexhaustible supply of the unholy fish; memories came flooding back of reading, somewhere, of American experiments in the Pacific. But the damn Brits had gone so much further—in total secrecy! The terrorist grapevine usually knew of developments like this; so much for friends, he thought bitterly. Wearily, he turned away, desperation flooding over him; more alone than he had ever been, he began the agonising process of swimming south-east, based upon a hazy plan for entering the Hamble river. But within minutes he knew that he might as well try for France; sobbing in agonised frustration, he turned yet again, making for the lights of the Southampton waterfront, a kilometre and a half away.

Perhaps, he thought vaguely, his luck might hold . . . there might be a Mick or two among the dock workers, or a safe house down in the red-light district. Not like the old days . . . when Southampton housed a whole company of Provos, to say nothing of a bomb factory or two. And all that had gone when the Dublin traitors sold out their country for a bucket of North Sea oil . . .

Now, he needed to rest more frequently, hanging inert on the dark choppy water, breathing with difficulty from bottles nearly empty by this time; on the crest of each swell, the lights seemed as far away as ever. He paddled feebly, each breath a torment, nursing the searing holocaust of pain in his back, drifting randomly now, strength all but gone; sometimes he sobbed, spitting out the mouthpiece, now flinging away his mask, now grinding out curses in a thin fluting voice . . .

10 Holocaust

In Damsel control, the Commander watched the main screen with ill-concealed suspicion, gnawing at a loose patch of skin on his left index finger. It was just a little too easy: the incident, from start to finish, had proceeded almost too well.

Perhaps he was giving his unit too little credit?

Maybe so. A launch from the Marchwood shore base was en route to pick up the bodies; they would have to get a diver down for the chap jammed under the dock gate.

He thought once more about that body. Limp, slack—that stream of bubbles slowing, stopping altogether . . . pity that Jack the Ripper was the only fish available carrying illumination gear; the Commander thought he would have liked to take another peep at that dead man . . .

He made a sudden decision.

"Bailey!"

"Sir!"

"Have you a spare fish available?" the Commander snapped.

"Yesser. Juicy Lucy and Suzie Wong are still at the subtug, waiting for the Marchwood crew—we can detach either one."

The senior officer sniffed. "I'm sure we can do without those damned names, Bailey. Oh, well . . . get one of them back to that dock gate and watchdog that third body until the Marchwood divers get there. And get me the chief Indian at BHLC—they'll have to be informed and maybe he can tell us what the hell's going on over there that's so important. And Bailey—"

"Sir?"

"I want a report on that body as soon as possible—it could easily drift away on the ebb."

"Aye, aye, sir."

The Duty Controller hurried away. Groping for his pipe, the Commander still felt uneasy—and he was certain they'd not heard the last of this night's work. Perhaps he'd left the interdiction a little late—but only because they could get no sense from the Duty Officer at Admiralty. And in any case . . . who would possibly want to wreck the *Albatross*? It was, after all, a passenger ship, not military—although he was sure, from what he had heard, that a military version would give the shrunken Navy the vital high-speed oceanic strike capability it lacked so badly. The Harrier-Carrier fleet was all very well, and the six Sea-Harriers carried on most British and WATO container ships pulled their weight. The whole business, it seemed to him, was old and slow and out of date, and aviation fuel cost so much today that a Special Finance Bill was needed in Parliament to fly a company of Marines out to Guyana or Corsica. Rumour had it that this new thing at BHLC cruised at some fantastic speed, although he discounted most of the rumours.

Perhaps . . . was that behind the raid tonight?

"Sir?

"We have a small problem, sir." The Lieutenant looked disturbed and apprehensive—as well he might.

"Go on, man!" testily. He'd been right, the Commander told himself. Christ!

"That third body—we've lost it temporarily. Must have drifted away, as you said, sir. I've three fish on search—we dropped Jack's marker buoy at the subtug and the Marchwood launch is there now."

"I see. Very well." The Commander got up, knocked out his pipe on the chair arm, dumping a hot coal on the floor; the Duty Controller winced and managed to get a shoe onto it . . . his damned floor would never look the same.

They moved over to the main screen. The dock gate showed in pale lavender, the dark olive-green shadow beneath dark and empty. The senior officer scowled, standing in silent rage watching the search deploy. Bailey pulled two more fish out of the Cowes reserve tank, sent them racing at flank speed up Southampton Water—representing more than fifty knots for a dolphin. The controllers worked their animals in over-lapping computer-programmed grid searches; Bailey, assuming the body had drifted, fed in details of tides and currents, concentrating the search on the sea bottom. The scuba gear, he thought optimistically, should pin the corpse to the mud like a lead anchor.

Minutes passed. Empty, unproductive minutes. Frequently, Bailey glanced at the face of his commanding officer, dark and lowering, and quailed before the thought of the inevitable Board of Enquiry, if that body wasn't found . . .

At Berth 34, the Continental Terminal, the early jetfoil flight to Le Havre–Cherbourg was filling fast. Passengers streamed on board; fuel tanks were topped-up with the synthetic alcohol fuel mixture based on vegetable waste and processed milkweed. It was shockingly expensive—yet still cheaper than aviation-grade Avtur.

The Captain swore he could run more economically on duty-free Japanese whisky, but the average jetfoil passenger ignored costs: 'if you want to know how much it is, you can't afford it—'

He ordered lines cast off at 04.00 hours, right on schedule; two hundred passengers, forty crew. In the main saloon, stewards began passing out pre-wrapped, self-heating breakfast trays, and the Captain stared out across the jet-black shimmering water towards the eastern sky: was there a giant glow of a false dawn? Daylight was two hours away—but the weather was fine: it bid fair for a good crossing.

"All engines ahead one third."

"All ahead one third, sir."

"Two points starboard—steady as she goes."

"Two points starboard—course one three five, sir," the helmsman said stolidly.

The Captain nodded. "Get Port Clearance, Number One."

Clear of the shore, Jetfoil Mistrall III began to build up speed: her micro-sonar scanned five hundred metres ahead of the knife-sharp foil pillars. Beneath the surface, the foils changed angle slightly and the ship rose bodily from the water, accelerating fast now up to the 40-knot mark. She headed away down Southampton Water and covered perhaps two kilometres before the port foil pylon struck McDowd, paddling feebly on the surface. The curved steel blade sliced into his belly, folding him neatly back across the pylon, killing him instantly; the water pressure held him pinned there and the onboard computer of the jetfoil sensed the change of trim, flashed a warning light and hooter alarm on the bridge.

The Captain opened his mouth to order an emergency shutdown, with a flash recall of a collision with a basking shark off Ushant the year before—and the computer acted swiftly to compensate the sharp yaw to port.

On the drifting French hovermarine, Claude Messignac was in a fever of indecision: detonation time had come and gone, the sea was dark and empty, his passengers long overdue. The deadline for waiting was a forgotten memory—he should be halfway to France by now, and his instructions were very clear: detonate on time, even if the team failed to rendezvous. But supposing they were still at the target?

Messignac shrugged, opened the storage locker, switched on the transmitter. He turned to his co-pilot.

"Get under way. Home for us, old friend."

He heard the fans winding up to lift speed, felt the craft tremble and thumbed the transmitter button . . . some instinct made him turn towards the distant shoreline, visible now in the crescent moon on the port quarter. Far away, a red ball mushroomed skywards, and he grinned: *his* money was safe, at least.

Seconds later, another and vaster explosion vomited skywards—a vast boiling nexus of flaming gas and smoke. Messignac frowned . . . only one detonation was anticipated . . .

With paralysing speed, the hovermarine was flooded with light from the patrol boat surging closer on full silent electric power—almost on top of them and riding a white bow wave. One of those new British steam-electrics with emergency rocket acceleration . . . Messignac knew there would be no running away from this fellow: he could wind up to 100 knots in ten seconds. He turned to the engineer, shrugged, made a twisting motion with thumb and forefinger; the other spat and said forcibly:

"Merde!", switching off the engines. They waited in self-accusing silence in the white glare of the searchlight, swaying gently with the motion of the craft.

On the jetfoil, events occurred with horrific speed. The plastique blew away her port pylon and half the bow in the twinkling of an eye. Barely half a kilometre from shore, abeam the Hamble Shellmex tank farm, the resultant swing was far beyond the capability of computer, automatic pilot and rudder to control. The foil listed hard to port, bouncing along on the ruins of the bow structure, her list advancing every second. The bridge crew were in a tangled terrorstricken heap in the port pelorus, incapable of stopping engines running at full power: conditions in the engine-room were indescribable. The 1,000-tonne craft ploughed up over the shingle beach, shedding remnants of shattered foils and pylons, and rammed her bow into a storage tank containing a million litres of high octane petrol.

An early workers' bus in the Hamble Lane caught the full fury of the deadly tide; the driver saw the surging wall of burning fuel, as high as a man's shoulder, advancing on a broad front across the fields, and jammed his foot hard on the gas pedal, screaming in sheer terror. The old sluggish diesel responded— too slowly; within seconds, bus and thirty-two passengers were incinerated; weeks later, only the scorched chassis would be found.

The morning wind from the south began to pick up burning debris, carrying it a kilometre to the cluster of high-rise suburbs, and the initial cataclysmic explosions rocked the city in a series of deep reverberating pressure waves after the nature of a 'stick' of bombs. Windows lit up . . . people peered out nervously into the scarlet sky and before they were fully awake, building after building ignited like Olympic flames, surrounded by torching trees and outbuildings. On the edge of the fire belt, vaporised fuel drifted down like lethal rain, coating every surface with an oily film which flash-ignited with flames still twenty metres away.

One after the other, the remaining 35 tanks on the oil depot boomed into oblivion, giant contorted fireballs leaping skywards, and the deadly flood rolled on, ever reinforced; zero plus fifteen minutes and the eastern outskirts of the city were engulfed in a sea of destruction. The suburbs—Weston, Bitterne, Woolston—were ablaze from end to end, a disaster of such staggering proportions that seventeen days were to elapse before the last flame flickered and died: three months before the last charred remains were slipped quietly into a plastic sack and taken away.

Without really knowing how he got there, Savage stood at the bedroom window, shaking with cold and shock, legs stiff and racked with cramp. Beside him Jan clung to his arm, trembling violently without cessation, and they stared incredulously at the sea of fire spreading out into the estuary below, like some ancient red Japanese fan; for long moments they were bereft of speech, until he turned, made her put on a robe. A fleeting thought crossed his mind and he stumbled into the lounge, drew back the drapes; the window faced south-east, towards the epicentre, and he saw at once that they were in real danger. Already, buildings were flaring in the heart of upper Weston, half a kilometre away; as he watched, a six-storey block much closer blossomed into a ghastly pear-shaped furnace . . . he could smell the reek of heavy fuel vapour, stronger with every moment.

"My God! Jan—hurry! Get some clothes on—fast! We have to get out of here . . . the whole place is going up!"

She stared uncomprehending.

"Come on, damn you!"

She sensed the fury in his voice and reacted instinctively: a hand slashed out and left a thin line of blood on his cheek.

"Don't you talk to me like that, blast you! You can't get me out of here like that . . . throwing me on the street . . . not for some damned fire miles away . . . get away from me!"

Savage felt the blood drain from his face. "Janny!"

She screamed hideously. "Sod off, Savage! This is *my* home and no-one throws me out of *my* home . . . NO! STAY AWAY FROM ME!"

Jan was screeching hysterically now; Savage backed away from her, making for the bathroom with some tortuous idea of finding a tranquiliser, and she flashed past him into the bedroom, slammed the door. He heard the clash of a bolt and he was at the door, pounding, shouting, pleading . . . something heavy being pushed against the door inside . . . incoherent screams and sobbing . . . he turned away from the door and buried his face in his hands. *Jesus God Almighty . . . help me . . . help me . . .*

Fumbling blindly, he found a jump suit, friction boots, pulled them on, tried the bedroom door again, shoving hard with his shoulder; it gave a little but held again and again . . . Savage recalled the fire axe in the lobby cabinet, fourteen floors down—the only one left by the vandals because it was outside the block warden's apartment.

In the hallway, groups of residents clustered round the windows like some Guy Fawkes night crowd watching fire-works, ooh-ing and ah-ing with each fresh fireburst; Savage tried to warn them of the danger and they laughed . . . don't be ridiculous, they mocked. What could possibly happen to an all-concrete and steel block seventeen stories high? There was no profit arguing with them—Savage limped to the elevator and was hurled to one side by a new rush of residents from lower floors, come to watch the fun. Alone, he made it down as far as the tenth floor and had to fight his way out past a horde of sightseers bound for the roof; they refused flatly to go down, invited him to join the party, passing round bottles and cans.

Twenty flights of stairs came very close to killing Savage: there was no strength in his legs and his heart, he knew, would explode like an over-ripe orange before many seconds passed . . . he staggered through the swing door, lurched against the wall, fingers scratching impotently, coming to a rest kneeling in a corner, coughing as if his heart were about to tear loose. He was aware, dimly, of the chattering excited throng milling around, waiting for elevators, of the flickering red glare through the big double doors, and suddenly there was no oxygen in the air and his lungs were bursting . . . he began crawling to the door, a hand, a leg, at a time, people falling over him, cursing him, and the door was closer, open and he was through.

Savage rolled down the shallow steps, ducking the slanting sheets of water flooding down the façade and he knew shockingly that it was not water but condensing gasoline vapour finding cold concrete and steel to reach a fluid state. He began scrambling away from the block, insanity pressing into his brain with indomitable pressure, and he could see nothing but visions of human torches, running incandescent figures in their last agonies, and far to the back of his mind, behind the fear, lay a single thought that would haunt him forever: he had left Jan behind . . .

A hundred metres from the block at the edge of the park, a concrete gully carried away water from a cluster of springs to the sea; he saw it when only an arm's length away and rolled down it, headlong, into half a metre of water. It tasted foully of filth and sewage but he went straight under like a diving porpoise, to absorb as much as he could into his clothing. His head came above water—and the sky opened up in a titanic white flare with a pressure wave that sent a thick young sapling sailing across the water duct above him with a hissing of air through the leaves.

Instinctively, Savage ducked under again, feeling the whiplash of radiant heat on the back of his suit . . . he scrambled frantically forward, straining for air, hands slipping and rasping on the slimy bottom of the duct, and suddenly he was in blessed shadow, in a flashing green-pink tunnel of bushes through which he could see the ravening flare of flames enveloping the tower block. Mini-explosions boomed, fifty, a hundred metres in the air as drifting concentrations of fuel vapour ignited, and the great building was cocooned with amber and red flames, standing in a spreading lake of fire and overhead, reflecting the nightmare below, a drifting nauseous cloud of smoke and debris.

He stared in mute impotence at the colossal torch until he became aware that here, too, he was far from safe: trees and undergrowth were flash-igniting, and he went away from the holocaust, sometimes walking, at other times crawling, dragging himself along, towing useless legs behind a body racked with pain. In later days he came to recognise that the shock reaction which stripped his mind clear of thought probably saved his sanity; he remembered nothing of the journey through streets of bedlam to the great bridge over the Itchen river, of fighting viciously with fist and body, to stay with the screaming crowds climbing the access ramp. There were dim, distorted flashes of twin streams of stunned survivors crossing the bridge, separated by the tight-locked convoys of ambulances and police cars moving east into the fire zone.

Already, an hour after ignition, there was some semblance of a relief operation working at the City end of the bridge; as Savage dragged himself the last few yards, climbing to a steel guardrail sticky with burned hydrocarbons, nurses and first-aid men were sifting through the human torrent of misery, ignoring those who could walk, seeking those with more than superficial injuries. He learned, much later, that in those early hours real injuries were in the minority: people caught by the fire rarely survived, and there was a thin trickle of twisted ankles, dislocated shoulders, sustained in the panic exodus. With a handful of others, he was bundled into an ambulance and came to rest in a long echoing corridor of the same hospital he had left, short days before.

A nursing sister recognised him; they left him to his mug of warm sweet tea and tranquiliser, and later, in a brief interlude between ambulance convoys, a harassed but cheerful Gillespie came to him.

"Bad penny turns up again, Mr Savage—eh?"

Savage gazed at the doctor with eyes still stunned by the immensity of the disaster.

"Dr Gillespie?"

"How do you feel? You've been very lucky, you know—lost a little hair, a little skin—but very lucky. I suppose you were picked up close to your home?"

The man on the stretcher grinned with a certain distorted pride. "Not on your bloody life, doc—must have covered two kilometres or more. Got to the City end of the bridge."

Gillespie frowned. "Remarkable. Couldn't have done your legs much good. I don't see your wife around—?"

"Jan? She's . . . she wouldn't—I tried, doc—God, I tried. She locked herself in the bedroom—thought I was trying to . . ." he broke off and turned his head away.

Gillespie said: "I'm sorry, Mr Savage—truly I am. There will be many more before this night is over . . . I must go, soon—more arriving every moment. One thing, very quickly—your own problem? The tests we did . . . I think we may have found something. Purely by chance—we irrigated your blood system with a chemical to show up on X-ray, looking for constrictions and deficiencies in the circulation. We found something odd near that neck wound . . . tell me, were you wearing any kind of insignia on your uniform shoulder the night you were shot?"

"Insignia?"

"Badges—specifically plastic badges—?"

Savage made a huge mental effort to concentrate. For Christ's sake, what was the man talking about uniforms for—in the middle of all this? Badges . . .

"Shoulder badge," he said slowly. "We wore a plastic shoulder badge—regiment. Green plastic—that's right. Why?"

"That bullet, Mr Savage, entered the upper arm, went on through the badge and into the neck, before moving away. I think there's a small piece of the badge buried in your neck, very close to the main nerve fibres, producing the intermittent paralysis and other symptoms. I'm sure your military people X-rayed you thoroughly, but it wouldn't show up on normal X-ray. Purely by chance, the plastic reacted with our chemical additive and produced some kind of mineral salt which did show up."

"You mean?" Savage said uncertainly.

"There's a letter in the post to you already—the sooner we get that fragment out, the better. I didn't like the look of it at all: there's a fuzzy halo round it which could be the start of a growth of some kind. Look—I must go, Savage—but when things settle down after this hellish mess, I'll have you in one more time. For the moment—rest easy."

Left alone—in the core of a ceaseless flow of patients, staff and survivors—it seemed to Savage that he had come full circle . . . it was as if he was an embryo reaching full term, about to enter a strange new world. It would be a world without a home—and without Jan. Perhaps even without a job, if the quacks kept him in hospital too long . . . there were too many people lined up for every chance. Well . . . maybe he could try somewhere else—maybe overseas?

He tried to imagine how life would be, fit and well again . . . God, supposing that damned fragment was responsible for *all* his problems? He began to appreciate that there was a chance—the faintest possible chance—that he might be a man again, in every sense of the word. But too late . . . if this had only happened a year ago . . . Jan . . .

He lay there on the stretcher under the red blanket, face stained with smoke and sweat, a cigarette burning, forgotten, in his fingers. He stared up at the ceiling with eyes that insisted on smarting and blinking, and a tear tracked down a smoke-blackened cheek, leaving a clean fresh trail like some new highway to a distant and brighter sunrise . . .

11   *A Deal is a Deal is a Deal*

Villa Borghese, Via Castellano, Palermo, Sicily
Eight Fifteen Local Time.

"Ajaccio 51–385?"

"Si."

"This is the International Operator at Messina. I have a person-to-person call for Don Ricardo Vicenzi on this number, from New York Operator Number Four. You can accept this call, Palermo?"

"Don Ricardo does not use the telephone personally. Who is calling?"

"The call is from a Signor Keyhoe, New York City. That is K-E-Y-H-O-E, Palermo—"

"Bene. You will wait . . ."

"Don Ricardo will speak now, Messina—"

"Go ahead, New York—I have your party on the line—"

"Don Ricardo?"

"I am he."

"Ah—you speak English. Wonderful. Listen—I have been dealing with your New York agent—Giorgio Fiumente . . . you still there, Don Ricardo?"

"I am here. You will speak slowly, please. I will understand. You speak of the business arranged by Giorgio?"

"Damn right I do, Don Ricardo. Say, what kind of operation

129

do you guys run, anyway? I read in the papers we've . . . blown it. In a big way. You unnerstand?"

"I know this. Mr Keyhoe. Our failure is regretted deeply. Your fee will be returned in full."

"Like hell it will. Listen, for me the deal is still on. I don't want no fee—I want action. We have about five weeks to deadline—you follow me?"

The line hummed gently for a long moment.

"Mr Keyhoe, we supplied materials and transport as agreed. You supplied the men. Perhaps *they* failed—not the material. But we do not argue with customers. Your money will be returned: the contract will be filled."

"Shove your money, Don. I don't care about that end. Listen—you know the objective—can it be hit before it leaves for America? The additional fee will be generous—"

"I told you, Mr Keyhoe. This is our responsibility now. We will retain your original payment pending successful completion. Which will be in fourteen days or less from this time."

"Yeah? You sound very confident, Don Ricardo."

The shrivelled little man in the dark worsted suit stared out across the bay, to the hills and the twinkling lights of the waterfront.

"We will try, Mr Keyhoe. To the best of our ability. This has always been enough in the past—"

The voice from New York chuckled. "Yeah, I guess it has, at that. Okay—I can leave it in your hands, Don Ricardo?"

"Yes."

The line went dead. The old capo di capo replaced the instrument he detested so much gently upon its cradle, walked round the desk and pressed the recessed button. Four sons . . . four telephone calls . . . four deaths . . . no wonder his heart still pounded at the shrill of a telephone bell, he thought sadly.

He waited patiently. At age 71 there was sixty years of waiting behind him, while other men did his bidding, and nothing would make time flow faster. Soon, a thick-set man with heavy eyebrows that shadowed his eyes came into the room. He wore black slacks and a black sweater and walked like a cat on soft

130

rubber shoes with a peculiar heel-lifting gait that hinted of crouching, subdued violence.

"Pietro," the Don said tiredly, "I want four soldiers available immediately to travel to England for an important duty. They must be in Southampton tomorrow morning and they must contact you here at nine exactly for instructions, leaving a number you can call back. They must have weapons and money, and be prepared for a stay of two, perhaps three weeks."

"Yes, Don Ricardo."

"And bring me the file on Giorgio Fiumente. I wish to know those with whom he arranged to have plastique supplied to a man named McDowd in Le Havre. The supplier, in the name of the Family, may have provided defective materials; the man McDowd and many others were killed."

"I understand, Don Ricardo. And the supplier?"

"Have someone take care of him. We must protect our good name, Pietro. And—one more thing—"

"Yes, Don Ricardo?"

"Fiumente should be reminded of the importance of arranging reliable suppliers. I know the man . . . he thinks and moves too fast . . . perhaps a little problem with a kneecap will slow him down a little . . . enough to learn his lesson."

"*One* kneecap, Don Ricardo?"

"Of course. You think I am a vindictive man, Pietro?"

12 *Lepe in the Dark*

Dr Gillespie, for no other reason than professional curiosity to determine a correct diagnosis, sent Donald Savage north, in the van of thousands of fire casualties, to a Manchester clinic owned by a personal friend of the consultant; a concentrated programme of tests and they wheeled a drowsy Savage down a gleaming corridor into a theatre; he lay, it seemed, in warm cottonwool, staring up at a vast circular light fitting, watched with detached curiosity as an anaesthetist inserted a very large needle into the back of one hand, and vaguely remembered starting to count.

The following day, Gillespie was pleased to take a telephone call, if only to find time to take a breath: the General was bursting to the seams with a ceaseless flow of casualties.

"Gillespie."

"Peter? Hello—Peter Lucas here—Manchester. Busy, I suppose? Really? I can imagine—we're taking overspill here, too,—as far up as Preston. Short of good burns men, as always. Yes. Now—your man Savage. We put him through yesterday. You were quite right, old chap. Nasty chip of plastic—about the size of a penny. Jammed up against the spinal column, compressing a ganglion. Must have played hell with his nervous system. And I think we got to it none too soon—well-establishing casing of fibrous matter around it. Could well have turned malignant—but there it is. Came out cleanly, easy as shelling a pea—but no wonder they didn't pick it up on X-ray: we checked with the Ministry of Defence, and they say it was a plastic developed in the Vietnam days for anti-personnel mines. Impervious to X-ray. Well—he should be all right. We'll send him back in a day or two—I would give him a week or so before you see him, but I can see no problems. Yes. What? Not at all. My pleasure, old boy. 'Bye—"

Nine days later, Savage walked slowly into his office and found Dee Purdy taking a call; she glanced up, glowed with pleasure at the sight of him and got rid of the caller quickly.

"Don!"

She came to him quickly, impulsively, hands on his shoulder, holding up her face. Off guard momentarily, he kissed her instinctively, a welcome-home kiss that progressed to something quite different; she moved back, pink-faced, in some confusion.

"Don—you look marvellous!"

She spoke no more than the truth: Savage was walking with near-normality, and the chest pains, the pins and needles, the leg-cramps, were becoming only bad memories. In his heart, he had not really come to grips with his changed situation; each morning, on wakening, there was the old intense premonition that he'd fall on his face getting out of bed. He thought the week in a Blackpool convalescent home had helped—it meant seven more days without having to worry where he would live. In a long but spasmodic telephone conversation with Jack Martin, Savage learned that only a blackened shell remained of his apartment block; that a week after the fire, clean-up squads were still two miles from the epicentre. That more than a thousand people, like Jan, were dead and thirty times that number in hospitals nationwide with burns and other injuries.

Martin, typically, had offered to provide a bed for the prodigal boss—but Savage was only too aware that the offer was more rhetorical than realistic: Martin supported a wife and three children, one of whom was an eight-year-old spastic boy. There was a perfectly good bunk in the back office of the Guardroom, and he could eat reasonably well—and inexpensively—at the works canteen.

He grinned cheerfully.

"I feel fine! What's new in Security?"

She wrinkled her nose despairingly. "Never mind business . . . sit down and let me fix you a drink. I heard about . . . the fire—your wife—" her voice fell away.

Savage nodded moodily. "That was some night—you were well out of it, Dee. Did you see it?"

"My God, yes. Some of us living on Lepe Beach walked up to Calshot Spit. We could see most of it . . ."

Years later, she could still not describe her feelings, that night. She had stood in night clothes and a thin raincoat, slippers sinking into the soft sand, staring up Southampton Water at the horror unfolding five miles away; she had to keep reminding herself of the distance involved, to keep in some perspective the awful dimensions of the tragedy. Even at that distance, it was light enough to read small newsprint, if she had wanted; worst of all, the smoky fall-out began to reach her—nauseous disgusting odours that defied description, until she could bear it no longer and retreated, gagging and retching, to her mobile home.

Savage said: "Do you know what caused it, Jan? I've heard nothing but rumours—"

"It was the jet-foil, Don—it went out of control and smashed into the Oil Storage tanks at Port Hamble. I've heard people say the boat exploded first . . ."

"Nothing to connect it with us, here?" he said slowly.

The girl shook her head. "I don't think so. But there was a panic meeting yesterday morning—Jack Martin was there. Have you seen him?"

"Not yet, Dee. How's David Perry? Everything all right with the *Albatross*?"

"Everything's fine," she said. "He thinks they can launch in about ten days time—they had some problems with the power plant after that awful business—"

"I know. Well—it doesn't look as if anyone's missed me very much—" he said ruefully. He got out of the chair, walked to the window and watched the movement in the Yard for a moment or two. Behind him, Dee said diffidently: "I missed you, Don—"

"Oh, sure," he grinned over his shoulder. "No-one shouting at you."

"Fool," she said happily. Perhaps she had said enough . . . more than enough, she thought. It didn't seem to matter. She stared at him.

"Where are you living?"

"In the Guardroom—temporarily. Don't worry—I'm all right," he said lightly.

Dee Purdy hesitated, uncertain of what the future might hold . . . perhaps it was too soon after Jan . . . perhaps not.

"You could do with a solid meal or two," she said at last. "You'd better come over to the beach this evening—I'll sort out something nourishing. About seven?"

"Sounds good, Dee. I can borrow a jitney, I expect. Thank you."

The girl flushed. "I think Carl Wayne would like to see you— should I ring him?"

"No—I'll go down there. See if I still have a job—" but his eyes twinkled and she stood quietly in the office for long minutes, staring at the door, her hand rubbing the side of her neck reflectively.

*

The Chairman's welcome verged on the boisterous. Jack Martin was with him, and they got up as Savage came through the outer office; there was a new secretary behind the reception desk, he noted wryly—a stern-face horsy woman or fifty or more, who started asking questions, until Wayne heard Savage's voice, took him through into the conference room.

"Don! Bloody good, man! Just got back? Fit to start work?" he bellowed.

Savage stared blankly at the Canadian. "I still have a job?"

Wayne jabbed Martin in the ribs. "See what I mean? You try to figure this guy out—I give up! Sit down, Don. How are you?"

"Feeling good. Thought I might be in the doghouse after going missing for two weeks—"

"Good grief, Don—forget it. Hell—you saved the *Albatross* when the reactor went sour—and then getting involved in that fire—say, I'm sorry about—"

He broke off awkwardly.

Savage said evenly: "I know—thanks. Jack—nice to see you. Everything under control?"

They made him sit down, and brought him up to date. Grainger, under arrest, had resigned—as had Betty Weiskopf, for no other reason that anyone could see, than she expected Grainger to implicate everyone possible. Julie van Heusen was in Holloway awaiting trial for offences agains the Industrial Espionage Act, 1985.

Savage nodded. "I heard that before I went sick. What about Chaffey?" The others exchanged glances. Wayne said defensively: "We thought it best to let him run loose for the time being, Don. We watch him constantly—so far he's behaved himself. What do you think?"

"I think," Savage said bitterly, "we ought to drown the bastard in a barrel of oil. I'd feel a lot safer. Still—as long as he's here and apparently unsuspected, his bosses might think twice about feeding in a complete stranger. You don't think he lost complete contact when Grainger was arrested?"

Wayne thought not. "Seems they usually have emergency channels in cases like that. The Special Branch is watching his home, reading his mail—so far nothing."

Savage nodded, deep in thought. "That jet-foil thing—"

"Yes?"

"Any connection with us?"

Carl Wayne nodded sombrely. "Strictly between us, Don, very much so. Commander Chisholm came in with an officer from Gosport last week. Seems that there was an abortive attempt to blow up our dock gates to destroy *Albatross*."

"Jesus!"

"We were lucky. The Navy picked them up early enough and intervened, but they think the jetfoil probably detonated some of the explosive involved. There were three men—they only found two afterwards."

"Who were they?"

"We don't know. No personal identification—they wore long johns under wet suits—no markings. But one of them was probably from the East—an Arab, North African, perhaps."

Savage chewed his lower lip, deep in thought. "You know that doesn't sound the sort of thing the Russians would mount. I mean—it's too much like a military operation. How did they travel? An air drop?"

"Mini-sub. Westinghouse—an American type used for working on oil-rigs." The more Savage thought about it, the less he liked the idea of Russian involvement. He said so, vehemently.

"Look, we know they're almost home and dry with their thing. Sure, they'd like to delay us—they damned nearly did, through Grainger and Chaffey. But what they need is a 'genuine' industrial accident—not a commando raid."

"What you're saying," Carl Wayne said incredulously, "is that there is someone else after our guts?"

"Doesn't it make sense? But who, in God's name?" Savage began rubbing his right thigh, realised that the gesture was purely habitual and forced himself to relax. "When you get down to it, Mr Wayne, who else could possibly be interested in wrecking the *Albatross*? This Company has held all the major patents of the hovermarine almost since Day One—"

Martin said sheepishly: "Call me stupid but I still don't know the difference between a hovercraft and a hovermarine—"

"Just ignore him, Mr Wayne," Savage said comfortably.

The Chairman looked at Martin and nodded. "All the same . . . I'm starting to worry about how many people know about

136

the craft—how many know she's nuclear-propelled. You know that, I suppose?"

Martin nodded. "But nothing else. Listen, I'm not sure I even *want* to know—" he grinned disarmingly. "Too many people getting in trouble from knowing too much."

Carl Wayne glanced at Savage. "How about you?"

"No idea. David Perry develops lockjaw every time anyone asks him."

The Chairman nodded. "Quite right too. But you two have done as much as anyone to get us this far—and in any case, we'll be releasing details immediately after the trials. Briefly, we use the reactor to heat up mercury vapour to about 4,000 degrees and pump it round a drive tube submerged under the craft. Sea water enters the front and is converted instantly into steam, which jets out of the aft end of the propulsor. Around 100 knots, at full working temperature, the water is vaporised some ten feet ahead of the intake—and the thing works like a ram-jet aero-engine. She's designed to cruise at about 300 knots—nearer 350 on a calm sea."

He grinned at the expression on Martin's face—lugubrious in the extreme.

"You'd never get me on a thing like that," Mr Martin said very firmly. The others laughed. Yet Savage felt the same way—and didn't have Martin's nerve to admit the very idea terrified him. He'd heard rumours . . . but 300 knots? Christ, if they struck a floating matchbox at that speed, it would ruin them.

Wayne nodded. "That's what I thought, too, Don. But she carries microsonar good up to 150 knots—hooked into the steering computer: if anything big lies ahead, the autopilot adjusts to avoid it. At higher speeds, we use a pair of drones linked to the craft by thin wires—you've seen them on trial in the river?"

"What—those torpedo things with needle-noses?"

"That's right, Jack. They keep station a kilometre ahead automatically, giving us ample collision warning. And of course, *Albatross* can stop in a very short distance. Even at that speed."

Savage stood up. "Mr Wayne, I could listen all day—but we have work to do. I'd like to talk to the Navy people—see exactly what they found, what they can tell us. One last point—"

"Yes, Don?"

"You don't think they've given up now—our explosive friends?"

Wayne shook his head. "No such luck. Whoever they are—and there are four or five companies in various parts of the world working on ocean-going conventional hovercraft—they're not about to call it a day. They wanted us bust—they've failed so far. Presumably, the requirement still exists. Thanks to Jack here, our security here is 100%, I think. In addition, the Navy tell me we don't need to worry about more underwater attacks. And they're running a surface patrol with launches from Marchwood."

Savage scratched his chin. "That only leaves inside problems, I would say. I'm going to pull Chaffey in, sir—I don't think we can afford the risk of having him running around loose. He may not have contacted anyone—but how do we know he hasn't been contacted himself?"

Wayne nodded sombrely. "I think you're right, Don. It's your decision—you know I'll back you all the way."

"Well . . . that's nice to know. Tell you what, Mr Wayne—"

"Yes?"

"As soon as the *Albatross* leaves on her maiden flight, I'm taking a few days off—if that's all right."

"Absolutely—how do you fancy a week or two in New York?" Wayne said innocently.

"Huh?"

"You're down for the first trip yourself, Don—with as many BHLC people as we can pack aboard."

"Christ!"

"Quite. They'll be drawing lots on the shop floor, but you, like most key personnel, are going anyway."

They turned. Mr Martin was laughing—great belly-laughs that made him hold his stomach.

"Don!" he gasped, "you should have kept your mouth shut . . ."

Carl Wayne regarded him thoughtfully.

"You're forgetting one thing, Jack—" he said carefully.

"What's that?"

"You're going too . . ."

*

138

The jitney whined and bumped along the rough track parallel to Lepe Beach, and Savage winced at times, trying to favour his various scars and half-healed burns. Far down the Solent the sun was going down over Portland harbour, and the Isle of Wight lay like some great black hump-back whale across the water. He was not at all sure he was doing the wisest thing,— with the trauma of the fire and Jan's death not two weeks behind him, he felt uneasy about becoming involved with people in general at the moment—and with Dee in particular; he was not a complete idiot, he told himself irritably, and he had known for many months that Dee seemed more than usually interested. Or—was he assuming far too much? Maybe she had been just interested, genuinely, in his physical condition: with him every day in the semi-privacy of their offices, she had seen, more than most, the difficulties he had faced. Again—after . . . Jan, it was conceivable that Dee was simply being friendly, helping him through an experience which time alone would effectively alleviate.

He grunted, jouncing around on the hard rubber seat, more than a trace of exasperation in his voice. He parked the jeep, thumped on the caravan door until Dee opened up, and stalked inside without as much as a word. He stood in the tiny lounge, indecisive and unhappy.

"Don? Let me take your windproof—" he sat down heavily and watching her moving around the warm, cosy room. A stranger to such contrivances, he found himself impressed by the comfort; double-glazed windows kept out the noise and cold, and the methane-gas central-heating system worked well.

It worked, she told him, on chicken manure—a row of eight 200-litre steel drums buried nearby with fitted lids, each connected by copper pipe to a big steel reservoir where the gas was compressed for storage.

"Sherry? Or some beer?"

"Can of banana beer, if you have one," Savage said shortly. The girl stared at him and retreated to the tiny kitchen, biting her lip. Was this going to be as difficult as it threatened? What was wrong with him? She knew Savage well enough to know that he would not allow ill health to impair his manners—and he did look so much better . . . perhaps he was missing his wife more than she had thought—yet knew that this wasn't so. She sighed, found a chilled can, brought it to him with a tall glass.

"I don't know why I drink this stuff," he said presently. "It's stronger than ordinary beer—but the taste! Yeuk—" and she laughed lightly at his grimace.

"I can do better than that for dinner. There's an old chap earns a living fishing from the beach—I got two lovely soles from him. That sound all right?"

"Mm-mm."

Alone, he sat moodily watching the TV with sound turned down, listening to the sounds of progress in the kitchen. What the hell are you worrying about, Savage? It's only a meal with a friend—no big deal. You don't have to come back—and you don't have to prove anything by staying. Is that your story? Are you going to stick to it, Savage? It sounds pretty damned weak . . . So what in God's name are you really worried about?

Angrily, he finished the beer, slammed the glass on the table and groped for a Split. Why don't you face it, you rotten cowardly bastard? Why don't you admit you're terrified of this girl— of any girl, dammit—because you're not a man any more. That damned slab of plastic . . . if only it'd gone into his bloody brain and finished the job properly. And that surgeon in Manchester . . . same as all the rest . . . "Your faculties may return in time, Mr Savage—" oh yes? In twenty years, maybe thirty? Christ on a crutch, I'll be too old to even think about women . . .

Involuntarily, Savage groaned in an agony of frustration—and became aware that the girl was standing watching him; her face was pale, set—a mask of concern, and he thought once more what a strange paradox she was: look at her! That hair was straight, unrelieved by as much as a wave. Her eyes weren't too bad—but a little too far apart, and she had that square jaw and wide mouth that so many American women seemed to have— it was almost a national trademark, he thought. And yet . . . and yet, when she smiled, she seemed to radiate something as real and intense as the radiant energy from the sun itself.

He got up slowly, stiffly.

"Dee—"

"Yes, Don?"

He clamped his jaws together in sudden resolve. "It's not going to work—"

"What isn't?" innocently.

"You and I here . . . you just don't know, Dee. For Christ's sake, I'm a clapped-out old man, half crippled—"

"No!"

"—half a nervous wreck. I'm just not ready for . . ."

"For what? Dinner?"

"Jesus!" he said viciously, "don't make fun of me, Dee. You're nice—you're trying to make it easy for me. I'm grateful . . . maybe later, maybe three or four months . . ." he ground to a halt, staring at her.

"You don't understand, do you? You don't even *want* to understand! Look—do I have to spell it out to you? If it's a man you want, forget it. That damned IRA sniper did his job all right . . . look, just forget it. Give me my coat—"

The fair-haired girl stared at him for a long moment. Presently, she walked into the kitchen, shut everything down and went back to him.

"Sit down!"

"Eh?"

"Sit down, Don Savage, or so help me, I'll knock you down! Shut up and listen to me . . ."

Dee took a long deep breath. "Who the hell do you think you are anyway? You think I asked you here to feed you up and climb into bed with you? Is that what you think? You've got a nerve, Mr Bloody Savage . . . more than that, you're just too damn stupid for words! Are you too proud to admit that you're still far from well, that you've just left hospital, that you need a little care and attention? You think after two years working together, I would stand by and let you sleep on the Guardroom cot, eat at that damned canteen? Is that what you think?"

She paused for breath, and Savage blinked. This wasn't going the right way at all . . . suddenly, he was in the wrong! He gulped; she was off again.

"Listen, I'm going to cook you the best meal you've ever had—after which you're going into the spare bed in there and sleep for at least twelve hours. No—" she clapped a hand over his mouth. "Don't talk—Mr Wayne called me today and said he wanted you out of circulation for three days at least. What the Americans call 'rest and recreation'. Just for once, you're going to do exactly as you're told. And for your information, I don't give a tuppenny damn if you're the world's best stud or biggest eunuch; I was asked to knock you into shape and, by crickey, I'm going to do it!"

He was left alone to gape at the closed kitched door. He thought, much later, that he'd been suffering from delayed-action shock; docilely, he ate his meal, rested with a cigarette while Dee cleared up, clambered into warm dry sheets and remembered little else until he woke in the dark quite hours to find her with him. He found he *wasn't* the world's greatest stud; he wasn't about to break any records. But somehow, in those secret hours, much of the unhappiness and insecurity and doubt seemed to drift away; remarkably, he found himself forgetting his own problems in helping Dee cope with her own inexperience and the early sun was staining the sky before they felt they had explored the situation sufficiently to warrant relaxing in sleep. His last thought, before sleep buried him, was that Dee's love-making was so much like her temper, boisterous, forthright— and extremely effective . . .

13 *The Concrete Bomber*

David Perry glanced round at the sound of Savage's footsteps, nodded and scowled up at the grey overcast, the fine drizzle.

"Morning, Don. Of all days we really need good weather—" the project manager said shortly.

"Mm-mm. How long to go before launch?"

"We'll be ready in a few minutes . . . hold on—" Perry keyed his radio.

"Bob—Perry here. The Met boys give a fifteen knot wind, high tide just after eleven. What's the hold up?"

The voice of the launch foreman came through with a metallic quack. "Nearly there—a few minutes, Dave. I have twenty men down here, shifting the last of the scaffolding. All mould sections are clear except the stern and at support blocks. Are the crew all aboard?"

"Checking now, Bob. Call me when you're all set—and don't leave anyone down in the hole—they'll get their feet wet when we open these gates." Perry walked forward to the edge of the dock, staring at the *Albatross* bridge. "Perry to Bridge—come in—"

"Dickie here, David. I heard. All crew on station—checking the PA system in a moment. I can't see the mooring line crews from here—" the Captain left the question unasked.

Perry said cheerfully: "They're all there—straining at the leash. Five minutes to go. All fenders in position?"

The Captain grunted—a strange and distorted sound over the personal radio band.

"Yes, Dave. Not much room to spare in the gates."

"I know it. I've asked Bob Foster to station a crew at each gate with more fenders—they're arriving now. Dickie, will you check both engine rooms on standby for waterjet start-up?"

"They're all set. All four Auxiliary Power Units running: full electric power to all busbars. Main engines ready for starting."

"Fine, Dickie. Stand by—"

Perry and Savage waited on the dock edge, staring down into the great rectangular hole. The giant cranes were lifting out the last load of scaffolding; they could see the whole sleek length of her now, glistening white superstructure, the hull painted a translucent anti-foul black. Forward, under the bow, in big gold letters: RMH ALBATROSS SOUTHAMPTON. Royal Mail Hovermarine . . . the big bird would carry the King's personal post to the President of America on her first flight in two weeks' time. Providing the trials went off satisfactorily . . . Perry swallowed nervously.

Beside him, Savage said: "She's really something, Dave—"

"I can hardly believe it . . . after two years. I only hope nothing goes wrong . . . it's been too damned quiet lately, Don.

143

After all that excitement. Did . . . things go off all right Saturday?"

"Jan's funeral? Yes thanks . . . I really appreciate your flowers, Dave—and the wreath from the rest of the lads was . . ." Savage broke off, eyes gazing out across Southampton Water, travelling slowly along the wrecked unrecognisable skyline, trying to determine just where . . . the block, he knew, had been dynamited after the fire, like most other gutted and unsafe buildings. Whatever had been in Jan's coffin, it hadn't been her . . . the authorities, in their wisdom, had provided something labelled Jan Shelley Savage, to bury as a symbol of that which had once been—but Jan, Savage knew, existed now only as minute hydrocarbons drifting in space.

Perry, embarrassed, turned away and his eyes widened in surprise.

"Hello, Commander! Come to see the fun?"

Chisholm was wearing an old and stained dufflecoat against the drizzle, but produced a smile. "We've a vested interest in this old bird," he said equably. "We would like to see her launched successfully—without any more mishaps."

"You don't expect any trouble?" Perry said anxiously.

"No—not at all. Things have been very quiet—but we're not relaxing in any way, Mr Perry. If it's reassurance you're after, you won't get it from me. Our friends—the Soviets and others—have invested a good deal of money and effort so far, without successs. If you were in their shoes, would you give up? Mr Savage?"

The Security chief shrugged inside his windproof. Perry rubbed his hands together irresolutely. "Don't make me nervous, for God's sake, Commander. Anyway—once she's afloat, they can't do much harm: the reactor's been worked up to operating temperature, and there's only some fitting out to be done. Any news from the Black Sea?"

·Chisholm smiled bleakly. "Depends what you call news. Last week, there was a sudden shut-down in all news contacts from the area. No foreign correspondents allowed within 500 kilometres. You can draw your own conclusions from that . . ."

Savage grinned, a wide relaxed display of relief. "I'm glad

you're taking things seriously, Mr Chisholm. To tell the truth, we'll all feel happier when she's finished."

"Quite right. A few craft like this, built to naval specification, could put the Navy back to where it was in 1945. And if RAZOR performs up to expectations . . . make no mistake. We've got a world-beater here; once the initial investment's paid for, she'll cost next to nothing for fuel. Believe me, we've taken precautions to ensure nothing's going to happen to this little lot."

"Such as?" Savage queried.

"Such as having a squad of our men aboard the *Albatross* from now until she sails for New York. Such as standing patrols round the clock—"

"We've seen the launches," Perry said quickly.

"Right. We also have diver patrols on the gates—day and night. Our friends aren't likely to try *that* again—but the way the Russkies' minds work, they might just think we might assume that—and have another go."

Savage laughed. "Sort of—I think what you think I'm thinking is not what you think I'm thinking . . ."

"Oh, put a bloody sock in it, Don!" Perry said exasperatedly. "That's very comprehensive, Mr Chisholm."

"Quite. In addition, we have security patrols checking every building and roof within three miles—just in case. And our American friends at Marchwood have two patrol boats on standby off Hythe Pier. To back up the four Navy hovercraft operating out of Gosport."

"Jeez!" Savage said faintly.

They watched Perry giving final instructions to the pump man in the gate house, making a final check of all stations. Presently—

"All right, Duncan. Open them up—"

Far below, they heard a remote splashing, growing to a thunderous rumble of surging water; four streams, each a metre wide, poured into the dock, crashing against diverting baffles which directed but failed to tame the green frothing torrents. It flooded around and under the *Albatross* and the vast bulk trembled and shuddered against the restraining cables. Fascinated, after years of familiarity with a dry empty dock, the men on the brink watched the level rising imperceptibly but inexorably, swirling black and oily around concrete pillars, solid timber support stacks, forming occasional vortices around which little flotillas of debris rotated like satellites in orbit.

It would take more than thirty minutes to fill the yawning chasm, and Savage became aware of the concourse of people which, like magic, had assembled around the dock. They were silent, unmoving, every head bent to watch the baptising of that which they had built with their own hands; to Savage, there was an eerie sense of unheard prayer, unseen dedication, in the mute, almost hypnotised crowd.

Beside him, Perry stirred.

"Dickie—Perry here. Bob Foster there on the bridge?"

"Here, Dave. So far, bloody marvellous. No reports of any leaks—she rocked a little when the first impact hit the support blocks—but solid as a rock now. No bilge-pump lights on at all—all compartments dry."

Perry sighed with relief . . . only four weeks behind schedule—a long, long haul. Soon, he thought with a trace of sadness, she would pass out of his hands, into those of the trials engineers, the operating crew under Captain Dickie Byrd . . . he remembered mistily the interminable conferences, the sudden panics, constantly changing design, delayed deliveries . . . the furious rows with sluggish sub-manufacturers, the impotent rage at wrong parts arriving at the wrong time. Incessant wheedling, persuading, cursing, praising, prodding . . . faces of men drifted across his mind—Jackson, the designer taken on trust but with forged references; Colin Bergman, the elderly carpenter found dead over his workbench, tools still in hand. Young Maisie the accounts clerk who had her premature baby in the Photocopier Room one morning without a word of warning; the four laminators who won a record £4 million on the pools . . .

"David!"

"Eh? Yes, Bob?"

"She's coming up fast. She'll float off in a moment or two—we're standing by to clear away the remaining mould sections and the supports—"

"Okay. Bridge, did you get that?"

"Affirmative, David. All hands standing by on mooring lines . . . SHE'S OFF!" Don Savage jerked his head round in surprise: the dull roar of cheers built up to a storm, hands waving, toilet rolls soaring in streamers in time-honoured salute. He swung round: it was true! *Albatross* lifted gently, bow and stern dipping regally to greet the turbulent flow freed by the great dock gates, now swinging wide to form a common water level. A strident bell was ringing somewhere, hooters blaring across the river; down at the Fawley terminal, jubilant deck hands experimented with the deep sonorous ships' siren until the Chief Engineer rose up in anger from below decks to send them packing.

The gates were fully open; the two tugs had her now, and she began to pass the little group of men on the stone jetty. Savage could hear, as she passed, the deep thrumming of her auxiliary engines, and he blinked, half-blaming the boisterous wind for the moisture in his eyes.

Dickie Byrd hung far out of his bridge window, watching the dock wall sliding past with critical eyes; as she went, the remaining mould segments at the stern broke free under blasts of compressed air, baulks of timber swirling in her wake, and as he passed, the Captain caught Savage's eyes and grinned insanely, the flat Gaelic face split from side to side. As if in salute, the sun broke through and something caught at Savage's heart, watching the beauty of her moving slowly out into the basin . . . they had gone through so much to reach this point, and he cursed himself for a sentimental fool, feeling the thickness in his throat.

Something made him turn, glance up and across; high on the roof of the Administration building he saw Dee Purdy, with a group of office workers, grinned at her frantic wave.

Perry was talking again to the craft.

"Shore to Bridge—give me your bilge indications—"

"All in the green, David. She's as dry as a bloody bone! Did ye expect anything different?" Bob Foster's Tyneside accent came clear and bell-shaped over the radio. Perry grinned. "Not really, Bob. Shore to Chief Engineer—?"

"Oates here. No problems to speak of, David. We have a red light on the port drone launching hatch in the side wall—working on that. APU's are running half speed, manoeuvring engines at tickover. All waterjets functioning fine."

"Thank you, Titus. Fine. Stand by—"

Savage and Perry swung round at the sound of running feet; far across the concrete waste Jack Martin's legs were going like pistons; a navy lieutenant in blue windproof ran beside him, carrying a hand radio. Commander Chisholm moved to meet them, concern written deep on his face.

Not more trouble, for God's sake, Savage thought dully. Lord, we've had as much as we can take . . .

"Sir!" the lieutentant was breathing very hard, but thrust the radio into Chisholm's hand. "Contact Panther Four, sir. On that empty apartment block—" he pointed across the sun-dappled water to a building on the city side.

"Panther Four—Chisholm!"

"Four here. Tell those people over there to get that boat moving, fast!"

Chisholm swung round. "Perry—?"

"Right! Perry to Bridge—come in! Urgent!"

"Bridge—Byrd here. What's up, David?"

"Don't stop to argue, Dickie—get her moving, quick . . .!"

"Huh? I—" the radio went silent and the group of men on the sea wall turned to Chisholm.

"Now, Panther Four—what's going on?"

"Lieutenant Griffiths here, sir. We briefed the local police to watch for anything unusual. An electric Panda crew in Weston saw a plain van with three men, pulling up outside this block. Men were dressed as builders, carried toolboxes, sacks of materials. That sort of thing."

"Go on, dammit!" Chisholm was breathing heavily through his nose.

"Panda crew played it smart, sir. Knew it was too soon for building work—checked with Control before going up to the roof. Found they were setting up a Black Widow—"

"A—what?"

"Chinese anti-tank missile, rocket-propelled, laser-guided. They were lining it up on *Albatross*—another five minutes and—"

The Commander broke in impatiently. "What kind of warhead, damn you?"

"Didn't I say, sir? Mini-nuke. Coconut size, one kilotonne. Enough to flatten most of Southampton. The police went in fast—one of the Panda boys is dead, the other with two rounds in the belly. The bastards had Kalashnikovs. We hit the roof just as they started countdown—we heard the shooting and took no chances."

Chisholm glowered across the mile of water, as if to stare the speaker in the eye.

"Are you saying they're all dead, Griffiths?"

"Two, sir. The third is on the way to hospital under guard. Took a round in the groin . . . we didn't bother to give him pain-killer. He may talk on the way, and we don't want him asleep."

"That's better," the Commander said grudgingly. "Very well, Griffiths. Written report within four hours. Well done."

Savage watched dumbly; the Commander gave the lieutenant his radio back and told him to stand by. "Sir," he said hesitantly, "you have them now—why the precautions—getting the boat away?"

Chisholm stared, barely concealing his irritation. "You were in Ulster—what was the basic rule for guerrilla attacks?"

"Er—always have a back-up. Good grief—I see what you mean. There may be another team?" Savage demanded. Perry groaned, standing nearby.

"Could be. If so, having the craft moving won't help—not with a laser sight. All they have to do is keep the red dot on target. But Griffiths is a good lad—he'll have teams on top of every building in sight of the river within ten minutes—he did the same job back in Karachi in '89, covering the evacuation. Nevertheless, Savage—I'm worried. I don't mind admitting it. This effort tells me one thing only: they're committed. They have to crack it, no matter how many times they try. Probably mercenaries on contract—no big bang, no pay. Mr Perry—keep that craft circling out there, until we get an all clear—"

"Yes, Commander."

Don Savage walked across to the edge of the sea wall, looking at the city skyline through narrowed eyes. It all made some hideous kind of logic: with trials starting immediately, and take-off for New York less than four weeks away, those bastards would pull out all the stops. The thought of someone less than a kilometre or two away, behind a nuke missile, no matter how small, twisted up his gut and scrotum in an agony of fear, and he felt physically sick; he felt an overwhelming urge to start running, away from that place. And slowly his fear turned to a solid grinding rage, a burning fury which would know no rest until this thing was settled, one way or another. He became aware that Perry and the Commander were staring at him oddly; his jaw ached and he thought he'd probably been grinding his teeth.

Chisholm stared at him grimly. "I know how you feel. Savage. You too, Perry. We're doing what we can—trust me. Tell me, Perry—how fast can she move on waterjet power?"

"I—she can get up to 100 knots in ninety seconds. That's hump speed—where she accelerates past her own bow wave."

Chisholm gnawed his lower lip. "Not fast enough, if they get a missile through. What about the main engines?"

"Christ, they haven't even been tested yet! No way."

"Mm." Chisholm looked away, lost in thought. "She's a sitting duck there . . . I'm going to alert the Americans at Marchwood—maybe we can get a patrol boat each side of her."

He began talking urgently into the radio. Moments later—

"Lima 53 to Chisholm. En route from Gosport with Lima 52. We have a radar track, unidentified, inbound from Yarmouth area, west south west of you. Over."

"Aircraft, Lima 53?"

"Affirmative. Southampton Airport reports no traffic expected that area. Stand by . . . we have a visual . . . four clicks from you, bearing 155 degrees. No height . . . contact is Canadian Cargonaut helicopter, Malibu Crane type, with underslung load. Approximate height 400 metres."

"On course for us, Lima 53?"

"Affirmative. Will pass about a kilo south of you." The listeners could hear the roar of the hovercraft's engines, at full throttle, above the speaker's voice. "Load appears to be large crate, Chisholm."

The Commander snarled. "Get that damned boat on the move, Perry!"

To Savage, standing on the sea wall, the action seemed to unfold with grotesque and hideous formality, moving pieces on a timeless chessboard gravitating together like a concerted attack on the Queen . . . vaguely, he heard the rich Irish brogue of Byrd, screaming on an open channel to his engine room staff; with almost painful sluggishness, *Albatross*'s engines started their run-up to full speed and she nosed out into mid-stream—sixty, seventy, eighty knots, foam and spray creaming round the great black skirts, like massive Venetian blinds, angled back from the centrehull bow.

He saw two American patrol boats between BHLC and the pier, winding round in a delicate curving acceleration; far to the south-east, at the entrance to Southampton Water, the two Navy hovercraft, true air-cushion vehicles, roaring along at maximum power in clouds of spray. And to the south-west, the helicopter lurched into view, and Savage could hear the regular "whop-whop" of rotor blades above the noises around him. Beside him, Perry said fearfully: "Oh, my God, Don!"

Now they saw it: the enormous bulk of the block of stained irregular concrete, swinging ponderously at the end of a cable—weighing perhaps two tonnes, Savage thought desperately. Instinctively, his eyes found *Albatross*: Byrd had seen the danger and the craft was heeling over in a desperate attempt to change course, the long extending sections of the starboard sidewall straining downwards to maintain contact with the water; Savage knew that the port sidewall, even fully retracted, would be deep in the sea, and the craft heeled, jetting spray twenty metres high around the stern.

Suddenly, his eyes were opened: Perry saw it too, and they stood there, speechless with dread, watching the chopper approach.

Chisholm swore, punched the radio TX button.

"Chisholm to Gangway!"

"I read you, Mike!"

"Take that chopper, Gangway! For the love of God, scratch him!"

"Yo . . ." the flat American twang seemed unaffected by the emergency. Savage watched, heart in mouth; the flying crane was a few hundred metres from target, slanting in and down to build up speed, the great cube bent astern by wind pressure. A slim pencil shape erupted from the leading US patrol boat: riding a fiery torch at the end of a long smoke-trail, it accelerated incredibly, curving into a double parabola through a 90-degree turn, arcing over, lining up. The chopper pilot, short of target by perhaps four seconds, saw death's wings opening to engulf him and jettisoned his load, pulling up and away in a near-loop, away from the fiery sword . . . a second later, Perry and Savage stepped back instinctively from the giant red flower blossoming overhead; there was nowhere to run and they stood transfixed, eyes staring up in mute horror. The fireball, shedding debris, slanted a mere hundred metres overhead, impacting the water offshore in a deafening roar; Savage dragged his eyes away from the spreading sea of flame, to the *Albatross*.

Heart in mouth, they stood—Chisholm, Perry, Savage and, further down the sea wall, Martin and the Navy lieutenant; in stunned silence they watched the huge block, rotating slowly like some discarded child's playblock, grey-white in the bright sunshine. The sea exploded into white foam, so close to the steep sidewall that Savage knew, for one dreadful moment, that she was hit—it towered as high as the radar mast above the bridge, *Albatross* sliding past like some giant black and white screen; a wide solid gout of water belched up, catching Dickie Byrd full in the face as he leaned forth, watching the tumbling mass. Savage caught a brief glimpse of the broad Irish face streaming with water, the stunned expression of surprise—and suddenly, he and Perry and the Commander were laughing helplessly, pounding each other on the back for relief, and *Albatross* was settling back into the water off-cushion, circling, and the Captain was leaning far out of the Bridge window screaming, "I suppose you thought that was damn funny!" and suddenly Savage knew that, for the moment, he would stagger away, sit down on a bollard and grin stupidly at the others . . .

14 *Make 'em Laugh*

The operation was a guaranteed success, by courtesy of the United States law enforcement system in which local sheriffs and police departments control their own bailiwicks, State troopers or Highway Patrols look after road traffic, the Mob enforces Federal Law, Unistate protects the nation's integrity—and no one has a goddam clue what's really going on . . .

At 8.30 a.m., Rochelle Hudson noted, from her garage door, the Navy gas-hybrid pulling up at the front gate. As she began to lift the up-and-over, she started to worry again about her daughter. Melanie was fifteen, deep into high-school politics and fighting hard for her threatened job of chief cheer-leader. Like most American teenagers, she was totally aware, suffering no hang-ups after her abortion the previous year—in fact she was planning a re-run, to trap the University of Houston graduate who had impregnated her (and four other candidates) in an attempt on the all-time Houston record.

Rochelle liked the look of the Navy lieutenant walking up the path. There were few presentable men in Rosenburg, fifty kilometres southwest of Houston—she believed, genuinely, that she was faithful to her husband when he was on sea duty: her casual affairs, in her view, were harmless, enjoyable and a damn good way of keeping in trim for her husband's infrequent furloughs. It was her job to keep him well and contented and fit for duty (she came from a traditional and very patriotic Navy family). Anything she could do to improve the quality, variety and proficiency of their marital bliss was good for all concerned, especially for her husband, who—let it be said—was always thankful when the time came round to return to sea duty. Where he could get a bit of rest and peace . . .

"Morning. Mrs Hudson?"

"That's right, lieutenant. Good-morning. May I help you?"

The officer was tall, broad-shouldered, with a ruddy face and the first signs of grey at his temples; Rochelle measured his broad frame with experienced eyes.

"Sorry to intrude—is your daughter Melanie here, too?"

"Why—yes. Right here . . . say good morning, dear—"

'Dear' stared at the officer, scowled and leaned against the porch stanchion, opening her comic book.

The officer grinned engagingly. "I have two of my own, Mrs Hudson—bless 'em. I wonder—could you spare the Admiral a moment—we have a number of families to call on, and it won't take but a short time—he's right there in the car—"

"Why don't you come into the house and I'll fix you some coffee?"

He spread his palms regretfully. "If only we had the time, ma'am . . . but the Admiral is conducting these little chats with dependents in the car—it has an autosecretary. Please?"

"Well—" Rochelle hesitated. "Very well . . . come on, Melly—and behave yourself, you hear? This could be very important for your Daddy—"

Melanie said, poker-faced: "Daddy can go take a long stiff crap in the Pacific—" Her mother winced, but the lieutenant merely grinned.

"Don't you worry, ma'am . . . the Admiral has a good sense of humour. This way—"

The woman climbed into the back of the car, nodding to the portly figure in medal-spattered blue uniform. The lieutenant got into the driver's seat and tripped the button to bring up the glass privacy screen.

"Thank you, Mrs Hudson . . . good-morning—" the Admiral bent forward to tinker with the recording-machine at his feet. "Just a few questions—this could be very beneficial to your husband's career. Just let me switch on this recorder . . ." he seemed to inhale very deeply; Rochelle had some three seconds in which to realise that the machine was hissing very loudly, before it seemed that someone dropped a black velvet bag over her head. Melanie, the lieutenant was delighted to note, hit the floor simultaneously, her head ricochetting off a corner of the tape deck with a satisfying thud. He grinned, turned on the air-conditioner, got the glass screen down, and the Admiral, face red as a turkey cock, wound down the window and took long satisfying breaths.

The lieutenant picked up the car phone, punched a pre-dialled number and got through instantly.

"Rosenburg High? Good morning. This is the Navy Department, Washington. Section Twelve, Personnel. I'm calling on behalf of Mrs Rochelle Hudson, eighteen fifty two North Parkside—yes, Melanie's mother. Lieutenant Hudson is in hospital in San Diego and we transported Melanie and her mother during the night to California. Mrs Hudson asked us to call you—she's still in flight—to say she may be away some weeks and not to worry. Pardon me? Oh, nothing serious. The Lieutenant had a fall aboard ship—broke a leg in two places. Mrs Hudson says she'll call you as soon as she gets back—yes. Thank you—my pleasure, ma'am. Goodbye—"

The Admiral draped a red blanket over the sleepers on the floor.

"Okay, Kelly—move it out."

The long black car accelerated sluggishly: the gas the Navy used these days is real crud, Kelly thought. He oughta complain when he dumped the car some place eventually. He drove very carefully, heading out of town and west; fifteen kilometres out, he turned right, moving across country to a point a little north of Bay City, looking for a dirt road on the right. Soon, the road twisted through a few hectares of cotton-wood trees to peter out in a wide clearing. There, ready and waiting, was the Bell-Fiat VTOL. The crew, in plain shirts and jeans, saw the approaching car; within minutes, the twin propjets driving ducted fans began winding up to speed, pointing, with the whole wing, skywards. The plane went up slowly, like a powerful elevator, and the wing began to tilt forward, with the plane itself, into the horizontal mode. It began to accelerate, the propellers stopping and feathering, the main jets opening up to full power, the wing swinging back to the high speed position.

Seconds later, it was a steeply climbing dot, heading southwest, out across the Gulf of Mexico.

With variations, the exercise was repeated that morning in many parts of America, including Oakland and Redwood City, California, Baton Rouge, Louisiana, Biloxi Mo., Tampa and Miami Fla. and Denver, Colorado. Thirteen family groups were lifted from the New York area alone; two from Niagara Falls. The climax was the removal of the Modesto brood from Hackensack,

N.J.—Catholic Lt. Charles E. Modesto took his religion seriously and his wife at every opportunity, relying on the rhythm method; maybe he had no ear for music. Whatever the case, it took a six-man crew to ship out Mrs Modesto and her nine children. Ten—if you count the 8-month bulge which threatened to launch itself at any moment.

The whole plan was conceived and executed with military precision, as if the phoney Navy men had really picked up some habits from honest-to-God sailors. All the packages found their way, in good time, to the deck of a small general cargo ship cruising north at a steady 20 knots, east of Galveston. Their quarters were good; the food better, and the children enjoyed a nonstop supply of candies, movies, popcorn and video TV. Their parents, for the most part, soon tired of fruitless speculation and concentrated on the apparently inexhaustible supplies of food, cocktails, poker and dice games.

From start to finish, the sheaves were gathered in just seven hours and fifteen minutes. And due to immaculate attention to their cover-up stories, no-one, as we have said, had a goddam idea what was going on . . . if they did, it would have become immediately apparent that the families, in every case, belonged to an officer or crewman of the USS *Sherman,* now lying in Hampton Roads preparing feverishly for the coming South Atlantic exercises.

At this stage of the game, it should be reported, The Banker had the situation well in hand . . . and had long since decided he'd rather look like Robert Redford. Or maybe Paul Newman? Maybe someone a little younger . . .?

Walter F. Keyhoe took a telephone call just after midnight in his bedroom overlooking Central Park West. He climbed off his wife, got into a robe and took it in the lounge.

"Keyhoe."

"Cody. Two pieces of news. One—everything all wrapped up, satisfactorily. No reaction—we're watching all media channels, coast to coast. Nothing."

"Fine. Fine, Cody. What else is new?"

"Number Two—I'm bushed. I'm gonna hit the sack, boss. 'Night."

156

"Goodnight, Cody." Keyhoe sat down at the writing table, opened a drawer and found a shiny aluminium tube almost a third of a metre in length. He carefully clipped the end of the monstrous cigar, stoked up some fire, lit it and sat back, relaxed and thoughtful. He'd been saving that cigar for three years, for a special occasion—and this was it. He chewed the end of the cigar, meditatively . . . those bums in Europe . . . they couldn't pour piss out of a rubber boot with the instructions printed on the sole. Well . . . he still held a few hole cards . . . he hummed a few lines of "If the wimmen don't get you, the whiskey will . . ." and sat quietly until the cigar was finished.

He went back to bed . . . his wife was long asleep—but what the hell?

"Wake up, you bitch! Time to celebrate! . . ."

"Jack? Savage here. Get down to the pier steps—there's a boat waiting for us."

"For us? Where are we going, Don?"

"Out on trials in the Channel—" Savage said cheerfully.

There was a pregnant silence. Presently—

"In that floating H-bomb?"

"Right."

"Me?" Mr Martin thought his boss was joking . . . he hoped.

"Come on, Jack. Stop bloody stalling. You know you can't wait . . ."

Mr Martin said explosively: "I can't wait! Don't hang about for me . . . another day, maybe. I'm busy . . ."

"Get down to that boat," Savage said severely, "and no foolin' about—you hear me?"

Savage grinned. He could hear the sound of heavy breathing, and wished for a moment it was a visiphone . . . Martin's face must be a picture. At last—

"Are you quite sure you haven't got me mixed up with two other fellers?" Savage bawled "BE THERE!" and slammed the phone down.

When Capt. Dickie Byrd was first shown the *Albatross* simulator, he had reacted typically and strongly. An experienced pilot of large conventional hovercraft, he could see no reason for "mucking about with models"—what was so different about the *Albatross*? Carl Wayne silently indicated the craft speed indicator and for once in his noisy brawling life Byrd was speechless. He was used to logs reading from 0 to 100 knots—and to craft which came fairly close to the maximum—but 0–300 knots? These fellers were crazy, for sure. The mere thought of covering five nautical miles of sea every minute made the hair at the nape of his neck stir.

The Byrd family were typical bog Irish in ancestry, going back to the potato famines and the exodus West, and they never forgot their traditions. Children were bred with gusto and a total disregard of the parents' ability to support them. God-fearing Catholics one and all, they enjoyed their natural talents for sex, violence and hard drinking under the shelter of the confessional; it was acceptable—expected, in fact,—that they would spend six days and nights sinning just as hard as they could go at it, because on the seventh would come absolution and the licence to start all over again Monday morning.

James 'Dickie' Byrd was no exception. He played a murderous game of Rugby at University until he was banned for life after wiping a foot down the face of a prone opponent. At school, not yet sixteen, he avoided expulsion by a hair's breadth for near-rape of an attractive and over-developed classmate optimistically christened Virginia. She was saved—in the nick of time—by a junior English mistress who, after watching closely, intervened at the critical moment, sent the girl packing, closed the gymnasium door and began to lecture the boy. The process required some two hours, after which she emerged red-faced and breathless; she left behind a grinning Byrd who heard no more about the matter.

Byrd, it will be seen, was a very experienced man. He knew about travelling at speed over water; he said they only had to hit a floating used condom at 300 knots and the thing would break up.

They told him different. They showed him the retracting sidewalls, the knife-edged sidewall blades which could be jettisoned if damaged, revealing back-up blades behind. They showed him the aerodynamic stabilisers and the computers which would keep the craft absolutely steady at top speed, and the sonardrones which would cruise ahead of the *Albatross* scanning for floating obstacles.

In desperation, he pointed out—reasonably—that no diesel or gas turbine could produce speeds of 300 knots. Of course not, they said seriously. That's why we use nuclear propulsion . . .

With which Byrd got up and walked away in disgust.

In later years he couldn't recall how they talked him into it—but now, standing on the bridge of the *Albatross*, it was too late to regret it. Beside him, David Perry was on the radio to their escort boat.

"Trials Control to *Albatross*—"

"Perry here, Control. We are 30 clicks west of Cherbourg. All auxiliary systems checked. We have a good C. of G. position and we have maximum all-up weight in ballast. Running through Stage Three checks on the reactor; thirty minutes to go to speed trials. Over."

"Understood, David. All your warning systems serviceable and available?"

"That is roger. Total trials complement 37 including crew, standby crew, reactor commissioning squad and observers."

"Okay, *Albatross*. We're recording now on telemetry—we'd like a full verbal commentary on Company Channel. Good luck—"

"Thanks, Control. Request you stand by at twenty-kilometre range. We don't expect problems but we'll feel a lot better. We confirm we have three Conditions: Green, as of now, prior to start of main engines. Amber: proceeding with trial. Red—we lock everything down, dump the reactor in deep water and abandon ship, using the inflatables to reach you. We have a clear radar scan for 200 kilometres—all we can see is you. No other traffic—"

"We aren't surprised, *Albatross*—the Navwarn signal went out two days ago. You're being given a clear run."

"Damn it," Perry said violently, "they think we're a floating bomb."

"They could be right," the Captain said dryly. "Sort of Russian roulette—with all barrels loaded—"

Perry and Savage stared at the Irishman in disbelief. How in

God's name could he stand there grinning like that? They shook their heads, left him talking to the crew and went off into the transverse corridor. The floor was still uncarpeted, the herring-bone pattern of reinforced plastic exposed, showing scores of access panels. Loose electric and hydraulic connections every-where . . . stepping carefully, they went off into the midships saloon. Only a single row of seats was installed—most of the deck space contained steel 200-litre drums of water ballast, securely lashed down; ceiling and lighting trims were finished and the subdued light emphasised the stark unpainted finish of bulkheads and partitions. At temporary panels, crews of trials engineers were setting up systems of monitor gauges.

To Savage, the scene was one of total confusion, but in Perry's eyes there was something strange and wonderful in seeing in the flesh, as it were, systems and components he had seen conceived on computer drawing boards. They went on off to the main engine-room, passing the auxiliary engine rooms housing the great lift fans and generators, driven by steam turbines fed from the reactor. Pressure within the underhull plenum chamber would be only fractionally more than atmospheric—but over the thousands of square metres of area, the pressure would raise the giant craft twenty metres above sea level.

They paused at the main engine-room gangway; the public-address system was booming.

"Mr Savage contact the bridge! Mr Savage contact the bridge! Urgent!"

He glanced at Perry, his eyes mirroring what each was think-ing . . . in the name of God, what now?

There was a phone station near the aft baggage compartment. "Savage here—"

"Don? Jack Martin. I must be going mad—I thought I saw Chaffey in the forward saloon!"

"Chaffey? He's in cold storage in London, for Christ's sake, Jack! It couldn't be . . . could it?"

Martin said hoarsely: "I—think so, Don. Couldn't mistake him. What threw me was the clothes—wearing white overalls and red safety helmet with visor—"

"Same as the EEC people—the reactor technicians?"

"The same. Thought it was odd—had his visor down to cover

his eyes. But I've spent so many hours watching him—I could recognise that walk anywhere."

Savage bit his lip. If Chaffey was aboard—they'd find him. What worried him most was—why? The damned Commie bastard wasn't here for his health . . . and why the forward cabin? Did Chaffey think that was a safe part of the boat to be, maybe?

"Jack? Listen. Have the Captain radio the Yard—I want to know if Chaffey's loose—one way or the other—"

"He heard you. What else?"

"I'm going to check with the EEC foreman—how many bodies he has aboard. They were all checked aboard this morning—I saw Garner at the boarding hatch. But if Chaffey's here, he got here earlier. It's up to us to find him—and damned quick. They're starting high-speed runs in less than fifteen minutes."

The voice on the phone changed. "Don? Dickie Byrd. The Yard's checking with the Defence people now—Carl Wayne says they were questioning him in London. Is that the little swine who tried to cook the reactor a week or two back?"

"That's him, Dickie. David Perry's on his way back to you— what about the trials?"

"I'm not winding up the main engines until we know for sure," Byrd said solidly. "And when you find him . . ."

"Yes?"

"I'd like a couple of minutes with him. In private—?"

Savage grinned. "Get in the queue, Captain! I'll check back to you—"

The EEC trials foreman looked worried—with reason. "We brought eight people aboard, including myself, Mr Savage. And we've all been here since we sailed—I can guarantee that."

"None of your people would want to go up forward, into the bow?"

"No way. If your lad saw anyone, it wasn't one of us."

Savage nodded, only partly reassured. Back on the bridge, he spoke to Byrd.

"Captain, I'd like everyone available to help—your standby crew included. I want a picket line across the boat from midships saloon, working forward, checking every possible place. Jack Martin and I are going forward into the bow, work back. We have to find this sod, if he's aboard. And I think he is—I know Jack here would not make a mistake like that."

The Captain nodded. "You have them. Listen, man—he could be armed. You haven't got any—?"

"Not a thing. Wish to God we did. But Chaffey's not a fighting man, Dickie. He's the snake in the grass type—won't take any risks if he can help it. The problem is—I think he's done whatever he came to do. I think he's hiding as far forward as he can—which points to the power plant again. Look—have Titus Oates start a search of the whole aft end. We'd better get started, Dickie—"

Moving carefully down the bridge access stairway to the main deck, Savage thought he had never experienced such despondency as he felt now; perhaps they had been too optimistic—perhaps they had miscalculated badly. In assessing the risks, he himself had made the fatal error of believing that, with *Albatross* launched amid the considerable Press exposure following disclosure of the dock gates and helicopter incidents, the Russians would write off their losses.

But suppose Chaffey was not so much an agent as a mercenary? Paid in advance to ruin the *Albatross* any way he could, he would be under heavy pressure to fulfil the contract; Savage's experiences in interrogating both Cuban and Libyan paid terrorists in Ulster convinced him that, if Chaffey had to finish off his job to stay alive, he'd give it his best try. But how?

Savage stopped at the closed hatch in the forward transverse corridor which gave access into the bow structure under the bridge, Martin silent beside him. They had torches alone, by way of equipment—they would have to suffice. He glanced at Martin. "Easy does it, Jack. Better slow than sorry—"

"I'm with you, there," Martin said fervently. "It's quiet—"

"They've slowed the boat down, headed into wind—it helps."

Inside, the Forward Electrical Bay was empty, a vast windowless compartment stretching the full width of the craft; Savage found a service light near the door, switched it on, and the circular opaque lens cast a netural flat illumination, in which they could see the banks of grey steel cabinets, head high, which housed the myriad printed circuits of the main electrical system. In their nostrils a faint smell of ozone mixed with the strong

162

background odour of new glass fibre which pervaded the whole ship.

Softly, cautiously, they moved away from the door, Savage on the right, Martin to their left. Both stopped frequently to listen; true to their training, they kept in sight of each other, neither moving until the other was in position. Savage found himself breathing slowly but deeply to keep pulse rate down— a Northern Ireland ploy he thought he had forgotten ten years earlier.

The compartment seemed empty . . . to be certain, they opened any stowage or cabinet large enough to hold a man but in the end they came to the centre of the floor, eyes questioning each other.

"Well?"

"Christ knows, Jack . . . I would have given odds he'd be in here somewhere."

"Can we get any further forward?"

"One way to find out," Savage said shortly. "Look for an access panel . . ."

They found a panel, almost at once, a metre-square hatch cover in the forward wall but the screwed handles were down tight; Chaffey could not have gone through and locked up behind him. Savage rubbed a finger behind the lobe of an ear, thinking . . . something didn't quite add up. Then he saw it . . .

"Jack—this panel—way over to the port side like that. Usually, if there's only one, the designers would locate it in the middle of the bulkhead."

"Eh? Oh—see what you mean. So there should be another one—no way! Not with that row of cabinets there . . . hang on,—it should be behind this big fuse board here, Don—"

They stood silent for a long moment, staring at the mass of fuses and switches and electrical components which covered the panel, a metre wide and man-high. Savage took a closer look. "Jack! Check this—"

The entire panel was hinged—logically enough—to swing out for access to the second hatchway into the bow. Except the panel was missing; when Savage swung the switchboard aside, they saw only a black rectangular hole.

Before he could even speak, Martin moved forward, switching

on the torch in his hand, to lean forward into the darkness. "I bet the bastard's in here, Don—I think I can—"

Savage knew that his ears were ringing, as if charged by high-voltage current, in the aftermath of the explosion; Martin was catapulted back against the switchboard, sending it crashing into some cabinet behind, and he bounced off the smooth metal frame towards Savage, his chest somehow distorted into the semblance of some giant poppy, from the centre of which a red tide flowed. Savage reached out an instinctive hand, felt the grim warm wetness for an instant, his back up against the wall in the old reflex action.

He stared down, in the garish flat light. Martin lay on his back, eyes wide open, mouth agape, an expression of sheer incredulity on his face, as if, even now, he could hardly believe that which had happened. As Savage watched, Martin's right leg flexed slowly from the hip joint, knee turning inwards, for an inch or two before sagging limply back into immobility.

Time passed. Savage, in the end, took his eyes away from that sightless face and squinted sideways at the black mouth of hell in the bulkhead . . . old in experience, he'd seen many dead men—and they didn't come any deader than Martin.

Later—much later—he would mourn his friend. Just now, he had a problem. He listened carefully, unwilling to move until he knew where Chaffey was, exactly; by moving sideways, it was altogether possible that the bastard could get an acute-angle shot along the face of the bulkhead.

Savage found his mouth was dry as dust, yet the palms of his hands were wet with perspiration . . . do something, Savage . . . don't just stand there . . . think! Presently, he began to note very carefully the position of the machinery in the compartment. He looked once more at the angles of fire from that hellish access panel . . . it seemed just possible that Chaffey— who could not know if the men who had found him had guns or not—might be more than careful, relying on staying well back in the bow compartment, watching the lighted square of the open panel. In which case . . . Savage began to whistle soundlessly between his teeth, slid down to floor level noiselessly and wriggled, flat on his belly, across the floor and behind the nearest cover—a transformer box, waist high. With every movement,

he winced, listening for the last sound he might ever hear . . .
it was, he thought, almost certainly a .45, an automatic—those
slugs impacted with something like half a tonne—which explained why Jack had . . .

At the closed entrance door, out of sight of the bow access
panel, Savage stopped, breathing deeply. For the first time, his
confidence was returning . . . he was back in the fields and
hedgerows of Ireland, stalking people who were stalking him
. . . he opened the main entrance door carefully, glanced out.
The corridor was brightly illuminated—but empty; far aft, he
could hear voices, the thrumming of engines, and the deck was
canting slightly as the craft heeled in wave and wind.

Savage glanced at the lights in the corridor and grinned without humour: it could just work . . . he left the door wide open,
felt for the light switch and the compartment changed abruptly
from brilliant white to dim darkness. Light from the corridor
poured in, forming a thick beam slanting at surrealistic angles
from floor and machinery.

Now he began . . . keeping close to the wall, ears straining
for a sound of any kind, he groped his way back to the closed
access hatch on the port side—the twin of that through which
Martin played and lost.

The dogs were aluminium handles which rotated on threaded
bolts; with a little bit of luck . . . he began unscrewing, face
contorted, afraid—no, terrified of the slightest squeak of tight
threads. But the fasteners, brand-new, were well greased, and
all four came free, each in turn placed carefully on the deck,
well clear. Now, it was marching well; back to the door, slowly,
with painfully exaggerated care, and he closed it firmly into
position, the thud of impact echoing round the electrical bay.
Now, Mr Bloody Chaffey . . . just assume, for a little while,
that I've retreated, gone for help . . . just a little while . . . long
enough for me to get my hands on that scrawny damned neck
of yours . . .

Cat-like, in the solid black silence, Savage found his way back
to the port hatch. Now . . . biting his lower lip, he grasped each
side of the light glassfibre panel and pulled, gently, almost
experimentally. It gave, a fraction of a millimetre, and he tugged
again, again, until it hung free in his hand. He pictured the

layout in his mind's eye, knew that a clear stretch of wall to the right would accommodate the hatch . . . set it down, checked it for security and straightened, listening intently. He leaned forward, in total darkness, until his head and shoulders were through the hatch, nostrils wrinkling at the admixture of smells.

He heard Chaffey move softly, far to the right. Here in the bow, twenty metres above the water and well forward of the sidewalls where the sea surged and washed, there was only stark silence, and now, ears straining, he could hear breathing. It was shallow, rapid, and unseen, Savage grinned wolfishly . . . the sod was frightened! Good . . . he'd give the murdering swine something to be frightened about, soon.

Noiselessly, Savage eased forward over the low sill into the bow compartment. He had no concept of its construction, groping with both hands before him, searching, feeling, analysing. There was no floor as such . . . a series of transverse semi-bulkheads reinforced the curved undershell of the bow, together with intercostal stiffeners which formed a honey-comb series of boxes, half a metre on each side. He groped downwards; the hull shell was at arm's length below; he would have to progress on hands and knees, across the matrix of square cavities, where the slightest slip or sound would trigger the stunning flash and roar that spelt death. Sweat broke out in fresh streams from every pore, and he waited, knees and hands braced, until the spasm ended, until he could allow his breathing to operate automatically, without monitoring.

His head lifted, tilted on one side, listening. Chaffey was ahead, slightly right . . . Savage began to move left, towards the needle bow, until he felt the vertical smooth wall of some kind of side lining, internal panelling. If only he knew a little about how this damned thing was constructed—and Chaffey had a head start there. He'd know every bulkhead, every compartment.

Delicately, in total silence, Savage began working his way round the curved bow, gritting teeth against the pain of knees grinding against unfinished structure, controlling breath and muscles with some vestige of self-discipline squeezed out from some long-forgotten reservoir. Ahead, the breathing, occasional movements, were as a beacon for him; Chaffey, he reasoned, must be totally confused. The killer knew, from the start, that there were two of them. One was dead. The other, presumably, had gone for help. But why the delay?

Savage thought grimly: you won't have long to find out, my beauty . . . just a step or two now . . . stopped, sensing the man's nearness . . . slowly, he thought, his eyes were acclimatising, and he realised that the hull, no more than six centimetres thick, allowed a tiny fraction of sunlight to penetrate.

Now he could see the vague image of a man against the faint glow behind: Chaffey was seated, legs dangling inside a narrow box between two frame members, leaning forward in an attitude of concentration, weight taken on his left hand, the other forearm almost vertical. Savage could not see the gun—but it was there . . .

He was close enough . . . none too soon, because he could hear voices now, coming closer. Chaffey tensed; Savage got his feet beneath him, took a gulp of air and lunged bodily, taking Chaffey on the upper right arm with a solid shoulder charge, grappling for the gun hand.

He need not have worried; with the impact, Chaffey was flung sideways and Savage heard two distinct cracks. The man's knees broke sideways, ripping away joint sockets, tearing ligaments and tendons, and the screaming began—long searing screams of agony, such that Savage, appalled, tried to clamp a hand over the man's mouth to stop the noise. Chaffey, reduced to a wounded animal, buried his teeth in Savage's hand, worrying away like some terrier for a moment before resuming that terrible agonised howling.

Light flodded into the bow; Perry, standing in the doorway a compartment away, felt a frozen vice closing around his guts, and he cried out, fearfully:

"Don? Jack? Oh . . . my God!" He tried to drag his eyes away from the body on the deck and became aware of Savage shouting behind the far bulkhead. A torch was on the deck—Perry crawled through frantically into the bow and crouched there, aghast.

Savage, against the screeching and weeping, shouted, waving

Perry forward—between them they dragged Chaffey out into the light, ignoring the noise when broken shredded bones ground together.

Suddenly, it stopped. Chaffey was out cold, head lolling, blood running from a mouth which the tongue was bitten almost in two. They laid him on the floor near Martin and got to their feet slowly, staggering like drunken men to lean against anything which would support them. Savage breathed heavily, stertorously, like a man near the end of a marathon run, hands flat against the wall, head hanging between flaccid arms, stomach heaving. He was *not* going to be sick . . . goddamit, he *wouldn't* puke . . . he was aware of Byrd, crew members flooding into the compartment, and turned at the outburst of noise.

"Get him off there!"

"Stop him, damn you!"

"Christ, he's choking the bastard!"

David Perry knelt astride Chaffey, both hands locked at the throat of the unconscious man; a thin trail of saliva ran down Perry's chin and he hunched his shoulders, fighting off the clutching hands, hands bearing down hard, mouth working . . .

Savage picked up the big torch, measured his distance and smashed it down an inch above Perry's right ear. The Project Manager sagged, collapsed, head resting beside that of the man he'd tried to kill. The faces, a finger-breadth apart, reflected two basic human emotions: anger, agony.

Savage stumbled into the bow compartment. Surprisingly, the torch still worked—he found Chaffey's gun, the wood handle cold and moist with sweat, and went back into the Electrical Bay. Perry was stirring; the Captain, face pale and drawn, watched a group of crewmen and engineers lifting the Project Manager to his feet, dazed and glassy-eyed.

Savage said to Byrd: "Get all these people out of here! I want Chaffey—" .

The Captain stared at him with narrowed eyes. "Don—you . . ." but shut his mouth, watching Savage's set jaw, blazing eyes.

The Security man said hoarsely: "Dickie, that bastard on the floor came aboard to fix us, once and for all. Our only chance

168

is to find out what he did. Now—are you going to get these people the hell out of here and let me do this my own way?"

Byrd glanced sharply at the gaunt man in stained jumpsuit. The eyes seemed withdrawn, recessed, and there was a feral glow deep within them, and suddenly, Byrd felt a cold wave of fear breaking over him and he was glad his name wasn't Chaffey.

Savage lost all restraint. "GET OUT OF HERE! ALL OF YOU! BEFORE I START USING THIS—" and he showed them the blued barrel of the gun. They took one look and hustled a confused David Perry out of the door; the last man closed it behind him and the group of six or seven men waited, bodies shifting to the roll of the craft.

The sounds came in quick succession . . . a moan, the mumble of a voice, a second and deeper groan and a scream that started at the top of the voice register, trying to climb still higher in a paroxysm of agony and shifting into a horrid long-drawn croaking from the back of the throat that sounded, if it were possible, worse than the scream. Voices again . . . silence, and now the screams came in quick succession, as if each was in response to a renewed question.

Instinctively, some of the men moved towards the door; the Captain stood solidly in their way, one hand elegantly leaning on the bulkhead at shoulder height. The men stopped . . .

Soon, the Electrical Bay was quiet. The door opened and Savage, face ashen in the artificial light, came through, closed it behind him.

"It's all right," he said heavily. "He put explosive of some kind down in the centrehull—near the main drive mercury vapour supply line. You'll find it all right, Titus—Number Seven floor hatch in the aft saloon. Plenty of time—it won't go off for another ten minutes . . ." he was speaking to empty air.

Captain Byrd watched the engineers out of sight before turning to Savage.

"You all right, Don?"

"I'm all right."

"Chaffey?"

"He's dead. Silly bastard . . . he couldn't take a joke."

Byrd said faintly: "Joke?"

"I was only pulling his leg," Savage said in a hard flat voice, and walked away down the gangway until the series of swing doors swallowed him up completely.

Towards evening, the hoverliner cruised slowly up to the Solent on waterjet power, white superstructure gleaming in the last reflected light of the sun. On the waterfront at Yarmouth, on the Isle of Wight, a middle-aged man in rubber boots, a duffle-coat and a red knitted skull-cap took a final look at her through binoculars, picked up his rod and reel and walked slowly back to the vandal-proof public phone. He slipped his credit card into the slot, watching the steel panel slide away to reveal the standard ten buttons. It took some time for him to punch out the number he wanted, through the International satellite coding, but presently:

"Mahler and Company, Geneva? Mr Kloty, please. Yes—I'll hold . . . Kloty? This is the Southampton office—Clostermann speaking. That ornithological specimen you wanted so badly . . . I'm afraid delivery will be delayed. Yes—our agent, it seems, did not make a contact and the bird is still free. What? No—we have no other agents locally, able to make the delivery. What—we'll fire the man responsible, of course. I'll take care of that . . . Kloty, I *know* our friends will be furious—but we have run out of options. Yes. Very well. Goodbye—"

Some seven hours later, Walter F. Keyhoe took a similar telephone call, hurled the offending instrument at the nearest wall, said 'Shit!' explosively and sent for Cody. While he waited, he gnawed the hard skin around a thumb-nail and occasionally mumbled incoherently into a clenched fist.

15   *General Rip-off*

For more than 200 years, it has been customary, in US warships, to locate the captain's quarters immediately below the bridge from which the ship was conned. When the *Sherman* left the Groton yard of the Electric Boat Company, her only concession to the exigencies of modern warfare was the high-speed compressed-air elevator linking the Captain's day room with the bridge—a contrivance triggered precisely by the Captain's weight on a pressure plate. Since the modern warship may have as little as sixty seconds' warning of imminent disaster—compared with perhaps half a day in the case of the old wooden two-deckers—the elevator could make the difference between annihilation and survival.

Commander Burdett preferred the companionway ladder in normal circumstances: if, when the time came, he was forced to use that goddam pneumatic rocket, he'd use it. But until then—

His quarters reflected the revolution in Navy thinking since Korea, Vietnam and the Gulf Oil War. A happy captain was an on-the-ball captain, and since the ship could stay at sea more than a year on an average cruise, the designers pulled out all the stops. The dayroom deck lay beneath an inch of rich blue pile carpet; the furniture was contemporary sequoia redwood encased in tough clear plastic, and both linen and cutlery were beyond reproach. Mrs Burdett, on her first visit to the ship, realised thankfully her husband hadn't left her for another woman—only a ship.

Commander George McShane Burdett, USN, contemplated the fact that his 44th birthday was only two days off, and found the concept sat disagreeably on his shoulders. The Annapolis Class of 70 had been, necessarily, a small one, and the contraction of the Navy after the Gulf War and the evacuation of Southern Iran had caught him unawares; promotion to Captain was deferred and he spent five years on shore duty in the new bases a liberated Cuba made gratefully available.

He turned off the shower, dressed and rang for coffee. Waiting, he stood at the Bridge Repeater Panel, checking the electronic status board and Watch Bill. He was a tall spare man, a metre seventy-five, and carried his seventy kilos lightly. In civilian clothes he looked like a stockbroker or lawyer—perhaps an accountant; the grey eyes were deceptively mild and he rarely raised his voice above conversational level. His officers were acutely aware of the man's magical faculty of unspoken communication: a glance, a nod, a quick look at a piece of equipment, was enough.

There were, perhaps, eleven thousand Commanders in the US Navy, of whom maybe two hundred were classified as being of superior calibre and suitable for command of nuclear vessels; less than twenty were currently at sea and, of these, it is probable that Burdett's PH file listed him in the top three.

"Sir—?"

"Uh—Harbutt. I'll be right there."

His steward hovered uneasily. "Sir—just coffee?" His Captain's ability to survive throughout daylight hours on liquids alone was not so much puzzling as downright worrying: this guy had the best boat in the Navy with a crew of two hundred, all of whom needed him around in full working order.

Burdett looked up. "Do we have to go through this every morning, Harbutt?"

"No sir!"

"But we just did—" Burdett pointed out.

"Yessir. Beggin' the Captain's pardon, sir—"

"Are we sure tomorrow will be different, Harbutt?"

The steward swallowed—with difficulty. "Yessir! Positive, sir!"

"Very well, steward. After ten months—I sense victory in the air. Or is it sausages again? Now—hear this, and hear it good: any more hassle about breakfast tomorrow, I'll kick your butt clear down to the stern rail. Do you read?"

"Aye aye, sir!"

ᐧ The Captain grinned, satisfied. "Okay. Now move your ass out of here, and pass the word for the Exec."

Harbutt retreated. The Commander sat down with a refilled cup and checked the paperwork on the desk; soon, a knock on the door heralded the arrival of the First Officer, Lt. Cdr.

Shelton Burns. The Captain kicked the floor switch and the door slid open, with a muted hiss.

"Morning, Number One."

"Captain. We have good weather, sir—nice to get back to sea again."

The Exec. stood with feet astride, black hair two metres from deck level and very close to the painted steel deckhead. He held his peaked cap firmly under the left arm, and the solid muscular body left little sea-room in the regulation sea duty coveralls. Burdett stared at the bleary blue eyes confronting him and grinned.

"You fit for duty, mister?"

Burns flushed. "I assume I look as bad as I feel, sir—?"

"That you do. Party?"

"And then some, skipper. Woke up in some double bed ashore this morning."

The Captain eyed his Executive Officer. "Surprise, surprise—" sardonically.

"Yessir. Five other people there, too. And they looked worse than I do. Sir!"

Burdett grinned unsympathetically. "Well—you'll have plenty of time to recuperate. You'd better see the Surgeon-General about that head—I doubt if you can get your cap on securely. You read sailing orders yesterday?"

"I did, sir. Ship closed up ten hundred hours, clear the buoys ten thirty, set course ten-forty."

"Right. We'll go through final details on the bridge nine thirty. What's our status?"

The Exec. considered. "At this time, sir, all systems go, save a malfunction on micro-sonar. Chief Yeoman Parker is working on it. All lines singled up: we're in radio contact with Fleet Ops., Commissat and Port Security. Both reactors hot, steam to all turbines. Engine room bells, intercom and emergency systems checked out. AOK. All hands aboard or accounted for, sir—except Lt. Phillips."

Burdett looked up sharply from his coffee-cup. "Phillips? Where in the blue blazes has he got to, Number One?"

"Not sure, sir. Your coxswain says he saw Dean Phillips in

the Yard, on the telephone, thirty minutes ago. He's not far away. I sent your launch with Swanson to look for him, sir."

The Captain frowned. "Goddamit, Shel—Dean's usually on the line. He knew the seven a.m. deadline; you'll have to write him up for this. We can't sail on exercises without our Chief Coding Officer, for Chrissake. Ensign Krause hasn't been cleared on Confidential Documents yet, right?"

"Right. But he could cut it, sir." The Exec. sounded less than positive.

The Commander grunted, got up and walked to the daylight port, staring out over the sun-dancing water towards Newport News, so that Sheldon Burns could not see his face. The Exec. would, ultimately, carry the can for Phillips's absence—although there was little he could do about it, personally. Goddamit, Burdett thought—why can't we clear port just once without some miserable son of a bitch fouling things up?

The desk audio bleeped.

"Captain?"

"Speaking."

"Lt. Clyde, sir. Officer of the Deck. Chief Swanson just checked in, leaving the jetty, sir. He has Lt. Phillips aboard."

"Very good, Clyde," the Commander took a deep breath, slowly and with some enjoyment. "Have Lt. Phillips report to my day room, please."

"Aye aye, sir."

Burdett stared at his First Lieutenant, with eyebrows perhaps four millimetres lower than usual—but Burns knew the signs and quailed inwardly. The Old Man lost his temper perhaps once a year at most—the last time during a practice salvage tow in which *Sherman*'s cable broke a straight three times in a row.

"I want you here when Phillips arrives, Mister. Meanwhile, check the INS and have our checkpoints evaluated. You know the rendezvous location?"

"Yes, sir. Thirty degrees north latitude, seventy-five degrees west latitude. Eight hundred kilometres east of Cape Hatteras, sir."

"Right. And first checkpoint?"

"One fifty kilometres east of Hatteras, sir."

Burdett nodded shortly. "Very well, Number One. Report to me with Phillips."

"Aye aye, sir."

When the door hissed and closed, the Commander sat down again heavily. He must be getting old . . . for a while, there, he'd almost blown a fuse. He picked up the photograph of Shirley Ann and the boys, taken three years previously: Colin, eleven, George Junior, nine. His wife smiled out from the print—one of the first with that new-fangled Stereo Twin camera, he recalled—it really did produce a fine three-dee picture. Shirley, he mused, was still a fine figure of a woman . . . just short of being a physical-fittness fruitcake, she kept in good shape. One of these days, Burdett told himself, he'd take some of the banked-up furloughs accumulated during the last 18 months . . .

"Lt. Phillips, sir."

The Commander looked up.

"Before I have the Exec. write you up, have you anything to say, mister?"

Phillips bit his lower lip. Slim, fair-haired, the Navy Reserve officer had impeccable qualifications for a Chief Coding Officer: UCLA master's degree in pure maths, honours graduate at MIT on the IBM/Honeywell-sponsored course in electronic cryptology. To Burdett—who could remember most ships without the aid of a computer—Phillips was new-style Navy: qualifications without tradition.

"Well, Mr Phillips?" acidly.

"Sir—I'm sorry. It was Sue Ellen, my wife—"

"She sick?" Burdett demanded.

"Well—no, sir. That is . . . I don't know, sir. I mean—I always ring her before we sail. She'd worry if I didn't."

The Captain breathed heavily through his nose: this was getting worse all the time.

"You never heard of Security Regulations, mister?"

Phillips shifted nervously from one foot to another. "Yessir." Burdett glanced at Burns, but the Exec. steadfastly refused to become involved, staring ahead rigidly. Burdett sighed. "All right, Mr Phillips. You phoned your wife—"

"No, sir. That is—I got no answer. I called a dozen times or more. I thought—maybe she's sick, or something—she always waits for my call. So I called Verna May—"

"Who in hot steaming hell," the Captain said faintly, "is Verna May?"

"I'm getting to that, sir. Next-door neighbour."

Burdett sighed. "Where do your family live, Phillips?"

"Pleasantville, New Jersey, sir. Near Atlantic City."

"Okay. Go on."

"Well, sir—Verna May says Sue Ellen went to Washington yesterday afternoon, with two Navy officers. In a Navy limousine, sir. She said Sue Ellen sent one of the officers back to leave a message with Verna while she packed her things. The officer asked Verna May to phone the school today, to say Jimmy would miss school for a while."

Burdett said slowly—"Jimmy's your son?"

"Yessir. But Sue Ellen doesn't know anyone in Washington, sir. Her folks live in Joplin, Missouri—she went home only last fall."

The Captain sat back in his seat. "That's it?"

Phillips gulped and nodded violently. "Sir! I don't know what's going on but I know Sue Ellen wouldn't leave without letting me know. She knew we were sailing today—"

Burdett scowled. "Seems like the whole goddam country knows we're sailing." But he knew the boy could have good cause to worry. Maybe his wife was with the Navy, maybe not. Worried men never gave their best and he was short of skilled code men; he made up his mind.

"All right, Phillips. I understand how you feel. And you did make the ship in time . . . I'm going to signal Washington to investigate. Meanwhile, relax, do your job."

The lieutenant saluted, relieved, and scuttled out. Burdett lighted his first cigar of the day.

"Well, Number One?"

"Usually only two reasons a woman leaves home, sir. Another woman—or another man."

"Huh?"

"She could have left him, sir—but I know Phillips. He's happily married, and he doesn't play around himself. You want I should signal the Pentagon?"

"Do that. Try Assignments Branch and Public Relations, for a start. Then Security. It all sounds crazy to me . . . keep Phillips informed—and stand by to sail."

"Aye aye, sir—"

The USS *Sherman* paid off her tugs, entering the Chesapeake; the Captain stared back at the receding coastline, gave his orders.

"All ahead two thirds, Number One. Course 128 degrees magnetic—work her up to sixty knots before engaging autopilot and INS."

"One two eight degrees, sir."

Burdett walked sedately into the starboard pelorus and stood gazing out to the south-east; great banks of cumulus cloud rode like frigates under full sail, heading out across the Atlantic, and the *Sherman* rode in serene stability upon the green sea. He sensed underfoot the vibrations of the turbines and water jets; he took no part in conning the ship and left matters confidently in Burns's hands. Burns was a first-class seaman, long overdue for his own ship, and the Captain eased the waiting as much as possible by leaving Burns in charge of the deck.

They were directed to proceed at standard speed to their rendezvous point in the North Caribbean, exercising en route all stations and armament in cooperation with land-based strike craft and units from the Harrier-Carrier fleet. The First Lieutenant got the ship settled down to his satisfaction, handed the deck over to Lt. Clyde and released the starboard watch below. *Sherman* was almost fully automated—if every man aboard dropped dead simultaneously, she would arrive two days later at the RV point with an accuracy of better than 50 metres plus or minus ten, turn into wind and hold position.

Just after four bells, Lt. Phillips reported to the Exec. with a bunch of signals forms in his hand. His face said it all.

OFFICE COMMISSAT NEWPORT NEWS

TO USS SHERMAN CF CDR BURDETT INFO LT. PHILLIPS USN

PRIORITY IMMEDIATE

REGRET ADVIS NO INFO AVAILABLE WHEREABOUTS MRS PHILLIPS AND FAMILY STOP. LOCAL

MILITARY POLICE MAKING ENQUIRIES ATLANTIC
CITY NJ STOP. WILL ADVISE STOP. J.F.MCNALLY LT.
CDR. SECDEP SECTION THREE ENDIT.

The Exec. showed the signal to the Captain. "Inconclusive,
sir. Doesn't help Phillips much."

The Captain nodded sombrely. "I agree. Well—nothing we
can do until Washington or Newport come up with better information. It's odd—women do the damnedest things, sometimes."

Burns grinned. "I'm glad to say, sir. But this isn't the usual
domestic walk-out. I had a word with Phillips—he saw his wife
less than three weeks ago and things were fine. Kid doing well
in school, wife with plenty of friends."

"Yes," the Captain rubbed hs chin reflectively. "All we can
do is wait. Keep the boy busy, Shel."

"Aye aye, sir. Got that in hand already—ordered a muster of
Confidential Documents for eight bells tomorrow."

"Tomorrow? That's a two day job, Number One!"

"Yessir. Like you said, sir—keep him busy."

The Captain concealed a smile—with some difficulty. "Just
make sure his feet touch the deck occasionally, Number One.
And have someone stand by the Collision Warning . . . tell
me—you believe in reincarnation?"

"Sir?"

"I mean,—in previous lives, Number One. You think you
might have been Torquemada or someone like that? Oh, skip
it—"

The Exec. saluted, walked out of the bridge to find Phillips.
Sometimes, he couldn't figure the Old Man out at all . . .

At four bells, morning watch, May 7, the USS *Sherman* was
some 300 kilometres south of Hamilton, Bermuda. She had
secured from General Quarters an hour previously, and the
Captain was reasonably satisfied with her performance: there
was still much to do—but holes revealed by the exercises could
be plugged with ease, via more rigorous training and supervi-
sion. He had been pleasantly surprised after the last exercises
off Iceland, at the improvement in dealing with air attack—
especially in regard to the Méxican ships; only in recent years
her oil revenues had permitted her to buy the best equipment

going, and they had been lavish in provision of unmanned aircraft simulating Cruise missiles. Burdett was perfectly sure his proximity fuses would have detonated the pilotless jets at least half a kilometre from the *Sherman*—but the crew were under no such delusions.

The Southland enemy figured the surest way of getting maximum exercise points was a wave of eight laser-guided bombs at sea level, under cover of the strike aircraft running in at high level—the *Sherman* battle computer had handled it—but only just. The Captain went down personally to congratulate CPO Warren F. Hardy.

"Damn fine intercept, Chief. Candy's done us proud today."

"I guess Computerised Anti-missile Negation and Destruct Intercept *is* kind of a mouthful, sir. Seven hits and a proximity detonation is pretty good. The eggheads at Groton swear she can handle up to sixteen plots—she was nowhere near overload, sir."

Burdett beamed. "Okay, Chief. Keep it up. Damn fine job."

He walked back to the bridge through two watertight doors; *Sherman* was cruising semi-submerged, to wash away the anti-radiation compound applied at the start of the exercises; the gooey gunge was spray-applied and stank to high heaven—but it would absorb 90% of radioactivity from any air burst near enough to contaminate the ship without actually destroying her. Once washed free, it left the *Sherman* virtually free of contamination.

On the bridge, Number One was waiting.

"About to call you, sir. Radio room reports a garbled SOS call, with heavy interference, bearing zero five five magnetic."

"Have you altered course yet?"

"Yes, sir. No identification—radio room is monitoring every other frequency. They report it seems fairly close, sir. Signal strength niner."

The Captain nibbled a finger nail pensively. "Probably some damned fishing boat out of Bermuda with engine trouble . . . bunch of goddam amateurs. Well—we'll check. Hold course to intercept and report any developments. I'll be in my day cabin."

"Aye, aye, sir."

Burdett stumbled wearily down the ladder into his quarters,

threw his white peaked cap onto the bunk, loosened his tie and sat down heavily. He reached for a cigar and cursed: the humidor was empty. He rang for Harbutt and delivered a reaming which left the steward white and trembling; the fault was remedied and Burdett chewed savagely to mangle the butt into an acceptable ruin.

"Bridge to Captain!"

"Goddamit. Yes?"

"Radio reports heavy jamming, all frequencies, sir. Multiple origins, positions unknown. And radar reports contact three five kilometres dead ahead."

"Very well, Number One. Coming up."

The Captain climbed the stairs, swearing fluently in fractured bordello Spanish.

He checked the radar repeater. "I have the conn, Number One. Right standard rudder, helmsman."

"Right standard rudder, sir."

"New course zero eight zero. Standard cruise depth."

"Standard cruise depth, sir. Steady on zero eight zero."

The Commander turned to Burns. "What do you make of it, Number One?"

"It's the only sighting in that quadrant, sir. Could be the distress ship. The radio interference—Chief Hardy thinks it could be several of our air-drop jammerbuoys—same type as used by the Brazilians, second day of the exercises. Vibration-activated."

"Are you telling me," the Captain said moodily, "that we can't turn the damn things off?"

"Affirmative, sir. Short of finding each one and triggering the destruct circuit visually. Invisible on radar—they float with only the antenna above water."

"Great heaps of gopher shit!"

"Yessir. Deep and smelly. Stand by, sir—"

Burns listened carefully, ear close to the audio box. "Thank you, radar. Advise range five kilometres."

He turned. "Good contact dead ahead five clicks, sir. Target not moving."

"Maintain course and speed."

"Maintain course and speed, sir."

The ship ploughed along under an overcast sky, in a sea which moved in long heavy swells with an ominous oily consistency; the glass was falling, and far to the south, along the Bahamas–Barbados Island chain, something nasty was brewing up, weatherwise. This cruise was going all to hell, Burdett thought discontentedly. That queer business with Phillips . . . and that outbreak of stomach pains which left half a watch incapacitated for two days . . . and now this.

"Radar reports target dead ahead three clicks, sir."

"Very well, Number One. Launch a telebird—let's see what we have here—" Seconds later, the two-metre wingspan minijet with a 3-dee camera in its belly roared up the ramp in the bow, dropped the booster and roared off in a tightly-banked turn to the east. Burdett walked over to the bridge consol to watch.

The picture steadied: the mud cleared away and the grey-green sea began flowing from the top of the screen to the bottom, the telebird holding a steady 100-metre altitude. The camera panned upwards under the First Lieutenant's left hand; in midscreen, an indistinct blur condensed, clarified, took shape.

"Target a single-stack ship, approximately three thousand tonnes, sir."

"I see her. Run the bird in for ident, Number One. Seemed to be smoking from the stern, do you think?"

"Affirmative. Looks like a fire aft of the bridge—smoke blowing due aft, sir. She's signalling—Morse, no less! In this day and age . . ."

"We do have someone who can read Morse code, I presume?" whimsically.

"Yessir—" snide old bastard, Burns thought, with some affection. "Clyde—take this down—"

S.O.S. S.O.S. FIRE IN RADIO SHACK SPREAD TO CREW QUARTERS. WE HAVE CASUALTIES HAVE YOU A DOCTOR ABOARD BARNES CAPT SS NORMANTON

The target was in sight now, on the grey horizon, smoke drifting down-wind.

"Very good, Number One. Pipe for Chief Swanson and the launch crew, the Surgeon and one medical rating. Mr Clyde, make to Normanton: WILL HEAVE TO THREE CABLES

ON LEE SIDE. MEDICAL ASSISTANCE ON WAY. RE-
GRET HAVE NO RADIO CONTACT DUE HEAVY
INTERFERENCE."

The USS *Sherman* slowed to a crawl, approaching the burning
ship; Burns took her round in a slow turn, bringing her into the
semi-submerged mode to facilitate launching the boat. Burdett
leaned over the bridge rail, water swirling only metres below.
Doc Newhouse was on deck, waiting; with him, a medical rating,
Ensign Hughes and Lt. Phillips, with Chief Swanson and three
hands. Burdett thought the Surgeon looked like death, even at
this distance—face chalk-white, patched with yellow, following
his cataclysmic stomach upheaval days before.

The launch cast off, the bow rising as Swanson hit the throttle,
heading her round to head for the *Normanton*.

They approached her lee side: Phillips saw that she was listing
perhaps five degrees, and the smoke was thick and acrid—God
alone knew what was burning up there on deck. He led the way
up the swaying ladder, scrambled over the rail. Smoke drifted
in whirls and eddies, and he blinked in shocked fear. The two
men stood with legs astride, swaying with the motion of the
ship; each wore black coveralls, rubber shoes. They carried burp
guns—new model Schmeisser 0.22 with the powered rotary
magazine holding 1000 rounds. Wordlessly, they motioned Phillips to stand against the hatch cover to watch, while they roped
in all six remaining members of the boarding-party.

A third man in green coveralls and baseball cap loomed
through the drifting smoke.

He checked a small notebook, stared at the Surgeon. "You—
Newhouse—over here." He looked sharply at the Lieutenant.
"Phillips, isn't it? Over here with the Doc. Coding Officer,
right?"

Phillips clenched his jaws and said nothing. The green-clad
man grinned.

"Okay, Lieutenant. We know who you are—"

Swanson made his move, going in low on the nearest guard,
who sidestepped and kicked the Chief in the ribs, sending him
into the scuppers. The guard lifted his muzzle two inches, flicked
the trigger . . . the gun said 'Blutt-r-r-t,' and the upper half of
Swanson's body became unrecognisable as a human torso. Slugs

whined in ricochet and the *Sherman* party ducked, swearing and crying out in fear.

Ensign Hughes looked sideways at Swanson, went down slowly on his knees and vomited comprehensively, noisily. The man in green watched impassively; when Hughes was done, he said coldly:

"All right—Phillips and Newhouse, this way. Rest of you go with Kelly here. Dead or alive—he don't care, either way."

They followed the green man helplessly, stunned by Swanson's death; the lieutenant glanced at Newhouse and realised the man was close to breakdown, and gripped his upper arm, to steady him. They were taken up a companionway ladder to a cabin, small, unventilated; there was barely enough room for the three men and they stood in silence, waiting. Presently a fourth man arrived, this time in a plain dark civilian suit. He spoke briefly to the man in green coveralls, sat down at the small table.

"Phillips . . . Newhouse. Nine and seventeen. You don't know why you're here—but you soon will. Ten minutes, you'll be on your way back to your ship. First—" he turned, switched on a CCTV. "See anyone you know?"

Lieutenant Phillips stared, mouth suddenly very dry. The camera was rigged near the hatch of a ship's hold; the lighting was excellent and he could see a crowd of forty, fifty people, all women and children. The camera panned left, zoomed in, and he was looking at Sue Ellen and Jimmy. She looked very tired and her hair straggled wildly; fastened roughly to her sweater was a taped '9'.

"Sue Ellen—" his voice was hoarse, indistinct.

"She's fine, Phillips. Take another look—the families of every officer and department chief of the *Sherman* is there, in our forward hold. Including this lady—" the camera found a well-built, middle-aged woman carrying the number '1'.

"Mrs Burdett—the Captain's wife. Seen enough?"

The lieutenant gritted his teeth and stared at the man in the dark suit.

"You're a dead man, mister . . . once the crew lay hands on you."

"Yeah . . . yeah. I know. I heard it all before. Nothing will happen to those people—if your Captain does exactly what he is told."

The Surgeon, Newhouse, licked his lips. "I didn't see my wife there!"

"That's right doc. She isn't. But see this girl near the foot of the ladder?"

"Debbie!" the cry was sheer anguish.

"Right. Daughter Debbie. You thought she was in Spain— we know how things are between you and your wife, doc. Chances are, you'd have asked us to drop her over the side, quietly. Now listen—no more hassle, now."

The speaker pulled out a video disc.

"This goes back with you, to the Captain. First, you tell him— no tricks, no radio calls. He's to fire a green flare when he's ready for visitors. Any time we hear a broadcast for help, we drop a kid over the rail. Capisch?"

The men nodded dumbly . . . on the way back to the *Sherman*, ignoring the flying spray, Phillips brooded on what he would do to these men if they . . . his fingers tightened on the video disc.

The Captain glared at him, down in the day cabin. "What the hell do you mean—they have my wife over there?"

"That's right, sir. And forty or fifty more—all the officers' families. In the hold. They killed Swanson—"

"Swanson? Dead?"

"Yessir. Gunned him down—he didn't have a chance. There are at least thirty of them, sir—Americans, mostly."

Burdett ground his teeth together in an agony of indecision. "And they want us to look at this video film? Shit, Phillips, it's like some lousy little TV soap opera . . . it *can't* be for real— Number One?"

Burns said carefully: "I think we'd best look at it, sir. There's a video player in the wardroom—"

They watched in shocked silence. There was no commentary: none was necessary. Towards the end, Burdett's shoulders were bowed under terrible responsibility; the news went round the ship like wildfire. Towards the end, there was a short prere-corded section. The face of the man in the dark suit exuded satisfaction.

"Captain, we have your people here—as you can see. Now

184

hear this: no attempt at communication with anyone—or a hostage dies. Next—eight-five armed men will board you any moment now. No resistance—same conditions as trying to transmit. Last—ensure every man with families aboard the *Normanton* knows about it. That way, we'll get along fine.

"Fire a green flare when ready to be boarded. All side arms to be unloaded, stacked in the bridge. Anything goes wrong, we dump all our passengers into the sea."

The screen went blank.

Burdett stared blindly at the wardroom wall, torn between concern for the families, anger at the supreme impudence of the *Normanton,* and a completely new emotion he finally recognised as helplessness.

"Number One . . . you know what to do. I'll be on the bridge—"

A few moments later—

"This . . . this is the Captain . . . now hear this . . ."

The PA system hissed through a hundred speakers in the ship, and upturned faces waited, listening to the strange sound of a man trying to speak . . .

16   *The Chromium Corvette*

"For the purpose of this exercise, Captain, you can call me Cody. I'm glad you decided to cooperate . . . this officer is?"

"Lt. Cdr. Burns—my Exec."

"Okay—let's get this thing on the road. First, total radio silence except your scheduled reports to COMMAT. You transmit only your position and status—ignore all incoming queries. You give these positions at the times stated—" Cody gave the Captain a sheet of typed paper. "Next—head for this location—42 degrees north, sixty-five degrees west. Six hundred kilometres east of Cape Cod. Get it into the navigational computer and lock in. I want the course and distance from this position."

At a nod from Burdett, the Exec. sat down, began punching keys. "Distance 1308 kilometres. Course 354 magnetic."

"Now," Cody said cheerfully, "that wasn't too bad, was it? Get this thing on course now, Burns. How soon can you get us there?"

The Exec. hesitated. There was so much he wanted to do— and so little he could achieve . . . "Around ten hours."

"That's what I figured," Cody said with satisfaction. "Okay— better swing out into the Atlantic, east of Bermuda—we have plenty of time. And keep that radar going, Captain—avoid all shipping—and send for Chief Hardy."

"Chief—who?" Burdett said, surprised.

"Hardy. Your Fire Control Officer. Move it—"

The Banker arrived, well briefed, on the bridge and stared at Cody, without a trace of recognition.

"You Hardy?"

"I am. Say, what the hell is going on here?"

"Shut up and listen. You know we have the ship's families in the bag? You do . . . well, there you have fifty good reasons for doing exactly as I tell you. Right?"

"Right—"

"Report to a man called Kowalski in Deck C, amidships, in the Missile Area."

" 'C'? The Arcturus bay?"

"You got it. Move—" and The Banker was gone, as if he had never been present.

"Now listen, Captain. Listen good. We have men all over the ship, armed. No-one misbehaves, no-one gets hurt. Routine normal, down to the last KP party in the heads. At dawn I want this boat dumped—right down to sea level, out of sight. We stop all radio transmissions midnight—they'll know by then we're not where we say we are. Next, we don't want no trouble from satellite tracking stations—you keep your temperature emissions below detection level on infra-red—understand?"

The Captain started. "How did you know about—"

"Shoot, Captain," Cody grinned, "we know as much about this tub as you do. Just make sure we're on station before ten a.m. tomorrow morning, Greenwich Time without anyone knowing we're there. Blow our cover, Captain, and I radio the *Normanton*—now, you don't want anything to happen to those nice people, do you?"

Burdett shook his head numbly.

"Good. I've sent young Phillips back to the *Normanton*—with your signals code book. From daybreak, he'll be reporting to COMMAT as if still aboard this ship. As far as anyone knows, *Sherman* is way south of Bermuda doing her thing."

The Captain said jerkily: "How long? I mean—you can't stay aboard for ever—"

"Don't worry: You'll have your ship back tomorrow—I promise. We just want to use her for a little while. Parting will be very easy—we batten everyone down below decks, give them a jab of a needle. Time you wake up and break out, we'll be long gone."

Sheldon Burns moved, restlessly, against the wall of the bridge. "You won't get away with killing Swanson, damn you—"

"Now, don't come the little hero," Cody said gently. "The way I hear, he asked for it. And you can't run an operation *this* size without crackin' a few eggs."

"What size?" Burdett said casually. The man in the dark suit grinned.

" 'Ask me no questions' " Cody quoted, and left the bridge to the two silent guards standing by.

Chief Hardy met him at the MIRV compartment. "We're on top of it—these guys are all with us—"

Cody stared around with consuming interest. On each side of the vast hold, each of five great caissons held an armed Arcturus ICBM; the main work was centred around the aft end, where obliquely-mounted launch tubes served the short-range Sea-cruise missiles used against surface ships. Hardy's gang had one needle-nosed projectile set up on an arming rack; he took Cody down to brief him.

"This thing," he said with pride, "Goes more than 1000 kilometres, carries a hot or standard warhead. Booster-launched, computer-guided until its own radar picks up the target. Locks on tight and—boom!"

"And for this operation?"

"We're setting up two of them, standard explosive warheads—ample for a small TSV—"

"Hold it!" Cody said urgently. "TSV?"

"Thin-skinned vessel. No armour—you know? We'll run in at around 3000 metres, to within five kilometres, until she locks on. The nose TV camera'll be working: you'll be able to see the whole thing."

Cody nodded, satisfied. "It runs in fast?"

"You said it. Near Mach 1 at low level—at which speed she can pull 19G turns. No avoiding action is going to help the target."

The civilian stared at the Navy man. "This thing we're after—it may be travelling fast—around 300 knots—"

Hardy sneered. "On the surface? Nothin' goes that speed on the surface, man."

"This one does," Cody said bluntly. "So make sure."

"Okay. So I make sure. Lissen—I'm more interested in knowing how we get outa here, once the job's done."

Cody said: "We have four Sea Chinooks aboard, right?"

"Right."

"We have four chopper pilots with us. They take sixteen of us off the ship at midnight, by which time we'll be off Dominica. They take us direct to Santa Domingo where we have a DC12B waiting. The plane will take you direct to Casablanca, where you find your money and plastic surgeons waiting. After that, you're on your own. Got that clear in your thick skull, Banker?"

The CPO controlled his anger with an effort; with the money he was paying, this guy could throw insults all day.

"What about the *Sherman*, after we've gone?"

"What about it?" Cody said sharply.

"I got a lot of good buddies aboard this scow. I don't want anything happening to them."

Cody said contemptuously: "You're too soft, Hardy. For all your rackets and bluster, you're too goddam soft. If you were a drummer, you couldn't beat the devil's tattoo on a cake of hard shit. But—just to get you outa my hair—I'll tell you. Everyone gets locked up below decks; everyone gets a needle and sleeps a while. They have the ship under conn, you're long gone—with your millions. Satisfied?"

"Not that I don't trust you, Cody—you know?"

"You don't trust any son of a bitch . . ."

"Who's arguing?" The Banker said truculently.

The *Sherman* ploughed on through the night at sixty knots, with only her bridge above water. In the office of the Commander in Chief, Atlantic, a confused staff of officers and WAVES tried to make sense of her signals and positions. The Atlantic plot placed her in the correct locality, but her transmissions were outrageously routine and one way only; she remained silent to all signals requesting status reports.

At midnight, all traffic from the *Sherman* ceased, and COM-MAT ordered a full emergency, diverting a total of nineteen surface ships, four submarines and a growing air effort into the area long known as the Bermuda Triangle—long proven a hoax but which continued to swallow without trace ships, aircraft and men. In local space, seven satellites were in orbit, so that one was always over the last known position of the *Sherman* at any time.

At daybreak, the *Normanton* crew locked in the automatic navigator, battened down the hatches on the *Sherman* crew members and families and departed in a helicopter brought up from the forward hold and assembled. After two hours and some 500 kilometres they landed on the deck of a Chilean tanker bound for Santiago—the long way round.

Lt. Phillips was finally very, very angry indeed. Quite apart from stealing his ship, these characters had kidnapped his wife and child, assaulted her in the process, used them to secure the surrender of the *Sherman*, and—worst of all—had killed Chief Swanson. He was not interested, as of now, why they wanted the ship. What he was interested in was the possibility of doing something constructive—and what he did earned him a Navy Cross, field promotion and the everlasting adoration of his wife who—it should be recorded—regarded him up to that time as something of an esoteric namby-pamby with more brains than sense. Besides—he was the senior officer on the *Normanton*.

He started by ordering a search of the aft hold, using his three ratings and Doc Newhouse. When all was gathered in, he spread it out for consideration. Like any initiative program test, the task was simple: how to escape from a ship's hold, without a ladder, via the deck hatch battened down ten metres overhead.

At one time, the hold had been partitioned; Phillips found quantities of timber in various lengths, three tarpaulins, two 5-litre cans of peanut oil (the purpose of which escaped him to the day he retired) and oddments of rope, flexible wire and chipboard.

To construct a rough ladder was no real problem for the ratings; with it, Phillips clambered up to check the hatch; it was too much to hope that it had not been secured tightly, and he was not disappointed. The huge box-like lid was lashed down externally to deck cleats.

His mind went into top gear. He lashed together three long baulks of timber, lifted them until one end was rammed under the corner of the hatch. The timber, intentionally, was too long to stand upright, and lay some 15 degrees to the vertical. He packed the upper contact point with timber and went to work on the bottom end.

This was greased liberally with peanut oil, as was the deck itself; half a dozen lengths of rope were secured to the lower end of the pillar and he mustered everyone big enough, to haul. Presently four teams of eight stood ready; the three ratings held a baulk of timber like a battering ram, and Phillips started the count. With each blow of the ram, ninety-six hands hauled, and the pillar edged forward. More peanut oil, more hauling, the seamen hammering in wedges to prevent the timber pillar from slipping. The pressure on the hatch was frightening, yet it refused to give; the people were exhausted. Phillips's mind went into supergear and he had a single enormous loop of rope constructed, one end round the baulk, the other around a steel deck support girder.

Through the loop, they passed a single heavy beam of timber and began turning the enormous tourniquet.

The families cowered in a sheltered corner, listening appalled to the groans and screams of tortured timber; the deck was making noises like static electricity and the great loop twanged like a giant Jew's harp with each turn.

The break took all of them unawares, despite unlimited audible warnings; the deck hatch broke away at the corner, the bottom end of the pillar whipped ponderously towards the stanchion, neatly removing the left foot and ankle of Seaman First Class Donahue, who received a Silver Star, a full-pay pension and divorce papers from his wife, who had already left him for a penniless piano-tuner from Boulder City, Colorado. As is often remarked, there is no accounting for tastes.

But the hatch was open—and a single bright star tracked to and fro in the aperture as the ship rolled.

Leaving the Doc. tending to Donahue, Phillips went back up his makeshift ladder to find the ship totally deserted. The radio, naturally, was in ruins, but he was still doggedly trying to make something out of the mess when the Surgeon came into the radio shack twenty minutes later.

"Phil—any luck?"

"Not a goddam hope, Doc. Christ, I'm a Coding Officer—not a radio mech. I can use a radio—but I can't build one. How's Donahue?"

"He'll make it. One of the women had a sewing kit—I got it straightened away as best I could. One of the wives is an auxiliary nurse—she can handle it."

Phillips cocked an ear to one side. "The engines are still running—we're heading roughly north. Doc, ask the ratings to go right through the ship—see what they can find. But make it quick: those bastards still have the *Sherman* until we tip off the Navy."

As Coding Officer, Phillips knew with some accuracy when certain US military tracking satellites were overhead the Atlantic; he lacked only the means to signal them—until the ratings showed him their booty. A previous cargo had required protection against ingress of animal and insect life: they found six partly-used rolls of metal foil.

Twenty minutes later, the decks of the *Normanton* were covered with brilliant foil; he slowed the ship down until she could barely maintain seaway, to stop dislodgement of the foil by wind. Just before one a.m, a Mars-Deimos orbiter tracked across Florida, down through the West Indies at an altitude of only 200 kilometres; it picked up the biggest radar blip ever relayed to

191

BuOps Processing Centre in Mobile, Alabama—who were already totally commited to the search for the *Sherman*. Soon, Navy patrol planes dropped a flare and found what became known as Phillips's Chromium Corvette. After that, things moved very quickly indeed.

The USS *Bluefin* broke all records to an air launch position from which she hurled a VTOL passenger jet at the *Normanton* and scored a bull. Phillips was airlifted back to the sub-carrier, where they strapped a Superharrier to his backside and aimed him for Guantanimo, Cuba. From there, he reported by phone to COMMAT.

Consternation! He passed on details of the hijack, nothing about the *Sherman* they didn't know already. The Commander-in-Chief was well-nigh pissed with fright and worry: voice slurred, eyes rolling.

"Why in hell don't someone find out where that goddamned ship is? Jesus, we have the best damn Navy in the world bar five, and we can't even find one shitty little old ship? Where've those miserable motherfuggin bastards taken her?"

No-one answered. They were all too busy asking each other the same questions. It was like a Signal Officers' jamboree—everyone on 'transmit' and no-one on 'receive' . . .

Only one—an insignificant inoffensive Lieutenant Commander in submarines—did anything positive. He got hold of a chart and began marking off concentric circles around the *Sherman*'s last known position; by that time—4 a.m.—she could have travelled 1600 kilometres, as far north as Washington, southwest as Cuba, south to Barbados and halfway to the Azores.

He explained his reasoning to the Admiral.

"Sir, I don't think they'll push her at full speed. They'd have to stay part-submerged, or we'd have had a satellite report by now. I figure she's hull down, travelling slow to keep the wake cool: that way, she won't show up on satellite infra-red Doppler. She's been gone 12 hours—sixty knots . . . say, around 1200 kilometres. If she's heading for land, I'd say the West Indies—but why head for land? They need her for something, right?"

"Yes . . . yes. Go on, man!"

"Sir, I think we can wash out the Eastern seaboard—the last

place they'll be heading for. Lastly, if she's heading out on a long trip, they know we'll spot her in daylight by the wake. If it's southeast, round Africa, we'll pick her up when she crosses the Recife-Monrovia line of static seabed sonars—we have her engine voiceprint. Same with Greenland, Iceland, Britain."

"You mean," the Admiral said slowly, "we have her boxed in some place?"

"Yes, sir!"

"I know you . . . what's your name? Where do you work?"

"Ellis, sir. I was in subs—I've been your personal ADC for eight months—"

The Admiral went a little cross-eyed. Then—

"Mm-mm. Yes. Always know a face. Never fail. So—whatever they're going to do, it has to be the North Atlantic?"

"That's my view, sir," Ellis looked a trifle crestfallen. Spoken out loud like that, it sounded kind of stupid. The Atlantic was *big!* Stupid . . . it reminded him of the Senator from Milwaukee who achieved instant fame by declaring the reason for so many unemployed in Chicago was that there were so many out of work.

He tried his luck again.

"We can check the Big Board, sir—see if anything special is going on in the Atlantic. Exercises are over—but these guys might be trying to start a war with someone, using the *Sherman*—"

The Admiral's eyes crossed again. "You think so, Ellis?"

"Could be Mexico, sir. They have a whole lot of new oil-wells down there." The Commander in Chief made up his mind. There was damn little else they could do, anyway. Information began to trickle through. All ships in the recent exercises were warned. Guantanimo, in Cuba, reported the *Sherman* families all safe, ashore, and a probe into the origins of the *Normanton* got under way. A probe which led into several interesting but sterile cul de sacs. And with the break of day came coffee and cookies, and the Operations Room took on an air of festivity until someone noted the electronic symbol which had appeared on the board without warning.

"What," said the Admiral, mouth full of cookie, "in blue blazes is *that*?"

They told him.

"*Albatross*? Hovercraft? Nuts. No hovercraft ever crossed the Atlantic. Really? Nuclear-propelled? Well, I'll be a ringtailed sunnuvabitch. Ellis—any connection, you think?"

"It's the only thing new on the board, sir. Say—wasn't that the British boat in the news lately? Around the time that city burned down in England?"

It was indeed.

A signal was sent to Admiralty in London; a reply was received, short, to the point and in the Admiral's view, extremely rude. The *Albatross* had been at sea for four hours, was due in New York in less than five more. The Admiralty has informed the craft by radio of the strange disappearance of the *Sherman* and would appreciate being advised of any further developments.

The Admiral shook his head, not yet totally convinced that the whole thing wasn't some stunt organised by the Republicans. There was, after all, an election coming up soon . . .

9 a.m. EST—May 8th

The *Sherman* lay semi-submerged, engines idling, maintaining her position south of Nova Scotia and east of Cape Cod. Hardy had earned his money: two Seacruise missiles, armed, waited in Tubes 5 and 6. The *Sherman* crew, to a man, were jammed up tight in any compartment with a lock, herded in at gunpoint. Two engine-room mechanics objected, despite the fate of Chief Swanson, and started to argue; Cody disliked the sight of blood and had them thrown over the stern rail. Being a compassionate man, he gave them lifebelts; as a result, they stayed afloat long enough to give Cody's men some target practice. Waste not, want not. That was his motto . . .

17 *Gone Away . . .*

There had never been such a perfect morning, Savage thought. And this was as it should be: for a while, at least, his job was done, and he stood with Dee Purdy, hand in hand, in the line of passengers waiting to board the *Albatross*. Somehow—miraculously, it seemed to him—they had come through a series of traumatic experiences which would leave them scarred for life, but this morning, deep inside him, there was a heady and intoxicating surge of confidence and well-being which communicated itself in some strange fashion to the girl beside him.

The man had come ashore after the trials, walking past Dee, Wayne and the others at the landing pontoon like a blind drunken man, walking stiffly with a possessive hand on the stretcher bearing Martin's body. Savage seemed lost in a world of private grief, into which Dee, like all the others, was unable to penetrate. The man moved, spoke, ate enough—barely—to stay alive, but he could not, or would not, talk to her about the trials, and their aftermath.

Fitting-out went on apace; the Security force maintained its tight grip on the Yard, but there was an all-pervading feeling that the war was over, and Savage, for the space of eight or ten days, delegated responsibility to his men, spending long hot days sitting alone on the beach, staring down Spithead, past Portland Bill, to the Channel and the broad Atlantic beyond.

Martin was cremated on the third day; Savage never discovered, nor bothered to enquire, what happened to Chaffey. Carl Wayne ordered a complete clamp-down on the events of that day, aided and abetted by Navy Security, and it was some years before the story became known. After the service for Martin, Savage began to come slowly out of his condition of delayed shock, and the week in seclusion with Dee did much to restore him to normality. A week after the trials, Dee woke one night, full of some unnameable dread that he was gone; she switched on the bedside light and stared at the man. He lay flat on his back, lost in sleep—but his eyes were wide open, staring unseeingly at the ceiling, and, to the girl, that was the greatest horror of all. Appalled, deeply disturbed, she sat watching him; presently, he groaned deeply, turned on his side and began sleeping normally.

For her part, Dee was happy in a way she had never believed possible; daughter of wealthy parents, she lived in isolation almost from the day she was born until she was 18. Her parents held an oddly distorted, psychopathic view of ordinary schools and insisted on private tuition and virtual segregation from other children. Yet such was the character of the girl that, despite a terrifying experience with two lesbian teachers at her finishing school, followed by a near-rape at the hands of her first boyfriend, she still preserved an innate trust of her fellow-creatures. This over-weighed, at times, her natural caution and reserve; she was capable of a great deal of compassion which, in other times and places, might have seen her on missionary duties in some far-off dry and wasted land.

Realistically, she was totally aware that her love for Savage was one-sided in the extreme: he was, at this point in time, incapable of any significant emotions. The compounded shock of the Great Fire, the business with the reactor, and now the loss of Martin, had reduced the man to something approaching resignation and acute melancholy. Time, she knew, was the only palliative—and instinctively, she knew there was no guarantee, even long-term. All she could do was stand beside him in all he did—and pray . . .

Carl Wayne stood at the main entry port in welcome.

"Don—and Miss Purdy—"

Savage nodded civilly. "Mr Wayne. We have a nice day for it—"

"Forecast couldn't be better, Don. When we're under way, bring Dee up to the bridge."

Savage nodded again, and they walked across the threshold into the reception area. How different it all looked now, he thought dully. He had avoided the *Albatross* since the day Chaffey tried and failed, but now the carpets were deep and yielding underfoot, the decor pleasing to the eye in beige and dark green. They turned left, towards the forward saloon, and found what seemed to be most of the work force of BHLC already there; David Perry came over with his wife June.

"Don—and Deè! We've kept seats next to ours—front row, on the port side. Marvellous view from there. I suppose he's told you what it's like—travelling at speed?"

Dee shook her head. "Haven't been able to get a word out of him, David. But I understand it's very spectacular?"

The Project Manager grinned. "Just you wait. And don't worry—she's as safe as the Isle of Wight ferry boat. But it's the most exhilarating and terrifying thing you'll ever experience . . . we'll have orders for a thousand of these things, Don. The Press is aboard in strength . . ."

Savage relaxed fractionally. "I can see. Seen Dickie Byrd yet?"

"The crew have been aboard for hours. That big Irish buffoon's in his element—you never heard such a story as he's telling the reporters. We should be off soon—listen—they're closing the side hatches. We'd better strap in—"

Dee's eyes widened. "Strap in? Like an airliner?"

"Too true," Perry said cheerfully. "You'll see why presently—"

The girl said worriedly: "I'm not sure I want to ride on this thing, Don—"

"Too late to worry now. Besides—like David says: this thing is built around safety. It's going to carry millions of people over the next twenty or thirty years. Come on—I'll show you how the seats work."

There were some 500 airline-type seats in the saloon, most of which were occupied; in normal cruise, they faced forward, but, as Savage explained, in the event of an emergency stop the seat back was unlocked, swung forward to reverse the seat. The occupant now faced aft—"because she can stop in a very short distance indeed, Dee. Just by cutting the lift fan engines and letting her sink into the water."

"You're trying to frighten me," the girl said diffidently. The men grinned.

"No chance of anything like that happening, Dee. Sit down—relax—"

The *Albatross* cast off lines exactly on schedule—a minute

before 8 a.m. Motoring out into Southampton Water, she moved majestically under water-jets power, until the needle bow pointed south-east, towards the open sea; Bryd brought her up on cushion with a firm surge of power and, on the bridge, grinned at the distant chorus of screams and laughter far aft.

He turned to the First Officer. "Ask Mr Perry and Mr Savage if they'd like to come on the bridge, with their guests."

"Aye aye, sir."

The girls sat close together in the crew rest seats; Perry and Savage stood behind the Captain's seat on the broad bridge, stunned into silence by the sheer magic of movement, twenty metres above the water. Shipping lining the berths and jetties saluted in a cacophony of hooters and whistles, and she moved on past the seared ruins of the city on the left, past the Fawley oil terminal on the right, around Calshot Spit into Spithead with Lepe Beach passing on the starbound side. Savage watched the tiny strip of open land, the huddle of mobile homes, and turned, winked at Dee: reassured, she smiled brilliantly.

Passing Calshot, Byrd started a surprisingly tight turn to starboard and the great hoverliner banked into the turn like any aeroplane, massive sidewalls extending and retracting to maintain contact with green water flowing past.

"Meet her, cox'n."

"Meet her, sir. Course two four five."

The Captain turned, caught his passengers' eyes and grinned. The sheer relaxed confidence of the man caught at the imagination and quite suddenly Savage realised that he was, quite unbelievably, present at the making of history. He could remember little of the trials after Martin's death: he had collapsed into a seat in the forward saloon, drinking the strong black coffee donated from an engineer's lunch-box, and the remainder of the day had passed as if in a dream. He could recall vaguely some impression of enormous speed and vibration underfoot, the harsh roar of water and far aft, the bass hum of engines—he could have slept, because suddenly it was evening and they were tied up at the pontoon and he was stumbling up the steep ribbed gangway.

"All right, then," the Captain said sternly. "Let's be getting this thing to New York on time. Right standard rudder."

"Right standard rudder, sir."

"Course two six five. Keith, stand by to launch drones."

The First Officer acknowledged.

"Launch!"

Under the hull, two long sleek cylinders emerged from side-wall apertures, sliding into the water like twin torpedoes from a bygone age, accelerating out of sight under two metres of water. Keith Bigg operated press-to-test buttons, got two green lights. The drones moved further ahead, unwinding their carbon-fibre control cables from giant spools, propelled by annular linear accelerators. They maintained precise position to the *Albatross* feeding back microsonar pictures of the ocean kilometres ahead. The scan showed clear; Keith locked the sonar into the computer and relaxed. Warned of any dangerous floating objects ahead, the craft would alter course imperceptibly to avoid collision.

Dickie Byrd nodded to the rest seats on the aft wall of the bridge. "Best sit down, folks. Acceleration starting in sixty seconds."

Over the PA system, the Captain's voice sounded relaxed, confident.

"All passengers and crew take your seats, please. Fasten all safety belts. No smoking. Acceleration to cruising speed will commence in sixty seconds. Thank you."

Ridiculously, Savage found himself sweating. He glanced surreptitiously at Perry: the project manager was gripping the arms of his seat tightly and Savage grinned, suddenly at ease. He wasn't the only one scared fartless . . . it made him feel better. Few people ever travelled at speeds exceeding 60 knots on water . . . for a heartbeat instant, he wished he was somewhere else, far away from this . . . this . . . hot rod? He restrained an impulse to laugh hysterically.

Throughout the craft, Acceleration Lights changed from green, to amber, to red: from astern came a deep booming roar, a vibration—or was it pure noise? Savage gritted his teeth. The *Albatross* surged forward, riding straight over the hump of her bow wave, perched on a vast continuous cushion of air, stabilised by the knife edges of sidewall keels only centimetres deep in water. He sensed a heavy subsonic rumbling, a resonance in every frame and bulkhead and quite suddenly, the white build-ings of the Portland Navy base hurled themselves towards the craft; the shoreline shrank and disappeared, the rocky teeth of The Needles were a white blur, a split-second image of white faces on the lighthouse balcony, and the *Albatross* roared on into the south-west.

"One fifty knots . . . stabiliser function normal, Captain."

"Thank you, Keith. Autopilot holding, cox'n?"

"We have a one-degree fluctuation either side of course, sir. Trimming it out now—"

"Bridge to Engine-room—report, please."

Titus Oates's voice was a little unsteady but controlled. "Clear green board, Captain. All engine-room repeaters on line, all systems go, main drive at half throttle, all temperatures steady."

Half throttle? Savage turned his head to watch the coast, two kilometres to starboard, winding past like a runaway travelogue film . . . half throttle? Jesus!

The Captain said imperturbably: "Very good, engine-room. Radiation?"

"In the green, sir. All detector systems checked and operative. We have a limited amount of vibration below decks—from the region of the main water intakes in the inner sidewalls."

The Captain rubbed his chin thoughtfully. "We had that during trials, Titus—it seemed to cure itself above two hundred knots. Very well—stand by for power increase."

He straightened up, stared out over the piebald sea, patched like a palomino stallion with brilliant sunshine and the cloud shadows. "Stand by, Number One—seventy-five per cent power, please—"

"Seventy-five per cent, sir. Speed one seventy . . . one nine five . . . two oh five—seems smoother now, sir."

"Hold her at two twenty-five, please. I want to get well out to sea on course before we open her up. David—what do you make of that vibration? Did you hear what Titus said?"

"I did. I'm sure it's a flow problem around the main water intakes, Dickie. We may have to redesign the intake profile after this trip—it's all very well using a model in a tank, but these things escalate as the square of the speed, damn them."

The Captain nodded in agreement. "you mean, like the Reynold Number used in scaling up results from models to real aircraft?"

"Something like that. I don't think it's critical, Dickie. It'll wait."

"It will bloody well have to wait," Byrd said firmly. "Cox'n, stand by for full power. Navigator, are we clear ahead?"

"Clear screen, sir. Out to 45 kilometres range. Wait one . . . faint contact distance forty, bearing two eight zero. Well clear on the port beam. And I have another, heading for Plymouth, I think—bearing zero six eight degrees. No problem."

"Bridge to Engine-room—opening up now, Titus. Status report every ten minutes until further notice, please. Number One—let her go!"

Keith Bigg pushed the big red lever all the way forward. The sun was higher now, reflecting in a million sea mirrors, and the *Albatross* thrust forward into the western ocean, trembling as she encountered the first long Atlantic swells; the sidewall shells were in constant motion now, riding vertically to contain the air cushion. Forward and aft, the 'venetian blind' skirts rose and fell automatically, and behind the sharp bow the stabilisers changed angle minutely and constantly to keep the hoverliner level.

She crept up towards the 300-knot mark; Savage, staring mesmerised through the bridge window, could not believe what he was seeing. The Cherbourg-Plymouth ferry seemed frozen in time as they ripped past, the water streaming along the *Albatross*'s sides in a grey-green blur; they were out into deep ocean now, sliding sleekly over the long swells, cutting through them as a knife slices through butter. The crew began to relax . . . Savage and Dee Purdy sat, hands closely locked, hypnotised by the velvet smoothness of flight. Somewhere out there, he thought vividly, the whole of America would be waiting for them, this day; he realised dimly that, in its way, the flight of the *Albatross* was as significant as the voyage of the Founding Fathers . . . what would they have made of this vast white projectile, hurling itself westwards with a thousand human beings cradled in its cavernous belly? This ship of the future that flew, skimming the waves at phenomenal speed? Savage thought that, in their way, the Pilgrims would have approved

. . . they overcame enormous difficulties themselves to reach
the New World—and by the Lord Harry, it had been no piece
of cake for the *Albatross* . . .

Eight o'clock, ship time. A deck launch panel opened hydraulically, and the *Sherman* extruded a radar antenna on a telescopic
mast; it soared noiselessly to a height of thirty metres and began
rotating. On the bridge, Cody, the Captain, Lt. Cdr. Burns and
The Banker watched with varying degrees of interest. Cody
ordered an extending search eastwards along a specified track;
dissatisfied, he had a telebird launched as backup, and the small
drone aircraft cruised in computerised curves at three thousand
metres, scanning the sea two hundred kilometres to the east.

The bird's camera transmitted a depressing and unchanging
vista of grey-green sea, frothing whitecaps; the sky was half-
overcast with massive cumulus clouds, but light conditions were
satisfactory; Cody felt buoyant, confident, on top of the job.
There is no more exhilarating feeling than succeeding where
others have failed, and there was no way he could fail now
. . . he had the ship, the weapons, the escape capability. All
he needed now was a single confirming blip on that radar repeater . . .

Hardy was nervous, unhappy. Things were happening, things
beyond his control, and since the crude execution of two ratings
over the stern rail, he began reassessing his own future. Over
and over again, the thought burst through into his mind . . .
why should Cody and his crew waste time, effort and particularly
a very large sum of money transporting a bunch of renegades to
safety?

The more reasons Hardy thought up, the more convinced he
became that there was no way he was getting off this bucket
alive. He avoided the accusing stares of his senior officers and
stared out of the bridge window, brooding unhappily. He would
have been even more disturbed, had he been in the Missile
Room . . . there, all eleven of his men lay face down on the
steel floor, under the guns of four guards; a fifth waited at the
bridge telephone . . . relaxed, a sliver of toothpick between his
lips, he swung casually a length of rubber hose, the lower portion of which was filled with lead. He contemplated the job he

would have to do very soon with complete equanimity: he had, after all, worked for eighteen years in an up-state New York abattoir . . .

Four hours out . . . the stewards had cleared away the self-heating lunch-trays, and Savage leaned back in his seat in the forward saloon, turned his head and grinned complacently.

"Feeling better, Dee?"

"If you mean, am I only half-terrified—yes. I'm sure they put tranquilliser in the lunch—"

He grinned. "Maybe it was the wine—good, eh?"

The girl shrugged. "Really, Don—I don't know why I was worried. Once I got used to the speed—"

Savage nodded. "That first acceleration was something, wasn't it? Hell, the people will flock to ride in this thing, just for the thrill of it. And a lunch like that on top!"

He looked up. Young Osgood, the Navigating Officer. "Yes, Ossie?"

"Captain's compliments, sir—could you and Mr Perry come to the bridge?"

The men stared up at the officer. "Problems?" Perry said quickly.

"Not with the craft, Mr Perry. Captain said, right away, please—"

Savage nodded, got out of his seat. On the bridge, Dickie Byrd looked round with lowered eyebrows and set jaw. He held a pink Radex slip in his hand.

"David—Savage—sorry to get you back here. But I thought I should show you this before I spoke to the Chairman."

Savage said: "Where is Wayne? Havn't seen much of him."

"He's with the MOD people—they're having problems with that funny black box. Here—read this—"

They read. The message was lengthy, unusually verbose for an Admiralty communication. In plain language—they must have thought speed was of the essence—and digesting the message, Savage was inclined to agree with Their Lordships.

"You know anything about this *Sherman*, Dickie?"

"No more than you, lad. Missile cruiser, it says. The semi-submersible type—cruises half under water as a protection against nuclear blast. The Admiralty people say it's only by way of warning—no indication that the hijacking of the beastie is connected with us. I mean—we've had our problems, but surely no-one would go to the length of pinching a warship?"

Savage glanced at Perry and shrugged helplessly.

"Sledgehammer to crack a nut," he said phlegmatically.

"Some sledgehammer!" Perry said, grinning. Shades of Churchill, he thought.

"Some nut, by God," said the Captain. "Now, would you mind giving me your undivided attention? No doubt this *Sherman* monstrosity carries a deal of nastiness—and anyone throws as much as a bag of murphies at us, travelling this lick, there'd be a noise to end all expensive noises. Well?"

They stared at him blankly.

"Well, we can't ignore it, that's for sure. We can do everything possible—I'll start the crew practising emergency drills, and we'll keep a constant radar watch. Ossie—I want that set manned every minute, now, d'ye hear? Maximum range. Keith, signal Admirality and ask for locations of all known surface traffic, 400 clicks each side of our track. Work up a plotting chart—I want to identify every blip that comes up. David, where's that man Wade of yours? Still working on his black box?"

"I—expect so, Dickie. I'll go check—"

"Do that, please. It occurs to me—if we can get that RAZOR thing working it could give us a sporting chance if that ship's really waiting for us. We're supposed to be doing trials today with that Harrier-Carrier—what's its name?"

Perry said: "The *Londonderry,* I think."

"'Tis a good Irish name at that. I'd like to know in the next few minutes what's happening with RAZOR, David. Can do?"

"On my way."

As if by magic, the craft came to life. Passengers, dozing somnolently after a fine lunch, found themselves practising liferaft stations, swinging seats over to face aft. In the Forward Electrical Bay, floor freshly cleaned and burnished, Perry squatted, watching the final stages of work on RAZOR—until Gabriel Wade crawled out wearily from a cramped compartment, wiped his steaming face and nodded.

"All set, David. I'm not really certain about the calibration—but once the system starts working, it is self-tuning. Keep your fingers crossed. What's the panic for?"

Perry said blandly: "No panic, Gabe. The Harrier ship is standing by to do trial runs, but the weather further north is lousy—they may not be able to meet the schedule."

"Um. Well—here's hoping."

"Will it work, Gabe?"

The Electronics Officer sighed. "It worked on the trial model . . . it should work full size. But you know Podd's Principle—"

"Podd's—?"

"Development of Murphy's Law. 'If an experiment works, something's gone wrong.' "

"That it?" Perry demanded.

"There's more. 'Any system that relies on human reliability is unreliable.' "

Perry said: "Goodbye, Gabriel. Don't blow it—"

"What? My horn?"

"The gaff. Just make the bloody thing work, that's all."

On the bridge. The Captain stuck a paper under their noses when Savage and Perry walked in. "The Americans have asked us for all possible help in discovering this missing tin can of theirs," Dickie Byrd said irritably. "And the first Sea Lord, in his ignorance, has postponed the RAZOR trial until the return flight from New York."

Behind them, Gabriel Wade said fiercely: "Christ on a crutch! After a year of development and three hours busting a gut to activate the system—I could spit!"

"Not on my clean deck, you won't—" the Captain said warningly.

Perry broke in. "Where are we now, Keith?" The First Officer looked up from his chart, checked the INS reading in latitude and longitude. "About 33° 42 west, 49° 16 north. Plus or minus a metre or two."

"On time?"

"Naturally. In fact, we are about nine minutes in hand—we have good winds. ETA New York 3.42 GMT—8.42 local time."

"Watch that radar, Number One."

"Aye, aye, sir. The computer's starting to feed in other shipping: two contacts due shortly: SS *Hasibo Maru,* tanker out of Rotterdam bound for Panama, and the *Windhoek,* container ship, New Orleans to London. Both well clear of track."

Time passed; coffee and soft drinks appeared at regular intervals, and Savage went back to make his excuses to Dee; he found her fast asleep, despite the commotion, and let her sleep on. Back on the bridge, he talked with Perry in a quiet corner; by now, the novelty of high-speed cruising had evaporated in part, and they were aware of the sea, streaming past the craft almost undisturbed by her passage, only as a background to more pressing problems

"It doesn't jell, David," Savage said worriedly. "I can't see the Russians sparking off an unholy international row by taking a US Navy ship at sea. God, it's enough to start a war!"

"True—" Perry agreed. "You know, we wondered all along if someone other than the Reds was having a go at us. Well—seems they are, Don. But who, for Pete's sake? What the hell can they gain? Of the four or five smaller companies in the hovercraft field, most are making conventional full-cushion vehicles—and not many of those. Not with oil the price it is now."

Savage was unconvinced. "Which leaves—who? Or what?"

"Damned if I know, Don. The way I see it, you can put the industrial espionage—Julie van Heusen—and Chaffey's efforts, down to the Soviets: the link between them and Grainger is very solid. The dock gate attack? Not Russia, it seems to me. If it was, they covered their tracks: the wet suits used were German, the subtug American, the explosive Italian manufacture. Not a thing to identify either of them."

"I thought there were three divers—?" Perry said, confused.

"Only found two. The third was probably involved in the jetfoil thing—how else could it have exploded like that?"

The project manager shook his head. Savage, he felt, was getting a little too close to things best forgotten. "So—it seems the opposition wants one more try—with the *Sherman*?"

"Could be, David. God forbid . . . those ships all carry nuclear stuff."

"Ugh!"

"Quite. Question is—would they use them—or conventional warheads? We can only wait and see—"

The First Officer was speaking. "Skipper, we have an unidentified blip, about 300 clicks range. Doesn't match with any scheduled shipping we know about. Almost directly south—and the *Sherman* went missing down near Bermuda . . ."

The Captain nodded bleakly. "Where's that Harrier-Carrier?"

"The *Londonderry*? She's a long way astern and north, skip. Ordered to hold her position and try an intercept on the way home."

Byrd scowled. "Sure, she's about as much use now as a foreskin at a Jewish wedding, by God. Perry—if it is the *Sherman*—can they hit us at this speed?"

The designer shrugged. "Your guess is as good as mine. But if they can hit supersonic aircraft running in at sea level, we aren't much of a problem . . ."

"What do you think they'll use?"

Savage chipped in. "We were just talking, Dickie. They'll have some kind of ship-to-ship missile, low level probably, trying to duck under radar. From what I've read, these people might have difficulty programming a nuclear warhead—and they won't like tinkering around with that stuff. My guess is a conventional warhead, low level."

The Captain bit his lip. "Why are they doing this to us? Why, in the name of God?"

The silence dragged on. Then—

"These missiles—they are radar-guided?" Byrd demanded. Gabriel Wade stirred, behind Savage.

"Controlled by the ship's Fire Control system first, I think. Computer programmes the missile on the target location fixed by ship radar, confirmed by satellite if possible. Once in radar range itself, the thing locks on target for the final run, disengaging the Fire Control system."

Byrd nodded keenly. "At low level? The range at that point can't be very great—"

"I would think . . . four, maybe five kilometres," Wade said cautiously.

The Captain ran a forefinger along the smooth aluminium frame of the bridge window. Maybe . . . just maybe, it might work. Timing . . . that was the thing. At last—

"Wade, can you activate that box of tricks quickly?" he said urgently.

"RAZOR? Well—yes. Yes—the system takes about twenty seconds to warm up." Savage started. The crafty old Irish git, he thought admiringly. "Dickie—you mean—?"

"Why not? We wait until the thing's in close range, disappear from its radar screen and start a right turn. What happens?"

"It misses!"

"We hope," Byrd said slowly. "We hope . . ."

Keith Bigg said urgently: "In to 250 kilometres now, skip. And I just fed the data into our computer: it has changed heading to an intercept course. Estimated point of interception—due south of Halifax, Nova Scotia."

Byrd wasted no time. "Savage—get on that PA system! I want everyone back to their seats. Call Mr Wayne—I want him on the bridge immediately. Advise an amber warning for an emergency stop. Number One, I want everything battened down in two minutes!"

Carl Wayne fought his way onto the bridge. "Captain—what's the situation exactly?"

"No time to talk, sir. Brief him, Number One. And clear everyone off the bridge who has no specific job—that includes you, Mr Hoffman!"

The fat little accountant standing with Wayne blinked. "Really, Captain—I—"

"GET HIM OFF MY BRIDGE!"

Savage took hold of the bridling finance director's arm. "Come on, Mr Hoffman—there's an emergency on—"

"Why won't someone tell me what's going on?"

"There's just a possibility we may be under attack again, Mr Hoffman—the same people Chaffey was working for—or maybe someone else. We don't know for sure."

The accountant's eyes widened behind the steel-rimmed spectacles.

"Oh, no! They wouldn't . . ." and stopped, a finger to lips like a child caught lying. Savage looked at the man, curiously.

"That was an odd thing to say, Mr Hoffman—'who wouldn't' what? And who are 'they'? "

"Eh? Oh . . . for goodness sake, Mr Savage—I meant that they wouldn't dare try again—whoever they are. My God—do you mean that? We may be attacked?"

Savage nodded, and the strange little man, face ashen, scurried away aft, back to the first-class lounge amidships. The Security man watched him go, a little frown wrinkling his brow. Odd . . . Christ, Savage—ease off! Relax! You'll be suspecting Dee herself of being an enemy agent next . . . He grinned self-consciously and found the girl in the port corridor, heading back to her seat. Her eyes blazed with anger—anger he suspected was only partially simulated.

"Don Savage—where have you been? Ever since we left Southampton, you've been disappearing without warning! What were you talking to that funny little man Hoffman about?"

Savage grimaced. "The way some poeple think, their heads must be full of cotton wool and seagull crap. I think there's some Kraut back in his family—still can't speak English properly. Just for a moment, there I thought . . . no,—no, can't be."

"Kraut?"

"Never mind, darling. Another word for German—almost forgotten now. Come on—back to our seats before that warning hooter starts blowing its head off . . ."

On the bridge, the Captain sat motionless in his seat, manipulating his crew like a well-orchestrated song-and-dance team. From some strange depth, the man had produced magically an aura of confidence and efficiency that spread out to envelop all on the bridge.

"Where's that contact, Number One?"

"Bearing three zero zero, sir. It's angling round to cut us off . . . approximate course zero. Range 215 kilometres. Stand by . . . two of them now! Small blip tracking ahead of the larger one. I'd say that's an aircraft of some kind, sir. Building up speed—I have a height indication too. It's climbing—1500, 1600 metres—still climbing."

"Very well, Number One. Maintain course and speed. Have we contact with Mr Wade below decks?"

"Yes, sir. Coming up on audio now—"

"Wade? Captain here. That thing of yours all set?"

"Yes, Captain. Thirty seconds from the time you signal, we have radar invisibility—" Byrd swung round in his seat. "Number One?"

"Forward blip is accelerating, sir! On intercept course! Range 160 kilometres."

"Give me time to impact, damn you!" the Captain said between his teeth.

Keith Bigg's fingers played with virtuosity over the computer terminal. "Speed of missile 600 knots—time to impact six minutes from now!"

"Two degrees starboard, cox'n. That's all we can manage at this speed."

"Two degrees starboard, sir. New course two six eight." The helmsman, a stolid ex-Navy bo'sun, chewed his gum steadily, oblivious to the electric atmosphere on the bridge. Byrd glanced at the man and smiled, satisfied. H'd picked the right one there . . .

"Maintain course. Captain to bridge personnel—strap in tight—this is going to be rough!"

"Three minutes to impact. Missile still on course—hasn't turned to meet our own . . . ten kilometres . . . IT'S TURNED! No—back on course . . . eight kilometres!"

Byrd said tightly "I figure it just locked on with its own radar . . . Bridge to Wade—NOW!"

"It's working, Captain!"

"Six kilometres . . . five . . . four . . . Jesus!"

"Captain—Ossie here: I can see it: Oh, my God!"

"Shut up Ossie: Stand by, cox'n . . . NOW!"

The helmsman hauled back on the throttle, cut the main lift fan drive dead. Far aft, the main propulsion engine was silent, mercury vapour bypassed down new passages to the vast emergency condenser. Throughout the craft, the emergency siren was shrilling deafeningly and, like a giant hand grasping the *Albatross*, the savage deceleration began. In their seats, Perry, Savage, the girls, were forced back in their seats by a force ten times that of gravity, and breathing became initially difficult, then impossible: they choked and coughed, trying to expand chests compressed by some unseen vice.

Stabiliser and sidewalls fighting to maintain something like a stable attitude, *Albatross* sank bodily down towards the sea, air cushion no longer replenished and disappearing fast; sidewall impact blades and the tough reinforced skirts ploughed into water suddenly as hard as concrete and the fierce deceleration went on. Byrd, pinned to his seat by straps as rigid as steel, squeezed his eyelids closed, terrified that his eyes would pop onto his cheeks with the massive deceleration forces working on the craft. Underhull, the great Atlantic breakers were free at last, smashing into the main drive unit, tearing at the aft skirt as if to rend it into the tiniest fragments—and still she slowed, ramming into the waves like some ancient battering ram, and her speed fell within seconds from 300 knots, to 200, 130, then 90 knots and quite suddenly she was at rest, and being flung willy-nilly by rollers five metres high.

The Captain caught a fleeting glimpse of a long black needle with mini-wings located far aft, an indistinct blob of a power unit underslung at the tail, arcing steeply down to the surface perhaps half a kilometre ahead . . . Byrd paled. some five hectares of sea erupted skywards, propelled by a ruddy crimson glow, and for a split second he flinched inwardly . . . nuclear?

He roared, "Full starboard rudder! Full ahead water jets! Full power on main drive!"

"Christ, Captain—the passengers—!"

"Sod the passengers, Keith—get that damned power on! Meet her, cox'n—stay clear of that bloody mess out there!"

From an almost stationary position, the *Albatross* reached 100 knots in less than six seconds, heeling far to starboard as sidewalls and stabilisers fought to correct the list.

In the saloons, passengers had no time to reverse seats; now they hung in their straps, hanging on for dear life, most of them too terrified to complain; of the rest, many contributed to the frenzied howl of terror and the noise rose to ear-splitting level, complementing the combined roars of main drive and water jets.

"Cut water jets, Number One!"

"Aye aye, sir!"

"She's coming up on the hump . . . back to 75% power!"

"Seventy-five per cent, sir."

Byrd hurled himself out of his seat to the forward screen. "We're clear—meet her, cox'n! Don't worry about course—just keep her under control!"

Keith Bigg reached the radar repeater, searched the screen quickly.

"God, skipper . . . another one coming in! About sixty kilometres . . . weaving a bit . . . I don't think they can see us . . . what's our course, cox'n?"

"Near north, sir—few degrees west!"

The First Officer kept his eyes glued to the screen. "Still weaving . . . no—it's on course again, skipper. Forty kilometres . . . speed as for the last one, about 600 knots. Thirty-five . . ."

"Captain here—Wade, damn you—that thing still running?"

"Yes, Captain. Did it work?"

Byrd breathed heavily. "First time, yes. But we have another one inbound—it seems to see us."

Silence. Audio box hissing. The silence spread round the bridge.

"Twenty-five kilometres . . . started weaving again, sir! It can't see us . . . what the hell are they doing?"

The Captain said tightly: "I think this one's homing on our wash. Infra-red on the *Sherman* picking up the heat emissions from the main drive . . . we can't cut it again, Number One— it'd kill half the passengers. Range now?"

"Twenty kilometres . . . weaving badly now . . . sir, I think maybe it's in acquirement range now—taken over from their Doppler—but it can't see us."

"You may be right . . . range now?"

"Fifteen—it's drifting away to the west . . . straightening now! It's got us! On its way! Twelve . . . ten . . ."

Hunched in his chair, the Captain's brain turned to ice . . . almost psychically, he could sense the dilemma facing those creatures in the *Sherman*. Lacking the missile radar lock-on, they would have to fly it by wire—from the *Sherman*. From about ten kilometres out—using their infra-red Doppler at some 300 kilometres range. He had time to smile: no one got that lucky!

"Stand by to turn hard port, cox'n. Range. Number One?"

"Eight kilometres . . . descending steeply to sea level . . . six
. five . . . on the port beam . . . four kilometres . . . falling
astern now! Three kilometres, curving in to dead astern . . .
Christ, you're leaving it late, skip! Jesus save us . . . two kilometres . . . God, it's close!"

"HARD PORT!"

"Hard port, sir!"

"Keep it on hard! Wind the bastard round—break it if you
like but TURN!"

The First Officer ran to the bridge end window, took a quick
look astern. He opened his mouth to speak and the sheer speed
of the missile forestalled him.

It flashed through the welter of spray from the aft skirt,
straight as an arrow, and the *Albatross*'s turn was taking her
round to port, heeling terrifyingly to starboard as the sidewalls
and stabiliser reached the limit of their effort. The missile
streaked up the glistening length of the craft, almost touching
the superstructure, and continued on, out over the sea off the
starboard bow. Byrd saw it as if in a dream, saw that the wings
of this one were vertical, like some jet fighter initiating a hard
steep turn, but to no effect: as the needle-sharp nose began its
losing battle to follow the *Albatross* round the turn, the tiny
triangular starboard wing of the missile, black against the sky
collapsed.

The fuselage began rotating very fast indeed, about its own
centreline; he saw the rudder, the power plant, break free under
tremendous 'G' forces, and the missile plunged into the sea,
only a hundred metres or so from the hoverliner.

But this time, she was broadside on to the blast; perhaps it
was only the fact that she was heeling far to starboard under the
centrifugal force of the turn that saved her. The shock wave
impacted with the force of a million fists along the starboard
sidewall, forcing her first into the upright attitude and then into
the deadly roll port, into the turn. Extending sidewalls could
not move quickly enough to compensate, and she began to lose
air cushion; the port sidewall bit ever deeper into the sea,
dragging her even more tightly into the turn, and the terrifying
roll to port accelerated. On the bridge, the Captain stared up

at the clinometer: from the neutral 'O' mark, the scales were marked in degrees, in green, up to 30. Past that mark, in red, the scale stopped at 40 degrees; according to theory, she would never recover from a list exceeding that figure.

Over she rolled . . . 15, 20 and 25 degrees . . . all Byrd could do was pray . . . now, as if to deliver the coup de grâce, the first of the huge waves from the explosion reached her, forced her over still more . . . 30 degrees . . . 35 . . . and imperceptibly, she dragged herself round the turn to port, until the epicentre lay full astern. 40 degrees . . . 41 . . . 42 . . . and she steadied, trembled violently in every frame and stiffener, still deep in the turn, and now the detonation centre was no longer astern but on her port side. The green surging mountains began to help, not hinder—booming against the superstructure inside the turn, and Byrd watched in disbelief as the clinometer retreated degree by degree . . . 35 . . . 30 . . . 25 . . .

Like some living creature fighting for its life, the *Albatross* fought free of the lethal grasp of the ocean. Byrd ordered rudder midships, and the sidewalls began to bite; water was cascading off her superstructure and decks and she lurched a little more towards the upright position.

Stunned, the Captain said hoarsely. "Power back to one-third . . ."

"Back to one-third, sir," the First Officer said painfully: his throat was still sore from vomiting when the list passed 40 degrees, and he avoided looking at the bridge floor.

"My God," the Captain said shakily, "are we after being afloat, still?"

"I don't believe it, skipper . . ." the navigator said, in a thin voice laden with emotion. Byrd turned, grinned at his crew. "There . . . now that wasn't so bad after all, was it?"

Slowly, they began returning to sanity . . . the First Officer began turning her back onto course, and for the first time they noticed the helmsman, face as red as a ripe tomato, sitting rigidly at the wheel.

Captain Byrd said warmly: "Bloody fine job, cox'n! There's a fine bonus coming to ye—I'll see to that . . ."

"Beggin' yer pardon, sir—" the helmsman said thickly. "Rather have a drink of water, sir—"

"Drink, dammit?"

"Swallered me chewing-gum. Stuck halfway down, it is . . . what's wrong, sir? You do look strange, Captain, sir ... ."

18 Coming Home . . .

"Ladies and gentlemen—this is the Captain. We apologise for the discomfort and stress of the last half hour—we are preparing an announcement to give you full details. Meanwhile, we have no damage, as far as we can determine; the *Albatross* is now proceeding on course and we shall arrive New York with no further delay. I know that you have gone through a terrifying experience . . . to tell you the truth, for a while there, I was a little worried myself. Please advise the cabin crew of any injuries—we have a doctor on board. Mr Perry, come to the bridge please. Thank you—"

"Yes, Dickie?"

"I put this thing of yours through the hoop, David—and I couldn't break it. Chances are, we may even be able to use her again. You both did a fine job on her—"

"Both, Captain?"

"You and the good Lord."

Aboard the *Sherman* far to the south, Cody contemplated the ruins of his work coldly, assessing what could be salvaged. All radar contact lost with the target . . . the only two ready missiles expended—who would have thought both would miss? He eyed Chief Hardy balefully. "You miserable cheating son of a bitch . . . you fixed those things to miss—right?"

He ignored The Banker's pleading intermixed with anger.

"Take him down with the others," he ordered. "And *fix* him—good . . ."

In the Missile Room, the hard-faced man with the rubber hose set the telephone back gently on its rest, hefted his weapon and bent over the first man in line, tied and gagged, face down. Clinically, he hit the Navy man above and behind the ear, near the spinal column and moved on to the next. He had no need to check his work. When the guards brought Chief Hardy in, the long line lay still and he leaned against the door frame, knees sagging.

The hard-faced man grinned, rubber hose resting in the palm of a hand.

"Next, please—"

The *Londonderry* and the British Titan sub *Thatcher* headed southwest with temperatures way over the red line: orders were very explicit. Ten minutes after the *Sherman*'s last helicopter lurched into the sky, heading for St Johns, Newfoundland, with Cody's private army, the *Thatcher* boiled over the horizon into visual and radar range. Her Captain, displaying extraordinary seamanship, got a party aboard the *Sherman* at the third attempt, losing two helicopters in the process; heavy weather was blowing up from the southwest and the *Sherman*'s deck landing area rocked like a rubber raft.

Once in possession of the facts, the Captain scrambled six Super-C Harriers after the helicopters now over the northern horizon. The last, with Cody on board, was actually in sight of land when the Moccasin heat-seeking missile entered its jet exhaust at Mach 2, reducing the whole to fragments the size of bottle tops.

Aboard the *Sherman*, the released crew started a top-priority check of their ship—fortunately. They found an Arcturus 20-kiloton warhead connected to a simple timing device, which was exactly 85 seconds from detonation when the Navy senior rating found it. Staking everything on a wild guess, he ripped out a bunch of wires, watched the clock tick down to zero—and suffered a fatal heart attack when the search crew stumbled into the compartment, slammed a door open. The rating received a

216

Congressional Medal of Honour (posthumously); the search crew received minimum 2 years KP.

And aboard the *Albatross*, hammering westward through a choppy ocean at 275 knots, the bridge was crowded. Byrd and his crew were preoccupied with reaching New York on time; Savage and Perry were standing with Dee and Mrs Perry, talking to Carl Wayne, the men from MOD and Hoffman, the accountant, discussing preliminary points about a Navy research project for a military *Albatross*.

The sun was still near the overhead position; the *Albatross*, sailing at 8 a.m. from Britain, would arrive New York at 4 p.m. ship time, 11 a.m. New York time; all through the craft, passengers were relaxing, talking with much excitement about the Captain's statement, looking forward to seeing the legendary gateway to America.

Carl Wayne cornered Savage for a brief word.

"Don," he said earnestly, "you've come through this thing so well. Shoot, I know you don't want to listen to a lot of guff. But we'd never have made it this far otherwise. That girl Dee—you're getting married?"

Savage smiled tiredly. "Could be."

"Well, fine," Wayne said, genuinely pleased. "Don, we have manufacturing bases, not only in England, but in Canada, the States and Mexico. This damned world's in such a stew, no-one can be really sure of anything—which is why I want a much better Security set-up than before. We were caught flat-footed most of the time—right?"

Savage nodded.

"Well, then—here's what I suggest. You move over to Head Office in the McGill Building, Montreal, and you set up a full Security organisation for the Group. Tight—like you had in Northern Ireland. Good salary, company house, car—whatever. Can you handle it?"

For once in his life, Savage was floored. He stared at the big Canadian. Quite suddenly, for reasons he could hardly understand, he felt an actual physical sense of relief—as if a heavy weight that had rested on his shoulders for many years had been lifted free. It feels, he told himself, as if you were thirty kilos lighter . . . just keep your feet on the floor, Savage . . . smile and say 'thanks'!

He stuck out a hand, smiled. "Thanks, Mr Wayne. I can handle it. Christ, I can handle it!"

Wayne laughed at the exuberance, the boyish enthusiasm, remembering how this man had looked only a few weeks back; Savage did not know, but twice, in conference, directors had suggested replacing him—proposals turned down flat by Wayne.

"That man," he had said, "can do the work of four men—even when he's only half fit. When he drops dead, you can replace him . . . not before."

Thirty minutes out from New York. The weather had broken through—the sun shone brilliantly on a glinting blue-green sea, and all round the horizon, the cloud castles stood poised, as if watching the fleeting arrow booming west under full power. She left a wide flat wake, an arrowhead of white foam, of which she formed the tip, and on the bridge Captain Byrd was in contact with New York Port Authority on radio. They had special instructions for him . . . tweleve US Navy ships had been detailed to keep the approaches clear—and they were overworked: every boat and launch on the Eastern Seaboard was determined to be there. New York, the radio said excitedly, had declared a public holiday; the mayor and the President of the United States were waiting in Battery Park, under the feet of the Manhattan skyscrapers, to welcome the hoverliner. The entire world, it seemed, was watching on TV, listening on radio.

Savage stood with Dee Purdy in the port wing of the bridge, half-aware of the buzz of conversation behind them; soon, Savage knew, Dickie Byrd would clear the bridge, but this . . . this was the moment he had been waiting for . . . from the moment he stepped off the *Albatross*, Savage told himself, he was a free man. Quite possible, he and Dee might never return to Britain, other than business trips. In this big continent, they would find room to grow, dig a new foundation. The past years, with the pain, the mental and emotional pressures—the Great Fire, Jan—Martin . . . it seemed like segments of a nightmare from which he had only now woken . . . he held Dee's hand tightly and they

218

stared ahead, watching for the first sight of New York, towering above the horizon.

"Sir?" the Navigating Officer hung on his heel.

"Yes, Ossie?" Wayne balanced easily on the thrumming deck, a hand on the shoulder of Bill Hoffman. With luck, he could expect a Government contract worth £500 million, perhaps more . . . Bill was an old hand at squeezing the MOD orange dry . . .

"Captain would like a word, sir—"

"Very well."

Byrd stood behind his chair, one hand on the leather back, the other holding the now familiar pink slip.

"Well now, Dickie?"

"You'd better read this, sir," the Captain said thinly.

Wayne unfolded the Radex satellite-relayed message: it was from Brewer, the Navy Intelligence man in MOD, addressed to Commander Chisholm aboard the *Londonderry* and repeated to Wayne, on the *Albatross*. It was short—and to the point.

INTERROGATION GRAINGER AND VAN HEUSEN REVEALS LATTER'S CONTACT IN BHLC WAS ONE WM. P. HOFFMAN. PROBABILITY HOFFMAN IMPOSTOR SINCE 1989 WHEN REAL HOFFMAN VISITED E. BERLIN. FINGERPRINTS CONFIRM. TREAT WITH EXTREME CAUTION AND ADVISE.

Involuntarily, Wayne turned his head. "*Bill Hoffman?* I don't believe it!"

Near the bridge door, the accountant blenched. He hesitated, took a pace back and Savage recognised the .357 Magnum Hoffman was holding. Standard SAS issue at one time . . . more stopping power than any other handgun. His mouth went dry.

Hoffman took off his spectacles carefully. The bridge was filled with minor and quite irrelevant sounds. He said carefully:

"Give me that message, Carl—NO!" Wane stopped, his eyes bulging.

"Aloud, you fool . . . everyone else, stand still . . . *read*, damn you—!"

The Chairman read the message aloud, and Savage's estimation of the old man went up two more notches . . . his voice was steady and controlled.

Hoffman nodded. "You heard—all of you. Treat with extreme caution. Never doubt it for a moment. Byrd, how much longer to New York?"

The Captain glanced at his Navigating Officer. Ossie said thickly: "Twenty minutes—maybe twenty-five."

"I see." Hoffman seemed to be calculating mentally . . . then—

"Back against the bulkhead —all of you, except the man at the wheel. It seems . . . as if my employment has been terminated, Mr Wayne—"

"As of now, you bastard—"

"No doubt. And the design of this craft makes it difficult for me to make a discreet exit. In any case . . . I don't think life in British prisons would appeal. In the Soviet Union we prefer an extended vacation—in the Gulag Archipelago. DON'T MOVE!"

The First Officer froze, one foot lifted from the deck; gingerly, he set it down, eyes never leaving the gun.

This bad dream . . . I'll never wake up, Savage thought grimly. If ever I do, I'll be back in that ward in Keswick hospital waiting for someone to stitch me up and send me back again. I was a fool to think that there was anything better than this kind of life . . . yet—it could have been so different. The inside of his head felt like a great empty cave in the centre of an iceberg: someone had to smash up that horrible little man, and it didn't seem as if there was anyone else around capable his thoughts dwindled down to two simple issues . . . how? And when?

He turned his head slowly, and saw on the far horizon the white towers of New York and he realised that *Albatross* was surging along now between two immense columns of ships, large and small, private, commercial, forming an entrance channel stretching nearly ten kilometres out to sea.

There were flags, and rockets, and the distant blare of sirens, and thousands of white faces lining the decks which flashed past like country stations on an express rail line. Byrd, he thought furiously, was leaving it very late to slow down . . . and he stared at Byrd and at Hoffman and he knew . . .

Hoffman had it figured . . . maybe he was right, opting for a quick finish in preference to a lifetime sentence in the Hard Place. And what a finish! His Soviet bosses would put up a statue for him in Red Square . . . Savage had a ghastly mental image of *Albatross* ploughing into Manhattan Island at Battery Park, a nuclear-powered juggernaut travelling at 300 knots . . . spreading death, destruction and contamination up Broadway, through the city centre, on towards Central Park . . .

A disaster of such magnitude that the death of the President and others would pale into insignificance beside the destruction of Wall Street and the business heart of America. Savage doubted, in that moment of revelation, whether any son of the Revolution had ever been given such an opportunity to strike a blow for Mother Russia.

Dickie Byrd said urgently: "Hoffman—for God's sake—we have to slow down!"

"Hold course, damn you!"

"I tell you—that's the Narrows Bridge ahead! The Bay'll be jammed with traffic!" Hoffman shook a dogged head, eyes glowing. In that moment, Savage knew the man had reached the threshold of insanity and passed within . . .

The thundering *Albatross* flashed under the arch of the Narrows Bridge, into the Bay; without instructions, the helmsman edged the wheel round to a northerly course in a long sweeping curve: at that speed, any turn of more than a half "G" would be fatal.

"Jettison the drones!" Hoffman yelled—an afterthought, Savage thought dully. Ahead, growing from a speck to an image, Liberty Island and the Lady with the Lamp. Scores of small boats. Some liner easing out of the East River. Further on, to port, Ellis Island, and the stupendous palisade of Manhattan mounted on the flattened tip of the Island itself . . .

Albatross streaked past the great Statue, Governor's Island streaming past on the starboard side and voices were screaming, Hoffman waving the gun frantically to cover each and every enemy, and David Perry's wife collapsing slowly in a dead faint.

Savage had the hazy feeling that Time had slowed down . . . he leaned forward in an attacking crouch, eyes never leaving the Magnum, surging forward, hands clawing, feet scraping frantically for traction and the gun swinging round fast, too fast, and a small voice in the back of his mind said quite calmly: "You're not going to make it, Savage . . ." and a fist the size of a mountain smashed into his chest.

His world was a world of utter silence and drifting shadows and the dull impact of his shoulder against Hoffman's knees and the soundless grating of face and shoulder along the deck and he was rolling with exaggerated slowness onto his back, head hard against the bulkhead. He lay still, with shocked eyes, not understanding why shadows of people were moving around and across him. A giant hand grasped him once more, heaving him like some rag doll forward across the deck until he lay against the base of the centre control panel.

His body felt . . . not quite right. He was aware, remotely, that *Albatross* was deep into massive deceleration . . . Dickie would do it all right, he told himself absently.

In the silence, the bodies around him ceased to move with such crazy contortions and haste . . . an arm went under his neck, lifted his head and he saw Dee, her eyes liquid with the tears she could not hold back. Yet through the tears, in that dear face, he sensed an emanation of love, and understanding, and—agreement? He grinned a little lopsidedly at her, and the grin stayed there, for ever.

Fiction

☐	**Options**	Freda Bright	£1.50p
☐	**The Thirty-nine Steps**	John Buchan	£1.50p
☐	**Secret of Blackoaks**	Ashley Carter	£1.50p
☐	**The Sittaford Mystery**	Agatha Christie	£1.00p
☐	**Dupe**	Liza Cody	£1.25p
☐	**Lovers and Gamblers**	Jackie Collins	£2.50p
☐	**Sphinx**	Robin Cook	£1.25p
☐	**Ragtime**	E. L. Doctorow	£1.50p
☐	**The Rendezvous**	Daphne du Maurier	£1.50p
☐	**Flashman**	George Macdonald Fraser	£1.50p
☐	**The Moneychangers**	Arthur Hailey	£2.25p
☐	**Secrets**	Unity Hall	£1.50p
☐	**Simon the Coldheart**	Georgette Heyer	95p
☐	**The Eagle Has Landed**	Jack Higgins	£1.95p
☐	**Sins of the Fathers**	Susan Howatch	£2.50p
☐	**The Master Sniper**	Stephen Hunter	£1.50p
☐	**Smiley's People**	John le Carré	£1.95p
☐	**To Kill a Mockingbird**	Harper Lee	£1.75p
☐	**Ghosts**	Ed McBain	£1.25p
☐	**Gone with the Wind**	Margaret Mitchell	£2.95p
☐	**The Totem**	David Morrell	£1.25p
☐	**Platinum Logic**	Tony Parsons	£1.75p
☐	**Wilt**	Tom Sharpe	£1.50p
☐	**Rage of Angels**	Sidney Sheldon	£1.75p
☐	**The Unborn**	David Shobin	£1.50p
☐	**A Town Like Alice**	Nevile Shute	£1.75p
☐	**A Falcon Flies**	Wilbur Smith	£1.95p
☐	**The Deep Well at Noon**	Jessica Stirling	£1.95p
☐	**The Ironmaster**	Jean Stubbs	£1.75p
☐	**The Music Makers**	E. V. Thompson	£1.75p

Non-fiction

☐	**Extraterrestrial Civilizations**	Isaac Asimov	£1.50p
☐	**Pregnancy**	Gordon Bourne	£2.95p
☐	**Jogging from Memory**	Rob Buckman	£1.25p
☐	**The 35mm Photographer's Handbook**	Julian Calder and John Garrett	£5.95p
☐	**Travellers' Britain**	} Arthur Eperon	£2.95p
☐	**Travellers' Italy**		£2.50p
☐	**The Complete Calorie Counter**	Eileen Fowler	75p

☐	**The Diary of Anne Frank**	Anne Frank	£1.50p
☐	**Linda Goodman's Sun Signs**	Linda Goodman	£2.50p
☐	**Mountbatten**	Richard Hough	£2.50p
☐	**How to be a Gifted Parent**	David Lewis	£1.95p
☐	**Symptoms**	Sigmund Stephen Miller	£2.50p
☐	**Book of Worries**	Robert Morley	£1.50p
☐	**The Hangover Handbook**	David Outerbridge	£1.25p
☐	**The Alternative Holiday Catalogue**	edited by Harriet Peacock	£1.95p
☐	**The Pan Book of Card Games**	Hubert Phillips	£1.75p
☐	**Food for All the Family**	Magnus Pyke	£1.50p
☐	**Everything Your Doctor Would Tell You If He Had the Time**	Claire Rayner	£4.95p
☐	**Just Off for the Weekend**	John Slater	£2.50p
☐	**An Unfinished History of the World**	Hugh Thomas	£3.95p
☐	**The Third Wave**	Alvin Toffler	£1.95p
☐	**The Flier's Handbook**		£5.95p

All these books are available at your local bookshop or newsagent, or can be ordered direct from the publisher. Indicate the number of copies required and fill in the form below   7

Name_____
(Block letters please)

Address_____

_____

Send to Pan Books (CS Department), Cavaye Place, London SW10 9PG
Please enclose remittance to the value of the cover price plus:
35p for the first book plus 15p per copy for each additional book ordered
to a maximum charge of £1.25 to cover postage and packing
Applicable only in the UK

While every effort is made to keep prices low, it is sometimes
necessary to increase prices at short notice. Pan Books reserve
the right to show on covers and charge new retail prices which
may differ from those advertised in the text or elsewhere